Cat

Scan

By

Geoffrey Mandragora
and
ML McIntosh

Rosswyvern Press

This is a work of fiction. Names, characters, businesses, places, events and incidents are either the products of the author's imagination or historical persons and events used in a fictitious manner. Any resemblance to actual persons, living or dead, or actual events is purely coincidental.

ISBN:
ISBN: 978-1-7329395-2-3

Geoffrey Mandragora
For Romana.
Friend, Beta reader, editor

ML MacIntosh
For Meowzah Al-Kitten

Acknowledgments

There are many people responsible for publishing a book.

I would like to thank my co-author ML Mcintosh for her invaluable insights into writing and plotting.

I would like to thank my wife, my first beta reader and greatest inspiration. Without her, I would have given up on writing before I really began.

Once again, they deserve all the credit for the things that work right. I, however, am solely responsible for inaccuracies, mistakes and errors.

Prolog
October, 1927
Twenty years before magic returned.

The dig foreman walked with a carefully measured gait, struggling to hide his excitement. He was well aware of the danger should he rouse suspicion. He entered the shaded area beneath a tarp, the smell of mildewed canvas enveloping him.

In the summer, the tarp provided welcome shade from the unforgiving Egyptian sun, but this late in the season it did little to temper the cold winds that were increasing with each day. Approaching a slim Englishman with a shock of unruly brown hair and wire-rimmed spectacles, he spoke barely above a whisper. "Effendi, we have found something."

Dr. Justin Childress's eyes widened at the words, but he fought to keep his emotions in check. There was only one reason his dig foreman, also the representative of the Egyptian Department of Antiquities, would have announced it in this way.

Gold.

During Childress's first season excavation, he dreamed of finding great treasures, but that thrill died under the weight of regulations and the threat of bandits preying upon such finds. It wasn't like the last century when Carter and Lord Carnarvon discovered the tomb of King Tutankhamen. Now Egypt had a reasonable, and reasonably honest, police force. But they were not here, not now.

Childress moved the papers in front of him and uncovered a map of the dig, displaying the carefully marked grid. This was not the Valley of the Kings. The families buried in this area were not nobles, but very high-ranking servants and wealthy merchants from the later kingdom. But there was speculation that some of those buried here may

1

have been involved in looting other burial sites.

He indicated the map. "Where?"

The foreman bent over as if examining the map, but quietly whispered, "Section seven, grid twelve."

The skinny archeologist made a show of looking at his watch. His mind raced. If he closed down this early, the men would be suspicious. Even the hint of treasure could turn loyal workers into potential thieves, but rumors were a greater danger. If the workers carried a tale of newly discovered riches back to their family members, or worse, to the town watering hole, the excavation could be destroyed. Families that profited for decades from the illegal antiquities trade would invade during the night, carelessly digging up the surrounding countryside and destroying its academic value.

He pursed his lips in thought. He'd been saying he wanted a full-scale excavation of the south end. No tombs there, but the apparent remains of a worker's encampment. Hundreds of men had stayed there over several decades. No chance of treasure, but a wealth of tools and daily artifacts. He could reasonably redeploy works there.

"Who knows?" Childress murmured.

"Me and Ahmed. The young one," the foreman answered.

"Where is he?"

"At the first aid station."

"Is he injured?" Childress asked, concerned. He felt mildly guilty about using such young boys.

"No, Effendi. He was not injured, but that was the most discrete way to put him under guard."

"Good work. Move the workers to the south and get our most loyal guards posted around the area. Send a messenger to the local constabulary, and to our cultural liaison. We will dismiss the men at five, and we will meet at grid twelve. The others should be here from town by then."

But they weren't.

The sky shifted from the light blue of day to a darker shade, looking as thick and navy blue as the Nile itself. Childress and his foreman met at the grid site. Eight stone steps led down to a chamber, with a hole already cut into the thick rock door that had stood sentry for a millennium. He poked an acetylene lamp through and stared.

The foreman spoke, his voice hushed and hesitant. He had seen others jump to conclusions before and knew a false report of a find could undermine his status. "What do you see?"

The archeologist chuckled and could not help but quote Howard Carter, when he was asked the same question by Lord Carnarvon.

"Wonderous things."

His gaze focused on a rough sarcophagus with gold paint and a few obvious gems, adorned by one remarkable piece. An amulet, gold inlaid with lapis lazuli, glinted in the flickering light, perched atop the crudely shaped outer coffin. It was in the shape of the ubiquitous Usekh collar seen in all Egyptian art. The amulet itself was a golden version of the winged Isis; but there was something… He felt a pull, a desire about the piece, unlike anything he'd felt before, almost as if it were magically drawing his very essence toward it. But, but of course, magic didn't exist.

Present day

Leslie Modeste looked over the mishmash of artifacts covering the long table. Outside, the San Francisco weather was dreary, and rain fell in a torrent as if a thousand fire hoses sprayed the building. She peered over her half-rimmed reading glasses. "Are *any* of these genuine?" she asked.

"Some," replied a tall man with the polite, but slightly distant, air of a funeral director. His name was Herman Schon, the court-appointed estate executor of the Childress estate. "Since Mrs. Childress died, the estate has been tied up in probate. We recently found a letter from Professor Childress indicating he wanted these donated to a local museum."

"Exactly,.." interrupted an officious little man in thick, horn-rimmed glasses. "That means us."

Ms. Modeste didn't care for Brad Minors, the representative from the museum board. They'd been forced to work together several times and each time she found his manner more grating than the last, but she ignored those feelings and focused on her work.

She bit her lower lip, adjusted her glasses and ignored the remark. "Any provenance?"

"No." The executor shook his head and frowned his frustration. "Professor Childress recorded in his journal these were things he" Schon paused to curl his fingers into air quotes— "'picked up' on his travels. And yes, he uses the quotation marks in his notes. He brought the collection here just before World War Two."

"He was British, yes?'

"Indeed, but…" Schon's face twitched in distaste. "He didn't want to return home because of the scandal."

"Scandal?" Leslie absently asked, her attention on the artifacts.

The tall executor sighed in disapproval. "Yes, he married an

3

Egyptian woman much younger than himself."

"How young?" Modeste deigned to give Schon her attention.

"Too young. But, to his credit, she was an orphan, bound to be sold to a local brothel."

Leslie cringed. "Yes, that makes it *so* much better." The sarcasm rolled off her tongue like venom. She didn't have to wonder how a British gentleman knew about Egyptian brothels and the operation of procuring the residents.

She wrenched her attention back to the display. "If there is anything genuine here, it will need to be repatriated." The stout woman scratched behind her ear. She was a dilettante as far as antiquities were concerned, but she was a well-trained Sensitive. Since the Great Opening of 1947 spilled magic into the world, any collection of potential mystical artifacts had to be inspected before changing ownership. If there was anything authentic in the late Mrs. Childress's collection, it would be the oldest pieces she'd ever worked with.

"Will this take long?" Minors asked with all the patience of a seven-year-old.

"It takes what it takes," Leslie said under her breath.

Thunder cracked outside and the lights flickered. She half-smiled, taking that as an omen. She gazed at the table, opening herself to any energies that might be swirling around and was surprised how strong she felt them. Any collection of mystical items, even fake ones, would give off a sort of background radiation, but this was something much stronger, and darker. No, only partially darker, there was a lightness as well. Two different artifacts?

She suppressed a shiver as she examined each item in turn. Spreading her fingers over the items, she felt a tingle. A twinge stronger than she'd ever encountered. Her hand passed over an Usekh beaded and adorned with plates of lapis lazuli and bearing the golden image of a winged Isis sitting on the hieroglyph of the Eye of Horus decorated with more lapis lazuli. A common enough motif. Her first impression was that it was either a reproduction or had been thoroughly restored. It looked almost new. "What do you know about this piece?"

"That one?" Schon gave a tight smile. "Mrs. Childress loved that piece and wore it until she died. We have a photo of her wearing it at her eightieth birthday. Her nurse thought she wanted to be buried with it, but as her strength ebbed, she begged the nurse to take it off her and have it added to the collection."

Leslie regarded the artifact and reached out again, this time getting closer. The piece had an aura of cold around it. Her smooth hand edged closer, and she jerked it back as if she'd been bit. She produced a

4

jeweler's loop from her sensible tweed jacket and held it up to her eye. "There's some odd markings on this amulet."

"What sort of markings?" Schon asked.

"Can't really tell, they're faint. Maybe just scratches in the soft gold." Leslie lowered the loop and looked into the distance, consternation on her face as she whispered, "I really hope they're just scratches."

"What's going on?" Minors demanded, showing his first interest in the process.

Leslie didn't answer him but instead fished a cell phone out of her pocket and hit a number on her speed dial, placing it on speaker.

"Yes, Leslie?" a voice answered.

"Dr. Kaufman, I hate to bother you, but I think I just found a level three artifact."

Minors scowled at the woman as she addressed the Grand Master of the Revealed Gnostic Elite, or Nogs, the most powerful of the mystic orders that sprang up after the opening.

"Oh," the man on the phone replied with a mixture of enthusiasm and his usual, baseline distraction.

Leslie bit her lip. "I don't want to be a bother as the convention is starting. Especially since it may be unnecessary. After all, I'm a sensitive, nowhere near mage status, and certainly not a sorcerer like you."

Minors rolled his eyes. The woman wrapped herself in her humility like a blanket that stank of faux virtue.

"Don't worry," Dr. Kaufman replied with a chuckle and Leslie smiled relief. "I would rather you call me with a hundred false reports than miss a genuine one."

These two, Minors thought, *are prime examples of the problem with the world today.* All that political correctness, fake humility and gushing politeness made him positively sick.

"Thank you," she said.

"It's what, a six-hour drive to Los Diablos? You can be my guest at the convention. I don't think you should fly with the artifact. Can you pick it up?"

"No, but I have a containment kit in the car."

Minors's ears perked up. He was not scheduled to go to the convention, a once every four years mystical gathering, and a party that rivaled Mardi Gras. But if the artifact was going there....

"Has anyone touched the item since Mrs. Childress died?"

"Only the caregiver." She glanced at the executor who nodded.

"If she is available, please bring her as well."

"Will do." Leslie sighed and disconnected the call.

She took little notice of Brad Minors slipping out to the hallway. He took out his phone and hit his speed dial.

"McConnel?"

"Who else would it be?" a frigid, raspy voice replied in a harsh whisper.

"We found one. It's here like you thought." Unlike Leslie Modeste, he displayed no uncertainty and was careful not to remark this was the twentieth some-odd time he'd been sent to find one. "It's just like the other times, too. But they're taking it to Kaufman."

"The supposed Grandmaster." McConnel's voice on the phone sounded more like someone stepping on dry leaves than human tones. "No matter. The convention has started. He will doubtlessly be very busy. We have an asset, a Giggle-O looking to be an RNC initiate. Not the most stellar intellect, but reliable. Play it quiet for now."

"Will do." Minors ended the call.

* * *

The phone in the man's inner jacket pocket vibrated, giving him a start. He glanced around, even though his office was empty, and pulled the unregistered phone out. "Cooper," he identified himself.

The voice on the other end chilled him as it spoke, harsh and crackling. "I have a task for you."

Cooper swallowed and absently pulled his keys from his pocket and rubbed the well-worn leather piece holding them; an old habit to deal with stress. He glanced around the room, still fearing someone else could be there. A task for McConnel could get him out of this mess he called a life.

"I need you to block any investigation about the theft of an amulet."

Aaron Cooper, the Commander of Internal Affairs at LDPD, grinned despite the chill crawling down his spine. "Of course, sir. I'm your man."

Chapter One

I closed my eyes; face pressed against the concrete floor as I tested the ropes binding my wrists behind my back. I opened my eyes. The cat, adorned in an ornate collar of gold and the lapis lazuli. was still there, idly licking herself.

"*Merde,*" I swore, reverting to my native Haitian French.

She gave me a long, meaningful gaze before she opened her mouth. "Meeeeeooooowwww."

As the plaintive sound hit my ears, I actually seemed to hear the cat say, "Such language." Chuckles the Clown must have hit me harder than I thought.

"I don't think you can reason with him," said the cat, still licking her paws.

"What, did you say?" I addressed the cat.

Again, the words formed in my head and I assumed it was the result of a concussion.

"Cats can't talk," the cat said as she walked away from me. "That would be stupid."

* * *

Three hours earlier.

Waking up late on a cool October afternoon, my first thought was that tonight was going to be tedious. My vampire partner, Vlad, scheduled a personal day, err night, so I scheduled an evening cataloging evidence from my last three cases, also prepping notes for the active ones. Too damn many active ones. My name is Delacroix;, Detective Lieutenant Delacroix, Los Diablos PD, Magical Crimes Against Persons Division.

My plan went out the window when the captain bellowed from his office door. "Delacroix, get your butt over here!" The captain was a

7

heavyset man with a florid complexion, short hair and a shorter temper. I've been told that he was far more pleasant to work with before a serial killer case three years ago set him against the FBI and cost him his partner. I was also told never to mention that case in any way.

"*Oui, mon capitaine.*" He hates when I lapse into my native Haitian French and, normally, I refrained around him; but the bellowing rubbed me the wrong way. I followed him into his tiny office and waited for him to plop into his chair before I carefully sat in the visitor seat.

"Fricken clown." He produced a cigar and chomped down on it. I have only seen him light one once. That time "words were exchanged" and the cigar was put away.

But, so far, I had to agree with him. Fricken clowns.

"Biggest convention in LD and we, her finest, let some chump Captain Spaulding wannabe steal the most special necklace in *history*, apparently. Amazing. So, what're your leads on this greasepaint gangster? Spill it."

I was puzzled. "I've been away and there is no case file."

The captain stared at me, cigar dangling from his lips like I'd said exactly what he expected me to. He opened a drawer and set a file on his desk. "Of course, you ain't got a fricken case file. Why would you? Everything you need is in here. That clown is still out *there,* and I need you to put him in *there*, yesterday." The cap pointed from the door toward holding with his cigar.

I knew the captain blamed me for letting the fool walk away, but I was sort of busy keeping reality together at the time. The prankster took advantage of a distraction and swiped an Object of Power. He'd been giving the whole department the slip since he acquired the damn thing a month ago.

"Our boy was laying low, until five days ago…" The captain sated.

I picked up the file.

I was out of commission for two weeks after the Nog convention and I'd hoped this issue would be moot. But now, the file had reports of someone in clown make-up getting into black magic mischief, and even though the missing amulet was supposed to be much more powerful, his actions were barely above the annoying hexkiddie level. Hexkiddies are super annoying but not particularly dangerous. Some adolescents find they have a bit of talent and find or buy spells created by real wizards and use them for stupid pranks to show off, maybe gain some notoriety. For most, the talent fades as their hormones adjust or they just get bored with it. Some grow into talent and have some serious life decisions to make.

The captain glared at the folder in my hands. "What do we know?"

"Not very much. I'll need to look at the file."

The captain jabbed a finger on the desk. "Well, it's suddenly urgent. Turns out the mayor's niece was a bank teller at one ah the places that got hit."

"Addison? The girl from the convention?"

"No, her older sister Madison. He's got a dozen nieces."

I went back to the file. The first page was a summary, and I read aloud, "A clown was using mind control on some bank tellers, forcing them to give him some money. But he didn't tell them to forget that he did it, or to forget his face. I think the clown get-up was supposed to be a disguise. But the techies cleaned it up easily enough. Still trying to match it in the system. We know what he looks like, but no name or identification." I looked up. "No offense to the report maker, sir, but there's nothing here I did not surmise the moment you said he has come to the surface again."

The captain jabbed his finger at the folder. "This is a list of his last five ventures. I want you to figure out where he's going to strike and get your butt out on the street staking it out."

"Not many banks open tonight."

The captain grinned. "See, I just got a tip from vice today. Seems he used his ability on two different working girls, taking both money and uh, services. They also got a report of him hitting a pawn shop and a floating high stakes poker party. Adding that data shows he's using the amulet roughly every twelve hours, probably a recharge time. So, we can expect him to hit someplace around ten this evening. Now, since this is their hot tip and their part of the dance floor, I want you to be sure to keep vice in the loop. Make 'em feel pretty, Del. Just this once. For me." He gave me a sardonic grimace and waved his cigar right back into his mouth.

"Fine, I will talk to vice," I said, my voice drooping at the prospect. I would prefer not to. I was not popular after exposing one of their people and have been actively suspicious of the rest since. The vice squad was the second most corrupt unit in the department, right behind Internal Affairs.

Malkin., He was a former vice sergeant revealed to be a homunculus, something like a Frankenstein's monster, and an agent for a group trying to control all magic. I exposed him, yes, but I failed to *catch* him. He was still in the wind. And that thought cost me a lot of sleep.

"You have two advisers waiting to brief you in conference room one."

"Advisors?" I regarded the captain with apprehension.

"A sensitive working for a private company that identified the amulet, and a guy from some museum in 'Frisco."

"What do I need advising on? I can talk to Dr. Kaufman. He will brief me. He had the amulet during the convention."

"Yeah, but these two have been separately breathing down my neck. You make nice with them and get them to go away."

So, this was not so much about penalizing me but rather removing an irritation.

The captain made a sweeping gesture to point out the door. "Go to vice first and get their list of places he's hit."

I straightened my shoulders and walked out. A chat with the vice squad was just what I needed to prepare to deal with the unwanted "advisors."

The squad room door was open, and I walked right in, then halted. There were two men talking. The first was Ted Gruber, the new guy. A rookie just two months after getting his detective shield.

The other was far more worrisome. Police Commander Aaron Cooper. The overall head of Internal Affairs.

They stopped talking at my appearance.

The commander squinted at me. "Detective Delacroix, the voodoo cop on the MCAP squad?"

I nodded. I long ago gave up trying to explain the word *Voudon* to the intentionally ignorant.

"I hear you did some good work with the convention issue, and the, uh, Macklin affair. It would be a shame if such a solid career got sidetracked by your, ah, associations."

Cooper had a leather key holder in his hand and idly burnished the piece with his thumb and forefinger. It looked almost worn through; he would need another one soon. He wore them out every few months. His department had a betting pool.

"What do you mean?" I asked, my voice neutral.

Cooper shrugged and gave me a cocky grin. "Just I've heard tell you've been associating with some religious zealots, and a notorious pimp. Tell me, they, uh, come from the same social circle?"

I shrugged. "I really do not know anyone who fits those descriptions."

Cooper glared at Ted Gruber and pointed at me with his key holder. "Here you told me he was a smart boy." He turned back to me. "Ain't you?"

"I try," I said, displaying the file. "I need the list of the vice targets

10

that might be vulnerable to hypnotism."

Gruber looked blank, but Cooper glared at me and the file. "They put you on the clown case? You must be in the doghouse. It's gone ice cold, the perp's gone. Yeah, there's been some robberies, but it's not the same guy. Tell you what, leave the file with us and we'll see what we can turn up. Help you out."

"*Non*, much as I wish I could. I have my orders, I'm afraid."

Cooper frowned and turned to Gruber. "Give him the list, then. Sorry the department's wasting your time, Detective Del."

Gruber handed me a sheet of paper. I thanked him, headed to the conference room, and entered to witness a man and a woman staring daggers at each other. When I entered, the woman also stared daggers at me. She sat at the table, her hands clasped, and her face scrunched up in revulsion. I never liked that look on her.

"Detective Delacroix," she greeted me in a stiff voice and gave me an even stiffer nod. "Of course, it would be you."

I returned her nod. "Ms. Modeste, of all the police departments in all of Los Diablos, you walk into mine, *n'est-ce pas*?" Any other formalities would have been hypocritical. She'd put on about ten pounds over the last years and took to dying her hair the coal black of her youth. Not that she was that much older than me, but she went gray young. The hard frown lines on her face were new, but not unexpected; she never cared much for smiling. Same fashion sense. A no-nonsense gray skirt and jacket with a white blouse. She had five matching sets. I knew that, because I had once ironed them. Poorly.

She unclasped her hands and jabbed her left index finger across the table at a timid looking man with dorky glasses. "This is Mr. Minors from the Imagine Different Museum in San Francisco." I sized up Mr. Minors immediately. He was not the submissive sort of timid, he struck me as resentfully timid, like a rat. Coy, acting non-threatening but really waiting for an opportunity to snap out at someone.

He rose like he was going to shake my hand but thought better of it and just stood there in an awkward state of indecision. "The missing artifact was left to us by the estate of Dr. Childress. We are equipped to store a level three artifact." At a grunt from Miss Modeste he added, "Provided it is not subject to repatriation."

"That is not my responsibility," I pointed out. "I will turn it over to our forensic sorcery department once I retrieve it, they will deal with that."

"You've not had a lot of success retrieving this extremely delicate magic artifact for over a month," Miss Modeste said, her tone biting.

I did not try to explain I'd been in the hospital for two weeks, or that I didn't have a case file before today. "I am working on it now. Do you have any information beyond Dr. Kaufman's notes from the convention? I discussed this in some depth with him at the time."

"I was not aware," Ms. Modeste said, her voice artificially polite. "That you were acquainted with the Grandmaster."

"We have met. If that is all, I will get to it I have a possible lead."

"I'm coming with you," Mr. Minors demanded with false bravado.'

"*Non, absolument pas.*"

"French," Leslie snorted derisively. She used to think it was charming.

"My partner is not available and there is no one who can properly escort you." I would have preferred to say "babysit" but this was already difficult enough. "Neither of you is a mage or above. I cannot be responsible. Good night." I turned to leave and almost made it to the hallway.

"But I—" Minors started but shut up as Ms. Modeste glared at him.

She turned that glare on me. "May I have a minute?" She did not wait for an answer but stood up and followed me out the door. She closed it behind her, leaving us alone in the hallway. "I just want to say you won't get an apology from me. Nor do I expect one from you."

"That is fine."

"And would it kill you to use a damn contraction?"

"*Puet être.*" I turned on my heel to make a grand exit, but she grabbed me on my right shoulder with her left hand and spun me back. Before I could protest, she said, "There's something else." Her tone went quiet and devoid of anger, but still not friendly. "Something I found out and do *not* want that weasel to know." Her hand still on my shoulder, she led me down the hall.

I cocked my head at her inquisitively.

"There was one artifact in the Childress estate that wasn't left to the museum because it isn't Egyptian. It's a Babylonian clay tablet."

"And this is relevant how?"

"The tablet was found in Egypt, in the same dig where the amulet was found, but it is much older. It wasn't translated until I looked at it, as far as I can tell." Her words came quick as her glance darted to the interview room. "It references the artifact, and this." She took out her phone and showed me a photo, a close-up of the ancient tablet. I could see the fine detailed restoration, her specialty, but the sigil revealed made my blood run cold. It was hard to make out, but I could see a pentagon. Unlike most mystical items, it did not have a star inside but a jumble of x's, #'s, and tiny circles. Just enough to hint what it referred to, and enough to know it was evil. "The old gods have not been a factor since the opening. "Ner—"

"Do not say that name!" Lesli snapped.

"That is nothing but a myth," I protested.

"So was magic, until it wasn't. What about the Egyptian gods? What do you know of them?"

"Magic was bound in Egypt over four thousand years ago. When the djinn were released, they imitated the gods they knew. The djinn are mischievous, but they have not tried to bring us a god of evil. I cannot imagine one of them acting as a Babylonian demon.

Look, Del. I am not happy with what happened, but I don't want to see you get hurt."

I pursed my lips. "You are calling me by my nickname? Well, now I know you are being serious," I tried to quip.

Her grip tightened on my arm. "Scared, Del. I'm very scared, and you should be, too."

I nodded my understanding and turned away. This time she did not try to stop me, and I did not look back.

Chapter Two

The weather here is weird and while it does not rain often in Southern California, we were getting about our annual average tonight. It would be a soggy time waiting for the clown, but what are you going to do?

With the added data from vice, I determined he was working a spiral pattern, starting from the convention center. Looking at a street map, I just had to figure out if he was looking for cash or a good time girl.

Vice gave me a sketchy list of games and girls, and I didn't know if I could rely on their information. I could call Chelsea, the "notorious pimp" Cooper referred to, but that could get awkward. She didn't visit me in the hospital, but did call several times. I was beginning to look forward to those calls.

I pushed my non-existent love life from my brain and studied the pattern. I identified a very likely target: a pawnshop open until midnight.

It was just after eight, so I decided to drive by my favorite coffee shop and get some caffeinated consolation for the night. That turned out to be the first of my mistakes. The perp struck early, and I pulled up to the likely target just as he as pulling away. A plump, blonde pawnshop clerk stood on the sidewalk and cheerfully waved goodbye to the thief.

I waited to let the ancient white van pull out ahead of me. It was dented in several places and the sides were covered in a cheap, garishly painted advertisement. "GRINS! CHUCKLES! GUFFAWS! Birthdays, Weddings, Corporate Events! I do 'em all!" Subtle guy, *mon dieu*.

"Ok, *Chuckles*. Let us see where you are taking that pretty girl's cash box," I muttered as I slowly pulled into the street after him.

14

Cat Scan

No need for a high-speed chase, the van was lit up and could be seen for a block. I would just follow him home and make the bust. That was smart. Not calling in for backup was stupid. I mean, he was just a clown, right?

Seriously, who expects a clown to get the drop on them? I was the lucky idiot who followed him to a self-storage facility on the outskirts of town. An old ramshackle block of individual units, most of which stood empty. The door to the unit was open and I entered, gun drawn. I felt confident he was unaware of my presence.

The clown might not be the brightest, but he was cunning, and I was overconfident.

A ringing blow knocked me out cold on the floor. As the grey, concrete floor faded to black I had a fleeting notion that I had royally screwed up.

I woke slowly on the cold damp concrete, my hands bound behind me, a cricket bat sporting some of what I suspected to be my blood laying several feet away.

Chuckles sat in a metal folding chair, his forearms resting on the chair back. He looked down at me, make-up hastily wiped from his face. A cat sat on the ground by him right beside an ornate Egyptian Usekh collar, they kind you see in pictures of gods or nobles. The adornment glinted with rectangles of lapis lazuli and was held together with gold links, but the winged Isis amulet was around the cat's neck supported by some of the gold and jewels He put the amulet on the cat? He was a sensitive so he must not be able to touch it without consequences. That was information I could use.

That was when she spoke to me. I shook my head. Not a smart move but I was trying to assess damage and understand why I imagined the cat talking.

"You better do something, he'll hurt you," the cat said very matter-of-factly, as if unconcerned by my endangerment.

"What do you suggest?" I thought at her, but she didn't react. Maybe her telepathy only worked one way. I shook my head again, not having learned my lesson. Nausea slipped over me. I repeated my question out loud.

"Who're you talking to?" Chuckles demanded.

"I was asking the cat for help," I retorted.

Chuckles chuckled. "Yer gonna be waiting a while for an answer, bro. Cat's don't talk."

"Yes," I agreed. "That would be stupid."

He stood up and walked over to me. He was maybe a little over twenty, with short blonde hair and a flabby, squishy, physique. I could see in his eyes he did not know what to do with me.

His options were: kill me, or mind wipe me.

My Haitian grandmother, a powerful mambo, raised me in the *Voudon* tradition, and I am a fully trained *houngan*, but aside from the ability to smell magic, I have no talent. For protection I have always relied on a few wards my *grand-mère* put on me but that wouldn't save me from an Object of Power.

The clown's cellphone rang. He looked at the incoming number and walked back out the unit door to take the call.

"He isn't very good at his magic," the cat continued, still facing away from me. "No telling what damage he would do trying to control you. Plus, you're a male. He enjoys hurting males."

"So, why are his targets female?"

"It's public. He prefers alone time with his male victims."

I shivered. "I am still open to suggestions," I said, struggling against the ropes that held me. Maybe making balloon animals gave Chuckles some experience with knots, these would not give.

The cat turned. She was some sort of sleek Siamese mix, her fur chocolate brown with sky blue eyes set in an obsidian face, with matching boots and tail. Once she faced me, I could see clearly her collar supported the amulet, definitely the winged Isis. Even without talent I could sense it was old. And powerful. "Wait. Am I talking to the cat, or the amulet?"

"I am not the cat," she admitted. "Well, I am in the cat, for now." She stopped and tilted her head to one side. "Maybe I am a cat. I mean I feel like a cat. I really don't remember much."

Outside the unit I heard a silly laugh and snippets of a ridiculous voice. Then I heard him clearly. "So, you are offering full RNC status? I'll be with The McConnel himself?"

RNC. I'd heard that somewhere before. Something to do with vice. I had no clue about McConnel but made a note to find out.

"Are you a demon?" I asked the cat, expecting a denial.

Instead, as the cat replied I felt her give a telepathic shrug. "I don't know. I live in the amulet, with the other. Westley doesn't know about us."

"The clown?"

"Yes. I don't talk to him. His brain is. . ." Shoulders moved in a feline shiver. "Eeeewwww."

Westley came back in, smiling. He stopped smiling when he saw me. "Why were you following me?"

"You robbed a pawnshop, and a bank, more than one actually."

He smiled and said with ridiculous self-assurance. "Those women

16

gave me the money because I was nice to them."

"You used magic to coerce them."

He tapped his forehead. "You can't steal it if someone gives it to you. She's the one who did the stealing."

I abandoned trying to explain reality. "Then I will arrest you because you just confessed to receiving stolen property."

He snarled at me and picked up the cat.

"EEEWW," she said. "I hate this part." I didn't know if she meant the magic, or his touch.

Westley walked over and stood over me. "You are going to forget that you found me."

I closed my eyes and concentrated. I did not feel any coercion. Yet.

"In fact, you're gonna forget you were even looking for me, hell you might even forget how to walk. That would be funny, watching you flop around." He scratched the cats' ears and grinned. "Like a weird kinda land fish, right Puffy?" He giggled as he scratched her head.

She cringed.

Then he touched the amulet, just the tip of his finger. Pain shot across his face.

I felt a mental chainsaw revving up. He was not going to surgically change my memories but rip out a chunk of my mind and he was going to enjoy it.

Chapter Three

The cat struggled and I felt a moment respite as Westley lost contact with the amulet.

"The power is not bound to him," the cat reminded me.

Information I could use. I rolled over and gave him a condescending glare. "You have to touch the amulet?" I smirked. "Using an unbound talismans could be...painful."

He paused. "Yeah."

"It burns you, right? You didn't bind it to you, *mon amie*?" I tried to move to a sitting position. I failed. "Without binding, then anyone who touches the amulet can use it. Even on you."

"I've been doing fine so far," he snapped defensively.

I attempted a shrug. "Suit yourself. But I could teach you a binding spell. No one could ever take your necklace it away from you."

He glared at me with suspicious eyes. "Why would you help me?"

"To keep my brain intact."

He shook his head.

"Once you bind it," I said, "you will have much more control. You can make me forget about you without additional damage. The police could take it away from you and you would still have the power, if the power was bound to you."

"I don't think it works like that," the cat said.

Boy, am I glad he cannot hear you, I thought.

He thought about it, frowning with the effort. "I'm supposed to give it to somebody."

"You could give it and retain the power."

"I don't know. They're not people you can cross."

"But," I said with as much authority as I could muster, "if the power is bound to you, you have bargaining power. You would be important because they would need you to channel the power."

"Wouldn't they just kill him?" the cat said. I was so glad the clown couldn't hear her.

He considered that. "This spell is simple, right? You're not going to try to send me off on a scavenger hunt."

"*Non*, all you need is chalk."

"What color?"

"It doesn't matter as long as you can power a circle."

He guffawed at me. "Anybody can power a circle."

I couldn't. "You won't be summoning anything. You just need to sit in the circle with the amulet in your hands. Not touching any other living thing while you say the words of binding."

"That easy?"

"Well, you have to wait for it to recharge.":

"Recharge?"

"Isn't that why you use it every twelve hours?"

He laughed until he snorted. "Recharge? You think you are so smart?"

"I have the Talent," he snapped, his voice betraying a deep-seated rage. "I can make it work any time I want to." He paused and glared at the amulet. "But I can only touch it for a few seconds."

"Does it burn hot, or cold?"

"Cold."

"Good, that is easier. You can wear gloves; you just need to touch it to your bare forehead seven times and say the words of binding. Just touch, you do not have to hold it there."

His brow creased and his mouth looked like he was chewing something. "One minute." He pulled on a pair of gloves and then he went for the cat. The cat made a half-hearted gesture to escape but he eventually snagged her and removed the amulet. He put the cat down and the animal slumped on the cold floor.

Chuckles stepped outside the unit.

I looked at the cat. She wasn't talking, just sitting there licking her paw. She stood up and padded around. "Meoow."

"Be careful." I heard in my head. The entity, or maybe my concussion hallucination, was still in the cat.

Westley came back with an oversized pack of sidewalk chalk markers.

I finally managed to sit up. "Hold the amulet and draw the circle around you."

He selected white chalk and drew the circle, free hand and almost perfect. Power circles don't have to be perfect, just complete, but the closer to a true circle, the more powerful. I cannot use magic, but I can sense it, and as he formed the circle, I could smell the enormity of his power, the cinnamon burn of strength. Big ability, small intellect; a very dangerous combination.

There was an awkward pause and he looked up at me. "Now what?"

"The amulet is dedicated to Isis and Ra," I lied.

"You mean Horus."

"*Non*," I shook my head. "Rookie mistake. The eye of Horus faces the other way."

"Horus is the left eye." His assertion was strong, but I felt just the tiniest waiver.

"*Oui*. You look at the eyes of Ra and Horus like on a face. Horus is the one on the left, but that's looking at it, if it were on your face, it would be on the right. You are the center of the spell."

He frowned and I had the impression he was not buying it, but his jaw was working again. He cocked his head to one side, considering. "What happens if I invoke the wrong god?"

"Nothing, there will be no power."

He frowned and I could almost hear rusty gears trying to decide. Finally, he gave me a little sneer. "Nah, man. I think you're tryna rip me off somehow." He took out his phone and started thumbing the screen. "Wow," he said suddenly, then looked up at me with a befuddled grin. "Reddit says you're not completely full of shit. So, how do I do this, Mister Egyptian Kitsch Expert?"

"Power the circle to keep the energy in. Hold the amulet in both hands. Say 'In respect of the power of Ra and Isis, I bind this power to me.'"

"In English?" he said dubiously.

"*Mais oui*. While ancient Egyptian would be more appropriate, the old gods understand all languages. Say that seven times, touch the amulet to your forehead each time, but pour your power into it."

He looked at the circle and waved his hand over the lines.

He started the spell and I worked to free myself again. The cat was, well, lying like a cat, collapsed on in a warm spot with no intention of moving.

I felt powerful forces building in the circle, more than one person should be able to channel. The cinnamon was joined by sharp, pungent pepper scent. I felt a cold chill at the thought of what might be in the amulet. Westley felt it, too, and he stared at the amulet with shining eyes. He made the first incantation to Ra and Isis. He was not going to be happy when it didn't work.

The ropes felt ready to give.

He continued the incantation, but I felt a presence. Something off.

He touched the amulet to his forehead for the sixth time and held it there. His grin widened and became more malevolent.

The cat still looked relaxed, but I could feel a wave of fear from her. "It has him." I mentally felt her tense and prepare.

As he started the seventh repetition, still holding the amulet to his forehead, the cat sprang into the circle.

This was not supposed to happen.

"This is not good!" the cat screamed in my head. "The other is present!"

The clown had made another rookie mistake. I told him to power the circle to keep the energy in. He should have used a bit more energy to keep everything else out.

The cat landed in his lap and a psychic wave flowed out of the circle.

The clown stood, ignoring the cat.

"No!" Another voice boomed in my mind. "In the name of Isis and Horus, I bind *you* to me!"

The cat shrieked and jumped away.

Westley screamed, then fell silent. He raised his head and chuckled. Not the silly sound he made earlier, but a real sound of relief and amusement. He no longer exhibited that "squishy" quality, now he seemed hard, cold like marble. He placed the amulet around his neck and looked at the cat.

I felt a chill and knew that what I was looking at was no longer human.,

She stood back up, walked over to where he was sitting, and bumped his leg with her head. A gesture I recognized as "Pet me, dammit."

Westley complied.

"You are not Westley, are you?"

"No, it isn't," the cat said dismissively.

I jerked my head in her direction. "Are you still in the cat, or in Westley?"

"I am content to be a cat, and I cannot compete against the other." She brushed her face against the man's thigh and rolled over to have her belly rubbed.

The entity smiled and idly caressed the feline. Whatever was in Westley now turned that wide, horrifying smile to me.

A few years ago, we were after a true psycho working in the black arts. We got him surrounded, but there were too many cops without magic familiarization training. The psycho managed to summon hellfire and incinerated ten men, but he couldn't control it. Even as it consumed him, he grinned. A hard grin of hatred. The look of a man with nothing left to lose and the desire to burn the world with him. That exact grin was plastered on what used to be Westley's face as it stood, careful to show courtesy to the cat, and looked around, dismissing me as harmless.

Oh, Leslie, there is indeed something here to be afraid of.

The entity considered its surroundings, examined the chalk markers and selected a black one. Eyes rolled back into its head, showing perfect white. It squatted and drew a large, perfect circle on the floor marking the cardinal points with lines that might have been cuneiform. Then, inside the circle, it shaped a pentagon. Westley's stolen limbs jerked, spasmed like a nonhuman frenetic dance. A mockery of ecstasy.

I felt cold terror. This was magic of the darkest sort. Power from Horus and Isis channeled to the will of a magician, or whatever entity this was, dedicated to death, chaos and war would bring bloodshed. Holocaust levels of bloodshed. Millions tortured. What the *hell* did I release?

I knew the legends, but the reality was too raw. I wasn't prepared to cope with something so overwhelming.

The damn cat recognized that, too, and was cozying up to him. *La petite chienne* was joining the winning side.

The entity smiled as it made the final sigil more ornate, an act of love. It was the one from the Babylonian tablet, but now complete and unmistakable.

Lips moved in an incantation, speaking words that made no sense to me. Likely it could speak ancient Egyptian, or Babylonian.

The entity paused and turned to glare at me. There was no trace of humanity left. Maybe a demon or a piece of an Egyptian or Babylonian god, but nothing mortal and nothing I wanted to deal with. A cold chill enveloped me as I realized I'd just been nominated as the sacrifice, but Westley had neglected to procure a knife. The entity snarled, deep-seated frustration until it caught sight of the cricket bat, something I was more familiar with than a Louisville Slugger.

An expression of cold joy spread, relishing the idea of smashing my skull for ritual blood.

The entity stepped out of the circle and grabbed my collar. I tried to squirm away, but it effortlessly carried me to the edge of the ritual space.

The being dropped me onto my face. I tried to roll over, but a powerful foot stamped the center of my back, holding me in place.

It stood before the black designs and raised the cricket bat in ritual benediction. The cat was right by its ankle, her tongue flickering in anticipation as she drew herself into a tense crouch. She didn't say anything, but I felt she was feverishly watching, waiting for something. Likely waiting to taste my blood.

Heat radiated from the circle. Soon flames filled the ritual space, swirling like a tornado.

He raised the bat and held the handle with both hands, ready to descend in a murderous swing.

Chapter Four

I clenched my eyes, anticipating the impact, and was surprised when he stopped his swing, staggered and bellowed.

The Siamese cat was entwined in his feet. It tried to kick her away, but she slipped behind it, let out a vicious yowl and clawed deep, bloody furrows into the entity's calf.

The cruel monster that now possessed Chuckles' body screamed.

The sound was a mixture of agony and shock. The entity probably had not felt pain in thousands of years. But it made a rapid recovery; smiling again as it hit the cat a glancing blow with the cricket bat, knocking the feline across the floor.

The cat froze for a split second with its back arched and hair standing on end. Her eyes gleamed with pure distilled rage as she laid her ears back. "I gave my body to keep the world safe from you. I will not let you go free now." She attacked, but with a combination of human tactics and animal fury, she feinted to the left, dodged the next blow and leapt onto the thing's chest, her claws scrambling to get to its face.

It screamed, dropped the bat and clawed at the attacking animal. It screamed again as it jerked the cat away, leaving angry, bloody streaks on its face

The cat wriggled out of the entity's grip and leapt away. The thing bellowed, reached down, picked up the bat and threw it at the cat. The feline dodged and retreated to a corner.

The circle of flames glowed brighter.

The creature was pissed and determined to hit the cat. It stomped across the floor to retrieve its weapon.

I struggled harder while I was momentarily forgotten.

The cat backed further into the corner. It must have been my psychic link to the cat, but I knew she was not afraid, just preparing her attack. She bolted from the corner and cut around the creature.

The entity bellowed and went after her.

She headed for the ritual space and dodged away at the last second.

It followed her, stopping short of the circle and spun to her, bat at the ready. It noticed me again and its attention made me feel ill.

The cat crouched. Then I saw her hunch her shoulders, preparing to jump.

The creature held the bat ready with its offhand outstretched to protect his face from the cat's oncoming claw assault.

The cat leapt, but she was only pretending to jump high; instead, she streaked across the floor and swiped a claw at the creature's foot. The thing jerked its foot back of the way and the cat missed. The creature kicked hard, sending the poor feline flying across the room where this time she lay silent. In fact, the whole room went eerily quiet. For a moment I couldn't even hear the roar of the swirling flame. I looked into the circle and saw the chalk line smudged where the entity had pulled away from the cat's attack. For a split second it had stepped over the outline and into the ritual space, releasing the built-up power.

It didn't notice its error and was looking around, puzzled at the silence.

The cat moved awkwardly to her feet then sat, idly licking a paw.

The thing bellowed and tried to step toward the cat, and then realized its back foot was stuck. Energy from the circle spilled though the marred chalk line and enveloped its leg.

I saw fear flood the monster-human's eyes, then resignation. Westley's body flew backward into the circle like it had been slammed by an invisible mac truck.

The roar of the flame returned and was almost drowned out by shrill screams from the thing that had once been Chuckles the Clown.

Psychic energy slammed against my being, mixed with the creature's frantic screams. The combination made me grit my teeth.

The screams silenced abruptly, or maybe I went deaf, but the psychic energy still pounded my body.

Green fire enveloped the thing, flickering across its skin and face but not burning it, yet.

A new blaze ignited along the drawn circle and surged toward the center. When the two columns of flame it joined, Chuckles' burnt flesh became a living pillar of flame.

I struggled against the bonds, certain they were loosened, but I still could not free my hands.

The pillar pulsed and grew, shooting up through the roof and shining into the heavens. Angry laughter filled the air. No, not an audible sound, but one I heard in my soul. And that maniacal laughter froze my essence. The entity that had inhabited the clown shed that appropriated mortal body, becoming some kind of fire elemental.

Living fire in the service of death.

Westley was consumed as the sacrifice; it no longer needed my blood to build its power.

The entity had no face, but somehow, I still saw it grinning at me. The flames danced, eager to slip from the confines of the circle.

Pulses of power gathered into a space that went beyond white hot, beyond the core of a star. The living plasma launched at me, then stopped at the edge of the circle. The breach that had allowed the entity to be drawn into the circle had not broken the seal completely, only changed it.

"Rookie mistake," the cat said.

Westley had created the first circle to contain energy, and the entity did the same, intending to use my blood to free the flames. A *physical* being could step outside the line, but not one of pure, remorseless, murderous energy.

The entity realized the problem at the same time I did. Red and green flames leapt about as like some monstrous Christmas display as it gathered even more power to escape the circle, and I knew that it was drawing on the power of the sacrifice.

The cat nudged me and used her paw to bat the piece of white chalk to me. I grabbed the six-inch piece with my teeth and squirmed to get around the circle. The markings at the cardinal points were the key, I had to deface them before the flames reached critical mass. Once the entity created the power, it would break free. The release would drive psychic living fire for miles. Worse, the psychic hatred would travel hundreds, possibly even thousands, of miles. Most people would not even notice, but the hundreds of thousands with any touch of the Talent would be filled with that cruel rage.

The being realized what I was doing, and the power grew into light beyond anything mortal man should see. Fortunately, it was still contained, and I could minimize the effect by looking away. But there were still spots before my eyes and halos around what I could see. The room was bathed in red like I was looking through a film of blood. I slithered and writhed my way to the abomination of a sigil drawn at the north point, then used the chalk in my teeth to obliterate it.

"Hurry," the cat said.

The flame howled rage as the dark energy pulsed, still trapped, for the moment. The glyphs were all equidistant, several feet between each.

I trained capoeira, a martial art built on dancing. We have a technique for folding and twisting our bodies to move. A ju-jitsu practitioner would call the move "shrimping." My practice gave me the ability to make my way around the circle quickly. The chalk gritted against my teeth. Good that it was not complicated to deface the sigils. The cat kept with me, mewing encouragement and nudging me along.

The last sigil defaced, I spat out the chalk, but my efforts seemed in vain, or at least too late. No more power was going in, but it was still working with what it had. It processed the last of the sacrifice and pulsed with ultraviolet heat that I sensed more than felt. Soon, he would focus all of that to break the circle from the inside.

That would release the full cataclysmic power.

But a circle broken from the outside, with such forces raging within...

I knew what I had to do.

I had to break the circle. Then the energy would, theoretically, rebound on itself, and the physical and mystical vacuum created by the heat should send the creature back to the prison it came from.

Theoretically.

The only physical thing I had to break the circle was me. I had to inch my body across the line before the circle evaporated. The creature had made the mistake of stepping over the line. Just like him, my body would be incinerated, but the entity would be gone.

I inched closer.

"I got this," the cat said.

I imagined her tiny feline body turning to ash.

But the cat did not throw herself across. Instead, she batted the conveniently available cricket bat with her paw, like a toy mouse, until she edged it over the line.

Nothing happened.

I was out of ideas as a strange howl assaulted my ears. A sound of a dozen freight trains roared over my head as the wind entered from the top of the circle, whooshing through the hole burned in the roof.

The wind initially fanned the fire, and the flames surged brighter. I cannot describe how bright. Even my clenched eyes seared in that intense brilliance.

Then the light was gone, and the room was silent. I slowly opened my eyes. At first, I only saw yellow, then that slowly gave way to swirls of reds and violets. My vision cleared unnaturally fast and shortly the room came into view. My vision was a hazy black and white and trying to focus gave me a headache, but the world was dim and still.

Slowly, but steadily, like watching a time lapse video, my vision fully returned, leaving halos around everything, the floor was restored, and the lines of black chalk smoldered. In the center lay the amulet looking untouched by flame.

"He was not a nice man," the cat said.

I rolled over to look at her. "*Non*, he was not. But Westley did not deserve that."

"I disagree; I tasted his mind. But as bad as that was, I've tasted the other's mind for longer than I can remember. I've done my duty. It is back in its prison."

"Duty?"

"It once possessed an important traveler, and I lured it into the amulet so the priests could bind it. It is my sacred duty to ensure it stays." She licked at the blood on her paw. "Westley's incompetence saved many lives. Besides, he didn't go anywhere, he's in the amulet with the other one." She mentally shrugged. "He is the guardian now."

"And you?"

"The amulet can contain two. Westley and the other. The cat allowed me to bind with her and I can stay bound to the cat, as long as she lets me."

"She lets you?"

"I do not have the power to possess an unwilling host. We made a deal. I get the food, she eats it. I had to interact with Westley, and she gets to sleep in a sun-warmed spot on his floor."

"And if the cat wants you to leave?"

A telepathic shrug. "I think I will finally die." She sounded sad, but with an air of resignation.

Chapter Five

The cat walked up to me, unsteady on her paws, as if she was drunk.

"Are you injured?"

"Everything hurts, but I think I will be okay."

The little ball of fur saved my life. "I'll get you to a vet," I promised sincerely. "Do you have a name?" I still lay on the cold stone floor trying to get my hands free. You would think that a magic fire tornado would have brought some attention. My sight was mostly recovered, the violets and reds faded, but there was still a halo around anything producing light.

"The cat's name is Cocopuff."

"And you?"

She sank down on her haunches and looked embarrassed. "I knew things, just a few minutes ago, but without the amulet... my memories are faded, disjointed, as if waking from a dream. I am a cat, but I am sure I've not always been one."

"So, what should I call you?"

The feline mentally shrugged. "What would be a good name for a cat?"

I looked at the amulet. "Isis?"

Her feline shoulders sank. "I think that would be tempting fate."

"Bastet?" I offered.

"Too obvious." She licked a paw. "What the kids today would call being basic."

I sighed and thought hard. "Pakhet?"

I could feel her mental grin as she translated. "She who scratches."

"I saw the way you tore into that thing." Now I felt her mentally...blush?

I redoubled my efforts to get free, twisting and wriggling my wrists until the cord binding them was wet with my blood.

Pakhet started to pace nervously.

I looked up at her. "You okay?"

"The cat is hungry." Pakhet said, a trace of worry in her voice. "She thinks I have violated our agreement and is considering casting me out. The only thing stopping her is the pain. She doesn't want to deal with that, yet."

I struggled harder against my bonds. "Can't you hunt a mouse or something?"

I felt her psychic sigh. "I don't know how to use cat senses. I don't know how to hunt. I just kept finding where the clown hid the kitty treats."

"Can you let the cat hunt?"

"She says that is not our deal. If she gets hungrier, she may be willing to deal with the discomfort, but not with me."

"*Merde*." I chafed another layer of skin off my wrists. The bloody rope was slicker, and I thought I felt more give.

I heard sliding metal. "Delacroix?" A familiar voice called out. I heard a metallic clatter as he tried to get through the door.

"Here!" I called out, then turned to the cat and spoke quieter. "Tell the cat I get her the best *damné* tuna she's ever had if she gives us an hour."

"Cocopuff. Her name is Cocopuff."

"Fine," I hissed. "You need to hide and let Cocopuff take control."

"She won't. The pain."

"How bad is it?"

"Bearable, for me."

"You have to get her to take control, it is urgent."

The cat's eyes glowed for just a second.

"I promise to feed Cocopuff with the finest of treats every hour, if she will just let you hide for a few minutes."

"Cats are not fond of delayed gratification," Pakhet said in anguish.

I heard a clatter as the door came free.

"She gets to pick the treats," Pakhet said with a tinge of hope in her mental voice. "And she wants a trip to the fish market."

"Fine."

"Meeeeow."

Alan, a forensic sorcerer with CSI rushed in. "He's here!" he yelled over his shoulder.

He was the reason I told her to hide inside. If Alan learned about

30

her, she would go from house cat to lab rat, he was far stricter with procedure than his boss.

Alan quickly cut me loose. I rubbed at my chafed wrists while he shone a light in my eyes, checking my pupils and making clucking sounds. While he focused on me, I saw Leslie Modeste enter, followed by the unpleasant Mr. Minors.

Leslie surveyed the damage. "What happened?" she demanded.

"Terrible things," I said.

"The amulet is here, and it looks fine," Minors pronounced, unimpressed by the destruction around him.

"Details, Delacroix," Leslie said with simulated patience.

I told her an edited version of the story without mentioning the talking cat. I owed the little bit of fur; as did thousands, though they would never know it.

She saw the cat, stooped and held up a finger. "Pretty kitty." She stretched out to offer the finger to the cat.

Cocopuff backed up.

"Do you have a home?"

"She is mine."

Leslie looked doubtful. "Since when?"

"Since I picked up that box with my things you left in a storage unit," I lied, allowing some of the bitterness of the memory seep out. Twice I have felt such emptiness; once when my first love, Renee, married another. Bound by her families wishes. And Leslie…

Modeste had three cats, and a horse, when we were a couple. They were her excuse to procrastinate after we agreed to move in together. "I realized I missed the cats more than you." Another lie.

I caught a glint of hurt in her eyes, but it was gone instantly.

Modeste's attention swung violently to Minors. "Don't touch that." She demanded as he waved his hand over the amulet. She left me with Alan and stomped away.

"Seriously," Alan said quietly, "since when do you have a cat?"

"She is my responsibility. It is a private matter." I looked up at him. "I don't suppose you have anything a cat would eat with you?"

He shook his head. "Sorry. Look, your pupils seem fine, but you got a bad lump on your head. Even with magic healing you can't take much more."

I nodded.

"We called an ambulance."

"My cat," I objected.

"We'll keep her for a few days at the shelter."

"*Non.*"

31

"You know the rules. Any living thing involved in a MDE has to be observed for seventy-two hours."

Merde, they were invoking the Magical Destructive Event protocols.

Another CSI carried in a plastic crate.

When Cocopuff saw the animal crate, she arched her back and hissed.

"Alan, *mon ami*, she is important to me. She was barely an observer," I lied. I do not like lying, but I was getting in my full allotment that night."

He gave me a suspicious side-eye. "Delacroix, I never pegged you as a cat lover."

I held out my folded hands in a beseeching manner. "*Tanpri souple*." The words once forbidden at Grand-mère's table tumbled from my lips. "That little kitty saved my life, once. You could say we bonded."

Alan looked around like he was about to do something furtive. "You have no idea how much easier this would be if that cat was never here, but rules are rules."

"And your boss?'

"Welles makes up her own rules." His shoulders shrugged. "Look, if I let you take her away, promise this isn't going to bite me in the ass."

"Promise. The cat will not be an issue."

"What cat?" Alan said. "Sorry, I don't know what you are talking about. I got a full crew going to be here in two minutes." He puffed out his cheeks. "Would be bad if they found a cat."

I struggled to my feet and walked over to Cocopuff. She let me pick her up.

Modeste glanced at us, as if sensing something. I held my breath, and her attention went back to the amulet. She glowered at the cursed necklace.

"I will take her out to the car." I intended to rush to my car, but all I could manage was a wobbling shuffle. I reached the car and got the cat stowed, just as headlights signaled the arrival of the team.

"Cocopuff is really hungry," Pakhet said.

"Ask her to give me fifteen minutes."

"She doesn't understand minutes, or hours for that matter. I've calmed her down with descriptions of the great food you are going to provide."

"Okay, Scheherazade, you don't have to go for a thousand and one nights, just keep the cat entertained for fifteen minutes." I closed the door. As an SUV pulled up to me., I was relieved that Lenore, chief of the night forensic team, was not one of the passengers. No way I could have hidden Pakhet from her, although she would be more understanding.

"Hey, Steve." I addressed her deputy. "Alan has my statement. I'm okay, but he insists that I go to the hospital. I got hit on the head again."

"I'll get an ambulance."

"Alan called one, but I don't need it."

"Aren't you supposed to wait—"

"I'm fine."

"We don't know that," Steve spoke over me. "You gotta lay down until the ambulance gets here."

"Alright," I snapped. "Let me call someone to get my car. Vlad's off today." That and the fact that the first glow of morning was on the horizon meant he was not an option. The whole event seemed to last minutes, but somehow hours had passed. No wonder the cat was hungry. "Just give me a minute."

I climbed into the driver seat of my car. Cocopuff yowled from the back seat, voicing her hunger. I ignored her and made a call to my workout buddy, and good friend, Gillian. I hoped she would understand me pulling her away from bed, and her wife.

"Del?" she answered, her voice thick with sleep.

"I need a favor."

"You got it."

"It may seem trivial but trust me it is vitally important." I told her where I was and that there was a starving cat in the back seat. My catus ex machina in this situation: Gillian was a real animal lover and proud cat mom, herself.

"I can be there in ten minutes with the cat food," she assured me.

I left the key for her under the floor mat and got back out. Gillian would hurry, because I asked, but could she get there in time?

* * *

I was released from the hospital late in the day. I met with Gillian and found Pakhet playing with Muffin, a frisky long-haired tabby. Although playing was not the correct term, more like analyzing, as if she needed instruction on how to be a cat.

I got her back to my place where she promptly hid under the couch.

My phone rang. Before I could say hello, a voice spoke in rushed tones. "Detective Delacroix?"

"*Oui*, Ms. Falcata." I smiled at the sound of her voice. Of course it was me, who did she think she was calling? Our calls were not that frequent, and though they had become friendly of late, almost intimate, she always started phone conversations with an oddly formal lilt. "I heard you had another concussion." She struggled to sound nonchalant, but I was pretty sure I detected a note of concern.

"I am fine. They insist I stay home for the next two weeks." Now I was the one trying to sound nonchalant. "Perhaps we could do lunch?"

"Sorry, Detective, but I'm in Chicago. It's a tricky matter. I might be several days."

"Another time?"

"Yeah."

I think she heard the disappointment in my voice. We talked a bit about impersonal things and then I pleaded exhaustion and hung up.

I sat on the couch, wondering if *la petite* was going to show. I should have gone to sleep. *Ma grand-mère* would know not to call if I was asleep. She always sent a psychic warning before she visited. I felt a tension in the air, like the quiet before an island storm. Pakhet felt it too and she nosed out from under the couch. The air shimmered and my *grand-mère*, or rather her astral projection, was sitting in a rocking chair in my front room. I never understood why she bothered projecting the rocking chair.

"*Bonsoir, grand-mère.*"

"English," she admonished. "It is our language now; we must be consistent."

"Yes, Grandmother."

"I am delighted ta see you are not dead." No matter how hard she tried she couldn't keep the island accent at bay. "I get da news reports, and your concussions seem to be too common."

"I'm fine. Just a headache. They let me out of the hospital."

She eyed the feline form skulking under the couch. She smiled. "And who is dat little one?" Then her voice changed, sharpened. "What is dat?"

"A cat, with an inhabiting spirit."

Pakhet crawled completely out from under the couch and studied my grandmother.

"What kinda spirit? A demon?"

"She says she's not a demon."

Pakhet nodded.

Grand-mère's eyes narrowed, and she smacked her lips. "Dat is exactly what a demon would say."

"She is terrified of being cast out. She can only stay with the cat's permission. I think that makes her rather un-demonic."

Grand-mère's projection looked satisfied, and she nodded. "So. She is like a loa, den."

"Yes, I suppose."

Grand-mère went on studying Pakhet and it occurred to me in that moment that if any human could win a staring contest with a cat, it would be my beloved grandmother. "But she is not like any loa I ever met; you agree?"

"I don't know. She was trapped in an ancient amulet. I think she was once human and female. Or I might perceive her as female because the cat is." I looked down at the cat.

Pakhet gave a shrug. "I was human, a person. I think I was female."

Grandmother steepled her fingers and raised them to her lips. "I knew I was coming ta you in a time of need, child. Now. You have in mind a resolution?"

Chapter Six
Two weeks later

"One moment, *s'il vous plaît.*," I said to the cat walking in front of me.

She stopped and turned her head, looking at me over her shoulder. Exasperation burned in her eyes.

"Pakhet?" I asked, just in case she was letting Cocopuff drive.

My ears heard a long-suffering meow, but in my head, I heard, in tones just as long suffering, "Yessss, what do you want?"

"If I am going to bring you to work with me, we will have to establish that you are well behaved. Obedient."

"Obedient?" she said, projecting her distaste into my mind.

"You want to stay in the apartment?"

"No. There is nothing to do there."

I gave a brief thought to my apparently hideous attempt to leave the TV on for her to watch. Her frustration about trying to use the remote built up and her displeasure was nearly a psychic shock aimed at me when I got home. "If you want to go with me, you have to pretend that you are only a cat. Once people accept you, you can stretch your horizon a bit."

I felt her sigh. "I don't think you know much about cats. Are you confusing me with a dog?"

I rolled my eyes. "This is my first day back." The healer took good care of my second concussion in a month. I was able to return to active duty after a mere two weeks with little more reminder of my ordeal than a low-grade headache if I focused too hard on reading. "So, if you will get behind me and follow me in, and let me pick you up, this will go easier."

Pakhet's turn to roll her eyes.

"Also, while we are there, I have someone I want you to meet. She may be in a position to help you with your...issues." I initially thought to ensure Pakhet never encountered Lenore Welles, but her lack of an amulet to retreat into if the cat objected was an ongoing issue. Cocopuff threatened to cast her out daily.

Her glowing green cat eyes narrowed. "You trust her?"

"With my life."

"And she won't lock me away?" Pakhet didn't sound convinced.

I had to admit, to myself, there was a slight possibility. Only slight, and only if Lenore thought people would be in a danger because of Pakhet's freedom. Lenore has been known to play fast and loose with the rules, if she thinks it's justified. "*Non*," I said, grateful Pakhet couldn't read my mind.

I felt a psychic frown as she considered it.

"Look, didn't I go out of my way to get a copy of your amulet made because you said it would make you feel more comfortable?"

She considered me for a minute. "Alright, I will behave, for now."

I sighed, picked up the cat—who was at least three pounds heavier than when we met. There was still about ten pounds of fish waiting for her, according to our bargain made that fateful night. Pakhet settled in my arms, her twitching tail the only sign of her unease, and I resumed my walk up to the precinct, Central Division, Los Diablos California police department. Inside the door, my favorite desk sergeant smiled up at me, her eyes framed by crow's-feet, furrowed among the other wrinkles in her face.

"Detective Delacroix. You're in awfully early." She paused and cocked her head to one side. "You are supposed to be here today. Right?"

"Good evening, Rosie. Yes, I have medical clearance. The captain called me in about some special project." I regarded my watch. "By chance, is Ms. Welles in?"

Rosie peered over her desk. "Is that your cat? Such a pretty kitty. What's her name?" The words tumbled out with more enthusiasm than I'd ever heard from the elder sergeant.

"*Oui*." The cat allowed me to hold her up. "She is called Pakhet." I scratched her behind the ears like I had the first week we'd been together. Since then, she'd become standoffish about her head scritches. I felt lucky to get this one in.

"Packet?"

"Pah-Khet," I said phonetically

"Oh. Nice collar." She regarded the winged Isis amulet around Pakhet's neck.

The reproduced amulet. Though it offered no real refuge, she was clearly comforted by the feel of the familiar object; though this one was made of brass and glass.

"Anyway," Rosie went on petting Pakhet as she spoke. "I don't think Ms. Welles ever leaves. So, yeah, she's in her lab."

As if summoned, Lenore Welles burst through the door from the back. "Ah, Del, the captain is waiting for you." Lenore Welles oversaw the night magical forensics team. I previously referred to her as The Great Lenore Welles, but that honorific felt too modest as I saw the depth of her power at work. Not that it had not taken a physical toll on her. She was barely thirty but looked older, especially around her eyes. When I met her, her hair had been raven's wing black and fell thickly to her waist. Six years ago. The powers she wielded gave it white streaks that eventually took over completely. She'd recently trimmed it into a short pixie cut. This afternoon it shone like pure silver, and I could not tell if that was a consequence of her magic use, or a cosmetic glamour. She was always working some kind of magic, and it gave off a powerful, penetrating scent that made me think of eucalyptus.

I consulted my apple watch. The clock face displayed on the screen let me know I had plenty of time but knew better than to protest. The captain was the type to always expect you to be ten minutes early, even if he felt no compulsion to arrive himself. He especially hated when you missed a deadline you did not know about. I looked at Pakhet and forced a smile. There was no possible good outcome of taking her into the captain's presence. "Rosie, would you be so kind as to watch Pakhet for a few minutes while I meet with the captain?"

The cat's head whipped around, and her eyes narrowed with evil intent.

"Please behave for the sergeant," I implored.

The cat gave a haughty flick of her head to dismiss me and settled back to let the desk sergeant keep stroking her.

We took about two steps when Lenore said quietly, "Okay Del, what's going on? That sure is an interesting, uuuuhhhhhh, cat and something you got there."

"*Oui*, there is indeed something odd about her. I need your assistance and discretion."

A smile played around her lips. "Ooh, Detective Delacroix, it sounds like you may intend to break the rules."

"Later, *s'il vous plaît*," I said to Lenore in a hushed tone. "Meet me in your office in five minutes after we finish."

She pursed her lips and nodded. The captain's door was open, and I knocked on the frame just as I noticed two other people in the office,

Ms. Leslie Modeste and Brad Minors. Leslie looked like she studied frumpy couture. The rumpled gray suit and lack of makeup implied that she was too busy to take care of the little things. Minors wore a suit and tie that made him look uncomfortable rather than professional.

"Well, it's time you two showed up." The captain glowered. "Take a seat."

Nice offer, but there was only one more chair. I nodded for Lenore to take it.

"Ms. Welles." The captain scowled at her. A scowl was actually his most friendly expression. "Have you finished the analysis of the amulet?"

Lenore leaned back in the chair, like she was in the most comfy place in the world. "A few days ago, actually."

"Why are we just hearing about this now?" Minors snapped.

Lenore gave a shrug, exactly as if to say to Minors, "I think you're nothing but pig shit." Then she continued to address the captain. "I was waiting for a consultation with an independent source."

"Like whom?" Leslie leaned forward, a gleam in her eye.

"Brother Kaufman, Grandmaster of the—"

Leslie cut Lenore off. "We know who Bobby is."

I blinked. The only other person to call him "Bobby" was Lenore, who was now studying my ex with one eyebrow raised.

"What does he say about the amulet?" Leslie prompted after Lenore absolutely seemed content to study her until we all turned to dust.

Lenore's expression didn't waver. "Just that he agrees with my assessment. It is a level three object of power."

"Which we are prepared for.," Minors said.

"But you shouldn't have it," Leslie countered. "The amulet is clearly a treasure of cultural importance in need of repatriation."

"*Might*, it *might* need repatriation," Minors retorted smugly. "There is no provenance that the item is not a modern reproduction. After all, the thing is in pristine condition. We don't know where he got it or when it was ensorcelled. Tell me, has any one of you great, mythic experts of the antiquities; has anyone checked to see if it's stamped 'Made in China?'" Minors waved his hands in a mockery of spell casting as he spoke, and I was frankly shocked he still had them by the time he shut up.

I started to ask him why his museum even wanted the thing if it was so clearly a fake when Lenore spoke up.

"We do know it's dangerous," Lenore said. "It is capable of holding two entities. We are sure that the clown is one of them, and the other is capable of enormous power."

"Of course, it's dangerous" Minors retorted. "That's what level three *means*. My only point here is that the museum is the rightful owners of the amulet, unless, of course, there is the unlikely determination it needs to be repatriated...to...some place."

The captain focused on Lenore. "Any reason why we can't hand it over to the museum?"

"No legal reason, no," Lenore said, drawing out uncertain words. "But ethically, it needs to be in a place where the sentient beings occupying the amulet can be fully researched and dealt with per law. The violent entity needs to be banished, and the clown freed to go to jail. Brother Kaufman has it now, and I recommend he keep it until we know more."

"Ridiculous!" Minors blurted. "We have resources just as good as the Gnostic Elite. And you've just admitted you have no legal reason to keep it from us."

The captain's mouth worked in a tight circle, and I knew he was wishing he had a cigar. "We will need to arrange a secure transfer. Ms. Welles, coordinate with the Nogs and make arrangements."

"Yes, sir."

"We will schedule the exchange as soon as possible. Delacroix, you and Ms. Welles will ensure that this goes smoothly."

"The amulet should not be moved at night," Lenore added.

"Then until this is settled, you both are on day shift. I'm creating a task force and assigning you two to deal with this. Any questions?" His tone indicated he did not want any. "Ms. Modeste, Mr. Minors. Good day. I want to have word with my people."

Minors opened his mouth to protest.

"I said 'good day, sir,'" the captain cut him off.

The museum director reluctantly stood, and Leslie practically shoved him out. As she exited, she studied Lenore, her mouth tight and I had no earthly idea what she was thinking. There was a time when I could accurately finish her sentences.

The captain gave a long-suffering sigh as he rubbed his quarter-past-four-o'clock-shadow and leaned all the way back in his leather desk chair. "I need you both to go home and be alert for the morning. Also, apparently the frickin' clown continues to haunt us. Seems he was associated with the RNC."

"RNC?" I asked. "I remember him babbling about an RNC at the storage unit."

The captain slapped his forehead. "You couldna opened with that? The Real Nasty Clowns are a serious problem.

My temper flared. "My apologies, *mon ami*, I asked him for context, but he was too busy beating me with the broadside of a Willow cricket bat to explain. Then he got possessed by a demon and then he exploded."

A giant, vast silence filled the room during which I began mentally packing my bags to head home after being extremely fired. Then Lenore snickered as the captain slowly stuffed his cigar between his lips.

"Well, allow me to fill you in, *sweetums*. They're a gang. And I need *you* to take lead in finding out the depth of their involvement in..." The captain waved his beefy hands at the office door. "...all of whatever this is."

"Me? Why not the gang task force?"

"First, we are not talking some street gang, but a very sophisticated operation."

"So, not a gang, if we're being accurate," Lenore added as she crossed her arms under her chest. "More like a mafia. The organized crime unit then?"

"Then it would be kicked to the FBI, and we would have to beg for crumbs of information."

I was in my head, trying to remember what exactly I'd heard after being beaten with the cricket bat. "I heard the clown say something about someone named McConnel?"

Both Lenore and the captain laughed.

"What?"

"The McConnel," the captain said with a grin. "He's a boogeyman, a scary story that keeps low level gang members under control. 'Don't screw up or The McConnel with get you.'"

"So, not a real person?"

"No," the captain said, but Lenore had an uncertain frown.

"I will need particulars."

The captain gave a dismissive wave of his hand. "You know what I'm about to say."

"Right, right. 'Talk to vice.' I have it," I retorted as I turned to go.

The captain slapped his hands on his desk. "Whelp, tell vice I said 'Tiddly do,' *sweetums*t."

In the hall I sidled up to Lenore.

"You shouldn't talk to that guy that way, it makes him less likely to give you what you want," she admonished me.

I replied with, "Very well. Meet me in five?"

She nodded.

At the front desk I saw Rosie idly scratching the back of Pakhet's head, and the cat seemed to enjoy it. I was wondering if she'd surrendered control to Cocopuff. She caught sight of me and, jerked away from Rosie's touch. She stood tall and aloof.

I smiled at the desk sergeant. "Thank you for watching her."

"My pleasure." She treated me to a sheepish smile. "It's none of my business, but I noticed that your cat doesn't seem to be fixed."

"Fixed?"

"You know, spayed? She hasn't got a scar."

I did not need the psychic assist to understand Pakhet's sudden hiss.

"I will think on it."

Pakhet yowled and "You will not!" exploded in my brain. Not a single voice but a chorus as Cocopuff linked with Pakhet.

I gathered up the struggling, proud cat, murmuring. "It is alright." I repeated that several times as I carried Pakhet down the hall to the forensics lab. I passed through the open door to see Lenore bent over a magical talisman. She looked up at me and smiled.

I smiled back and slowly closed the door behind me. "Now a good time?"

"I was waiting for you. What gives?"

I checked the door was fully closed and set Pakhet down on the ground. She backed away from both of us, her hackles rising, and she let out an anxious meow that trailed out for several seconds. The words formed in my mind. "Her mind is not right. I can taste something intolerable."

"Calm down," I addressed Pakhet in my most soothing tone.

"She's not wrong." Lenore said.

Chapter Seven

We both stared at her, me with my mouth agape.

"What?" Lenore put a palm on her own chest. "Sorcerer." She pointed at the cat. "Unshielded psychic projection." She stooped down, smiled and addressed Pakhet. "You might think you're speaking point to point, but you are indeed broadcasting, though, other than your intended target, it would take a major talent to hear you." She held up a hand. "I can help you with that."

Pakhet backed away, her back arched and tail straight up as if the offer was a threat.

Lenore stood and scratched at the front of her hairline, crimson nails stark against the short silver-white hair. Her eyes rolled left to right as she pursed her lips. "Okay, let's put everything out in the open, alright?" She closed her eyes, grappling for her words. She rubbed her temples, as if she had a sudden headache. "You brought this cat to me because you trust me, yes?"

"Yes."

"And because you think we are friends?"

"Am I wrong?" I asked, suddenly wary of her tone. "In a way. I really like what we have. Your lovely naivety is, well, sweet. I trust you, and I respect you. I am sure *you* are my friend, but Del…" She took an exaggerated deep breath and closed her eyes. "I can never truly be your friend."

That stung. "Is it my lack of power? My position?" I asked, trying to identify my insufficiency.

"No. I know it's a cliché to say, it's not you, it's me; but this is the truth." She gave me a wan smile and looked like she was preparing to jump into ice cold water. "I am incapable of being anyone's friend."

43

She held up a hand to stifle my reflex reaction. "What I've liked about you is how non-judgmental, and oblivious, you are. Up to now you accepted your version of me, but I have to set things straight. I always liked I can tell you anything." She took a deep breath and let it out slowly as she shrugged. "But your perceptions of me are way too kind." She rubbed her hands together and her face tightened into clinical detachment. "The label isn't important. Sociopath, psychopath, antisocial personality disorder. Whatever." Another shrug. "What I'm saying is, I have no sense of empathy. My... psychological emotional status is private, but not a big secret. Our bosses know. Many mages can only achieve my level with a complete and total lack of caring for others."

That admission suddenly made sense. Another powerful mage warned me not to allow her around artifacts that might temp her. Also, during one of my astral conversations with my *grand-mére,* in response to her reminder that she was depending on me for great grandchildren, I suggested I might approach Lenore for a date.

Grand-mére's face had frozen at the suggestion. "No! Dat child is not for you. You leave that girl alone." Her words had sounded pleading, but also like a warning.

I returned my mind to the present. "No empathy?"

She flipped her hands out in a frivolous motion. "Not a bit. No conscience whatsoever about how my actions help or hurt other people. Don't worry, I'm not the thrill killing kind or anything like that. I obey the law and work to do the right thing. Not because I care about anyone else, but because my life is simpler and happier when things are calm, and order is kept."

Her words carried a firm note of candor but elicited a sense of unease. "And if you thought I, or someone would disrupt that order, then what?" I tried to match her bluntness, but a note of concern slipped out with my words.

"The best thing, for both of us, is to avoid that possibility." Lenore raised her thick silver eyebrows and smiled, an impish grin.

She clapped her hands together and rubbed them. "OK! New topic in three, two, one..." She squatted down next to Pakhet. "I saw the original of that amulet. This one has no power, so the entity lives completely in the cat?"

"*Oui.*"

"Not talking to you. Pakhet?"

Pakhet crouched on the floor, her tail flipping indecisively. "I share the body with the actual cat, who goes by the name of Cocopuff. We have an agreement. I find food, and Cocopuff eats it."

"But you were previously in the amulet?" Lenore pressed.

"Mrs. Childress calculated that I'd been there for over four thousand years. When she wore the collar and I worked up the nerve to speak to her, she taught me about the modern world over the last fifty years. But only as a companion, the feline form is the only body I know. Memories of my human body are vague."

"You were not the entity that tried to break out."

"No, that was the foreign demon that invaded my land. It was my honor to lure it into the vessel and then hold it there.":

"Is it free now?"

"No. Westley fell into my space. Anyone who wishes to release the demon must first remove Westley. The difference is Westley will want to be removed. He is a reluctant guardian.

Now Lenore looked at me. "You saw the entity."

"*Oui*," I may not remember everything. Westley gave me a thump with a cricket bat."

"So, I heard," Lenore said absently. "I hope the healer I sent helped you recover?"

I nodded. "But our current problem is that Pakhet, is not a demon. I think she is the equivalent of a *loa*."

"The spirits you invite in during your *Voudon* rituals?"

"*Exactment*. Like the *loa*, she can only stay in the cat with the cat's consent. In the past, if the amulet was removed from the host, she was drawn back into it. If the host kicked her out, she would also find refuge in the amulet."

"But now she is separated from the amulet."

"Yes, and the amulet can only hold two entities, so it is full."

"And if the cat kicks her out?"

"She thinks she will die."

Lenore bit her lip. "She may be right," she sighed. "Or she might not. Oh, Delacroix. It would be simplest to euthanize the creature." She held up her hands at my shocked expression. "No, I'm not recommending that, just stating straight, unemotional fact. Bespelling the amulet copy as a shelter might be possible. I'll need to do more research. You say she's not a demon?"

We both looked at Pakhet,

I was surprised the cat managed an actual shrug.

"Okay, I'm gonna go on the assumption that she is not a demon or Egyptian goddess, for now."

"Seriously. There is a chance?"

Lenore shrugged. "There are legends of Egyptian gods torn to pieces and those pieces interacting with humans."

Pakhet spoke up in a cautious, tentative tone. "I do not recall my life before the first time I was released from the amulet, or much before Westley called me out. But I am sure I wasn't a god. I think I might have served a god."

"We will put the god speculation aside," I said. "What do we do now?"

"High Magick is the only way to create a haven for her." Lenore sighed in resignation. "You know, Bobby might do it."

"He will insist I give my oath to the order."

"Is that so bad?"

I shrugged. "Perhaps not. The little one saved my life."

Lenore stood. "I'll get the ball rolling."

"And you will keep this quiet?"

Lenore glared at me as she dismissed my concern. "Of course, I will. I don't need people thinking I'm talking to cats."

Chapter Eight

I headed down the hall, Pakhet trailing along while managing to
look bored. I was halfway down the hall when I saw her coming. I was
looking forward to seeing her again, but not with Pakhet. I turned to
scoop her up and take her back, forgetting that it is impossible to scoop
up *la petite* without her approval.

I stepped back from her denial of my advance, sucking at the cut
on my finger. I heard a chuckle behind me.

I turned to see Chelsea Falcata. Today she was dressed in her para-
legal suit, a knee length blue skirt and blazer with a purple silk blouse
and comfortable shoes. She has Talent and frequently uses cosmetic
glamour charms. But I have seen her real look. I don't understand why
she feels she needs to change it so much, or maybe I can. She has no
attractive features. Her hair is a curly blonde tending toward frizz. Her
face is asymmetrical with her eyes spaced too far apart. She always
moves with a masculine, restrained power. And she is slender, well-
muscled, with just the right amount of curves.

So, no individual features one would consider attractive, but the
totality was, well, incredible. Her beauty was ageless, breathtaking. But
her glamoured version was conventionally pretty, and not nearly as
exciting.

"Not a great start if you're hoping to compete with the K-9
division." She put a fist on one hip and gave me a saucy smile. "Or is
this your emotional support cat, 'cause that's not a great start, either."

"*Non*, not exactly. That implies ownership, well, she is sort of a
partner, but not like that," I answered as Chelsea stooped and reached
for Pakhet.

The little beast leaned toward her to be petted, eagerly allowing

Chelsea to rub her back and scratch her ears.

I looked at the ceiling to avoid admiring the way her blouse now revealed significant cleavage.

Pakhet purred. A deep, full-throated purr like I had not heard since our first week together.

"Such a sweet little girl." She looked up at me still nursing my finger. "I guess you just have to know how to treat her." She vigorously scratched Pakhet behind the ears. "He does treat you right?"

Pakhet stopped purring.

Chelsea stood up, but Pakhet continued to rub against her ankles in the most overt display of affection since she was trapped in the cat.

"Ms. Falcata," I ventured tentatively. "I need to get together and pick your brain."

"Oh?" Her voice sounded interested as she smoothed her skirt.

I glanced around again. Against my better instincts I trusted Chelsea, but the vice department was after her. I knew that she was the pimp Cooper referred to. She represented several sex workers in the city. Vice called her a pimp; she would say she only provided physical and legal protection.

"Something called the RNC."

"Real Nasty Clowns," she almost spat as her glamour flickered. "Human trafficking, drugs, extortion. They live up to their name. They are a conservative's wet dream. A completely legal, well-funded interest group that traps young women into prostitution and leaves them at thirty, looking like sixty, with a drug habit."

"Well, the clown that owned this cat was going through an initiation into the RNC. Personally, I don't think he was bright enough."

"Probably not, but he might still make a good soldier. They prefer their low-level clowns to be more loyal than smart. Anyhow, the real RNC are hard men to find. They hide among the Giggle-O's."

"Giggle-O's?" I asked.

"The fans of several misogynist rap and metal bands. The have big festivals where they have women work the crowd."

"Seriously?"

"Seriously. They allow tents at the gatherings and have a very complicated series of scouts, so no one interferes."

Pakhet continued rubbing against her ankles as Chelsea spoke.

Her voice suddenly sounded like she tasted something foul. "The festival girls are better off than their hotel girls."

"You ever hear of The McConnel?" I waited for her to laugh. She didn't.

48

"That is a mystery. I think it's real. But what it is, I don't know." Chelsea bent over and gave the cat one last pat. "Call me after 6 a.m. tomorrow, we'll set up a time to meet before your shift."

"After my shift. On days for a bit."

"So, you're off this evening?" She cocked an eyebrow. "You could buy me dinner."

Her suggestion was a sword that cut both ways. I should mention that if having a working relationship with the woman Vice openly called "a notorious pimp" was tricky, having a *personal* relationship was, well, trickier... She saved me, once, and I felt I owed her, but there was also something else. I liked her company, felt relaxed around her and thought way too much about her. It was true, she called me every day while I was laid up in the hospital, and I know she called the nurses and badgered them for "honest" progress reports. I did not quite know what to think about that.

"I would be happy to, in a professional capacity," I said, trying to convince myself.

"Then it's a date. Meet at seven-thirty? Where do you like?" She stood up and brushed imaginary cat hair off her suit.

"The Port-au-Prince Café?"

"Caribbean cuisine?"

I flinched. "Sorry, my comfort food. We could go somewhere else."

"Oh no, it sounds lovely. See you there."

She smiled and I detected a hint if of shyness beneath the glamour as she turned and walked to the holding area.

Pakhet watched her go. Her eyes narrowed and her face scrunched up.

"You okay?"

Pakhet physically meowed, a long mournful sound. In my head her voice seemed very far away. "I have never seen a human with so much sadness." Psychically I got more than the words, the cat managed to project Chelsea's feelings.

"Chelsea? She has some family tragedy in her past, but she seems to be handling it."

Pakhet's head swiveled, and her eyes bored into me. "No, she isn't." Her tone would not tolerate disagreement. "She is using her anger to hold it at bay, but it is ripping her apart."

I could feel her project Chelsea's internal turmoil at me. It felt like a rumbling in my gut and felt the repressed anger. I shook It off. You are an empath? You can project emotions."

Pakhet looked at me and rolled her eyes. In my brain I heard,

"Duh. Just like her. I just have more experience. You know. About four thousand years of it."

"You said you could taste minds; I was thinking it was more superficial."

Pakhet ignore me and stared down the hall after Chelsea was gone.

"She needs someone like me." The words in my brain were sad. Before I could reply she continued. "But for now, I need you and your help." She did not sound happy about it.

I went to the office I shared with my partner and checked an almanac tacked to the desk. Sunset in another hour, Vlad would be in about thirty minutes after that.

I was reviewing details about the incident and Pakhet was napping when Vlad appeared. He enjoyed the effect of arriving at vampiric speed and just seeming to materialize. I ignored the entrance and checked the time, forty-five minutes before my meeting with Chelsea.

"They tell me you're workin' days." His accent was less Transylvanian and more east Los Diablos.

"Just for bit. You will not get a new partner."

"Good. I almost have you house-broken. Speakin' ah things that might shit on my floor, what's with the friggin' cat?" he asked. "Don't you know I'm allergic?"

"You are dead."

He screwed his face up and waved me away. "Oh, whatever."

Pakhet stirred and I physically heard a blood chilling feline yowl that mutated into the meanest, most frightful hiss that could emanate from a tiny, fuzzy creature. Her ears went flat against her little head and she put so much force into the hiss that it came in spurts. Vlad, incredulous, bared his fangs and hissed in return.

And there was I, trapped in the middle of a perpetual hissing contest between my vampire partner and a *loa*-possessed cat. That's when the psychic force slammed into me and nearly sent me reeling out of my seat.

"What have you done?" Her voice exploded in my head.

"What, what?" I shouted back.

Vlad quit hissing long enough to smart talk to me. "Hey, take it easy, there's no turds on the floor, I'm kiddin', jeez! And you! Shut up, fer crissakes!" Vlad bent over and launched into his usual litany of old vamp noises as he pulled a Red Cross pint bottle marked "POTABLE" from his mini-fridge. He set the bottle on his side of the desk to bring it up to room temperature as Pakhet lowered her hiss to an incensed belly rumble. "I just mean I didn't take you for a cat man. You pick up a stray, or something?"

He once tried to use a hot plate, but the captain forbade it. Said the smell was awful. I could not smell it, though. Strange how the air flow in the building went from Vlad's desk straight to the captain's nose. But, as everyone says, "That's just LD weather."

"Not a stray. My, uh, companion." I closed my eyes as the cat let out another physic yowl. Pakhet was pressed against the door frame, ready to bolt, her back arched and hair standing in a spikey mess.

"What is the problem?" I hissed at her.

"Vampire!" she snapped back.

"Friendly vampire, my partner."

Vlad's eyebrows rose. "The day walkers really did a number onya, didn't they?"

"What?'

Vlad pointed at Pakhet. "You're kinda holdin' parley with a cat."

"You and him…?" Pakhet seemed confused.

"Work together. Besides, what do you care? He only drinks human blood."

She glared, her eyes burning with flared anger, as if I had seriously insulted her. Then she relaxed and started sullenly grooming herself.

I returned to my chair.

"You gonna to fill me in?" Vlad sipped at the bottle; his face twisted in a grimace of distaste.

I noticed the blue "day old" band around the bottom and clucked my tongue. "Your diet has gone to crap, as you say, in my absence, Vlad."

"What?" he demanded. "Fresh AB neg every day, in this economy? Fer Crissakes."

"That stuff is no good for you," I chided. "You need fresh to keep your strength up."

"What's it gonna do, kill me?" He upended the bottle and gulped the contents even though it hadn't had a chance to warm. He wiped his lips on the back of his hand and sniffed suspiciously. "Maybe it will at that. More like 'week old' by the scent."

He grimaced and belched. Then he hit himself in the chest with his fist three times "That stuff doesn't go down smooth."

I filled him in until Lenore arrived.

"Del, can we speak privately?" She gave a sidelong glance at Vlad.

"He knows about the cat."

"Was that wise? You know what they say, the best ways to spread information are telegram, telephone, tell a vamp."

"Bite me.," Vlad snapped, but his heart wasn't in it. I think he sort

51

of liked her teasing him with vampire stereotypes.

"Okay," Lenore went on. "I've texted Bobby about your cat problem."

By Bobby she meant Archabbot Robert Kaufman, leader of the Order of the Gnostic Elites, or Nogs. It was considered an honor to be invited to join the order, even as a lay brother. I hadn't declined the offer so much as put it off. After all, the official initiation, including the tattoo I felt a little squeamish about, was going to take most of a day. And I had clowns to catch.

"And?"

"How much are you ready to pay?"

I sighed. "Whatever I have to."

"Okay, I've done my research. To shape the amulet, we will need at least half an ounce of 24 carat gold."

I grimaced. I wasn't keeping up with the price of gold. I think I'd heard on the news that it was somewhere over $3000 an ounce. I would need to take out a loan. But Pakhet did save me, putting her own life in danger. She must be walking on eggshells, terrified that Cocopuff would kick her out any moment.

"I'll find the money," I muttered.

"Talk to Bobby first."

I nodded and reached for my cell phone.

"Not here," Lenore said quietly. "Let's go out to your car and you can call to see if he is willing to help."

I looked at Pakhet.

Vlad cleared his throat. "You guys go. I'll take care of the little fur ball. Make sure she doesn't drop a steamer on my immaculate floors."

I looked at Pakhet and swore I saw her nod. "You sure?" I asked her.

"I tasted his mind."

I guess the vamp was now feline-approved.

I shrugged my overcoat back on. Lenore joined me in the dark lot illuminated by yellow lamps. I felt a twinge of anxiety about being late for my dinner with Chelsea. I wasted no time and hit the speed dial.

Dr. Kaufman answered on the third ring. "Hey, Delacroix, what's up? Saw you on the news, what were you doing? Fighting a demon?"

"*Non*, not a demon, I think, but I cannot say what it was."

A sharp intake of breath from the other side. "That's not good."

"I am looking for help."

"Anything I can do, just let me know," Kaufman said in a reassuring tone.

"I need to find an inexpensive way to get at least half an ounce of

24 carat gold." The strained tone in my voice was equal parts making the request, and my response to Lenore rolling her eyes.

"No cheap way to do that. What is it for?"

I hesitated. "There is an entity that has lived for millennia in a talisman. They have been blocked from returning to the talisman."

"Where is this entity now?"

I slumped my shoulders. "In a cat."

A sigh on the other end of the phone. "Not a demon? You're sure?"

"*Oui*, not a demon. More like a *loa*; it cannot stay without the cat's permission. We are concerned the cat may kick her out."

"Her?"

"Female entity, we think. She saved me the other night."

"No mention on the news about a cat…"

"I, uh, removed the cat from the situation." I almost felt his grin over the phone. Kaufman liked riddles and contradictions, but most of all he liked being in control, and having reserved information was his idea of control.

"Hmmm. Spirit trap or can the entity leave at will?"

"At will."

"Tell you what. You bring the cat in for us to examine, and we will cast the amulet."

I scrunched up my face. "I am not comfortable with the 'examine' stipulation. What if you decide that sheltering this entity is unwise?"

He didn't answer, which was his answer.

"If you want to supply the gold, I would—"

"Alright," Kaufman let out his breath. "I will promise to cast the amulet and ensure that the entity is safe."

"No caveats?"

I heard his reluctance. "No. But if I do the ritual personally, and there is a future issue, we will be in a better position. Also, I don't know how far to trust Lenore."

We were not on speaker phone, but she glanced at me and snorted. "Love you too, Bobby."

"Very well. Tomorrow too early?" I asked.

"Let me check my gold. I was going to give you a Krugerrand, but those are only 22 carat. I have a presentation medal from an event a decade ago. It is 24 carat, and at least 43 grams."

"How much will you sell it for? How much for the ritual?"

"The only price for the gold is for you to acknowledge your place with us. As for the ritual, that will be compelling enough to be its own reward. That working is a rare one and I will have plenty of volunteers to help."

He gave me a few things necessary to prepare and I made a list. I didn't know how Pakhet would feel about getting her chest shaved, even just a bit. "Let me get her ready. It needs to be early; I am temporarily working days. Have to be in by 8 a.m."

"That shouldn't be a problem. I'll cast the amulet at midnight. It should take about three hours to consecrate it. Bring the cat in at dawn. It'll take about an hour to get her settled. Good thing I have the other amulet," he added, and I could hear his triumphant smile through the phone.

"Yes, about that. I've been ordered to hand that over to the museum guy."

"Yeah," he replied, now disgusted. "I know. We can deal with him after the ceremony."

I hung up, wondering what it took for the leader of the Order of the Gnostic Elites to call a ritual "compelling."

Chapter Nine

I stopped by the washroom and freshened up as much as possible. I would prefer to go home and change, but the phone call with Dr. Kaufman made me late. Event

The door opened.

"Delacroix," an overly friendly voice called out.

I winced. That voice belonged to Ted Gruber. I could never tell if he was always trying to be that friendly or if the forced inflection was meant to be sardonic. It was how he always greeted everyone, like a game show host that was about to open fire on his audience.

"I hear you have date tonight!"

I would like to know where he got that information. "*Oui*, a business meeting with an informant."

Gruber sniggered and leaned against the sink so he could look me close in the eye. "Yeah, every date with that floozy is a business meeting. You're breaking the first rule of banging hookers, man. Never feed 'em. They'll follow you home, like a cat."

Well, at least I knew the sarcasm was intentional. I straightened my tie in the mirror. "I know of her associations."

"Half the squad's had her, not bad if a little bony." He gave me a leering smile. "Make sure you get her to name her price, then you can threaten to arrest her and get the milk for free."

"She has no arrest record."

"Milk for free…" He called over his shoulder as he left.

His words angered me more than they should. I knew little of Gruber's character, and I'd trust Chelsea over him any time. He was lying, trying to get my goat. And yet…

I made it to the restaurant and found her waiting for me at a table.

She spruced up for the date, her hair and makeup were still glamoured, but more elegant. She rocked the "little black dress." A bottle of red wine and two glasses decorated the table; hers was already filled with wine dark enough to resemble Vlad's lunch. She stood as I approached, giving me a glance of well-toned legs in precarious heels.

"Nice to see you, Detective. Did you have a chance to take Pakhet home?"

"*Non*, she is spending the evening with Vlad, I will pick her up later." I paused. I felt more than awkward, almost frightened. "Uh, Ms. Falcata…"

She frowned, a moue of disapproval. "I think it's time you call me Chelsea." She smiled and I felt the fear drain away, but the awkwardness remained. "I've been waiting to learn your first name."

"My friends call me Del," I said as I sat across from her. I rested my interlaced fingers on the table.

"Del…" She said the name delicately, as if trying it out. "You sound odd. You're being very stiff; am I making you nervous?"

"*Non…Oui*. Yes, I am nervous."

"No need to be." Her tone was sincere as she reached across the table to lay her hand on mine.

I didn't mean to clench my hands tighter. She must have felt that, or saw something in my expression because her eyes narrowed, and she leaned forward.

"You are giving off a very strong, uncomfortable vibe. Look, this is just a meal, we have to eat, right? If you don't want to tell me what's troubling you, that's fine, although I am certain it has something to do with me."

"*Oui*. It does. Someone in vice found out we are meeting and Gruber told me…things."

She sighed, took a drink of her wine and swept her hair back. "I'm sure he did. And what he told you bothers you? A deal breaker?"

"It is not that, it is the uncertainty. I need truth from you. There is too much gossip, and I know most of it is *connerie,* but does one see the shore from a sea of lies?"

Chelsea rolled her eyes and put her hand on her wineglass like she was hanging on for dear life. "You can say bullshit in English."

"Can I interest you in tonight's specialties?"

I jumped in surprise. I had not heard the waitress approach; it was if she glided up silently. She smiled, displaying her fangs. So, she did glide up. I was unaware the restaurant had vampires on the wait staff. She was pale as moonlight and as thin as a rail. Her face looked young, but her eyes were old. Her long black hair fell over her shoulders.

"Tonight," she announced, "we have *Fwa Di ak Bannann*, beef liver cooked with plantains, and *Woma Boukannen*, a grilled lobster."

She passed us menus.

Chelsea waved her away. "I'd love to try the *Woma Boukannen*."

"Of course."

"And I will have the *Kalalou Djondjon*," I ordered from memory. My grandmother would cook this dish whenever I was feeling sad. It was my usual order.

"Very good." The waitress smiled again, and I felt her influencing me to order something more expensive to bump up her tip, which wounded me. I would think they knew me here well enough to know I was a good tipper, anyhow. Between *Grand-mère's* protection and my own innate will, a non-magical asset, the influence flopped, and her smile wavered. The jury is still out if it is a telepathic thing, or a reaction to pheromones. No one has even decisively confirmed if vampires can project the effect at will, or if it is a reflex.

"Well, I'll will be back with you all in a minute." She slipped silently away.

Chelsea watched her go; her eyes sad. "It wouldn't be necessary if we just paid people what they're worth."

"Pardon?"

She nodded in the direction the waitress went. "She wouldn't have to try to glamour you if she was just paid what she's worth. And that's on us as a society." Her eyes fluttered to the table, and I saw her cheeks redden.

I took a moment to reply. It was clearly something that mattered to her, and I truly agreed. The undead were not subject to the minimum wage laws; since they are literally immortal and there is free blood available from the Red Cross if you qualify for a SNAP card, which most vamps do. Vlad was lucky enough to be above the poverty line, if not by much.

Which meant I lived comfortably, if not extravagantly, in Los Diablos County while my partner, who did the exact same job as me, essentially lived in squalor.

"You were about to tell me what is bothering you?" Chelsea asked, suddenly eager to change the subject. She sipped at her wine with the intense interest of the overwhelmed.

I blinked, trying to reset myself emotionally. "I just wanted to talk about being honest with each other. I do not wish to insult you, but I will need you to confirm or deny things."

She leaned in very close and spoke in a low tone. "Let me guess, you want to know if I'm a prostitute." She closed her eyes, and I felt her tension. "The answer is I was. You see, my family has a history—"

"I know about it. Your sister was Laura Falcata. The Blood Red Rose, the papers called her." The crime was horrific, and the public reaction nearly obscene. When Chelsea was twelve her mother was sick, no father. So, her older sister worked as an escort, and her gruesome remains were found dumped in an alley. It is one of Los Diablos's most infamous murders. The killer was never caught and the victim supposedly never identified. Of course, the second half of that story was for the papers. The department helped the family keep a low profile.

"My sister..." Chelsea said in a distant voice and dropped her glamour spell So, she had taken the time to make her face and hair almost as nice at the glamour. She looked at me to gauge my reaction to the change.

I smiled my appreciation.

She returned a shy smile and continued, "I was twelve when Laura was murdered. Fourteen when my mother died. And I always knew what I wanted to do with my life. Protect the vulnerable, and sex workers are about the most vulnerable. That's why I went into pre-law and took karate and studied practical shooting as a sport."

"You own a gun?" I felt a worried twinge.

She paused. "I'm not going to lie to you. Yes."

"Permit?" I had no concern about how she might use a gun but was very worried what could happen in a situation with vice.

"Denied, but on appeal. Courts are backed up so I should know something next year."

"Do you carry it?"

Her eyes crinkled in that mischievous merriment she had. "I'm not gonna lie."

I clenched my eyes shut. I did not wish to make trouble for her. I demanded truth and she was giving it to me. I just was not sure what to do with it now that I had it. "But why be a prostitute?"

She took a moment to sweep her hair back again. Without the glamour the locks fell back into exactly the same spot. "I couldn't just show up one day out of the blue." Her voice had a bite in it. "The girls would see me as some know-nothing goody-two-shoes and the pimps would be after me. But if I already had a reputation..." She shrugged. "The police buried my sister's identity, supposedly to protect our family. I could maybe create confidence by telling them about Laura, but Mom wouldn't have wanted that, me dragging Laurie's memory through the mud. Mom spent half the last two years of her life seeing her child's ghost around every corner of the neighborhood. I can't tell you she was just seeing things, either. Who knows? So, yeah. I spent a year working as an escort and a street hooker. I used the name Regina. I made sure that every girl on the street know who I was and I wasn't going to let the pimps screw with me. I ensured the vice cops all knew me."

"No arrest record, though. Seems lucky."

"I prefer it that way. I bought my way out with cash and services."

I choked on my table water. "You admit you bribed the police," I said in a whisper.

Chelsea gave me the look. You know the one. When someone has taken the last cookie and they have no regrets. "No, they committed a crime *with* me and then let me go so I wouldn't talk. So, it's really more like entrapment, of me, with a sprinkle of some well-deserved blackmail, the laws on which are very blurry in this state—but now I really am talking shop. Look. I'm not comfortable with what I did, but I'm also not ashamed. Most of my clients were just lonely. Only the cops were abusive jerks. So, deal breaker?"

"I am a police officer. It is, how you say, what I am, not what I do. I cannot ignore crimes."

"I see."

I back-pedaled at the hurt look on her face. "Not ignore, but I will try to understand. I need to think about it." That was a lie. I knew how I felt about her, and the vamp influence brought that feeling to the surface. I would be lying if I said her past didn't disturb me, but it did not dissuade me. But I felt worried that telling her would be rushing things. Since our earlier adventure I thought she felt the same way, but, like I said, I have a hard time noticing when someone finds me attractive.

I saw Chelsea's head bob up and I turned to see the waitress bring us a basket of bread. She laid it on the table and moved away, sliding like a wraith.

"But we are here to talk about the clowns." I tried to change the subject before I said something stupid.

Chelsea took another sip of red wine. I could see she was trying to hide hurt feelings.

I sighed. "*Mon ami.* We are friends. I trust you and I can understand why you felt you needed to do these things. I do not hold your choices against you. I wish there had been a better way. As a friend, I am sorry you had to go through that."

"Don't feel sorry for me," Chelsea said, her eyes flashing with anger. She let out a breath. "That was a bit harsh." She nibbled at her bottom lip as she regarded me, and her gaze softened. "You mean well.

But I never asked anyone to feel sorry for me. I don't feel sorry for me. When you become aware of the crimes committed against women, not just sex workers, you get sensitized to how people react to our experience." She looked up and cocked her head to the right. "I'm a survivor, not a victim."

I glanced up to see the waitress approaching with a large tray professionally balanced on one hand over her head. The dishes piled on it easily required more strength than her lithe form should have, but, you know, vampire. As she neared the table, she brought the tray down with a graceful swoop and with practiced ease delivered our food.

"Enjoy your meal." She smiled. I felt a tendril of influence.

I looked back at Chelsea. She seemed oblivious. Perhaps the waitress assumed, correctly, I was paying, and it was better to flatter me with her attention.

"Thank you," I said, trying to convey back to her that, indeed, I would tip her well.

Chelsea waited until the waitress was gone to speak. "The RNC," Chelsea said slowly, "are protected. Vice is on their payroll, as well as Internal Affairs. Making any move against them could end your career, or life."

"That seems a bit extreme."

She rolled her eyes, then stared directly at mine. "I know they've made witnesses and victims just disappear."

"Maybe they just paid them off and they left town."

Chelsea looked at her grilled lobster with an amused smile, the meat already separated from the shell. "I thought I was going to get to break it open." She sighed and her amusement vanished as she gave me a hard look. "You can't be that naive."

No, I couldn't. I took a moment to enjoy the scent of the black okra stew in front of me. For a moment I was home, in *ma grand-mère's* kitchen. "How many people are we talking about and is there any evidence?"

"Three working girls that I know of. The RNC doesn't keep women over thirty. Most they just abandon with no money, not prospects and a drug habit, like I told you. Sometimes those women get the treatment they need and then want to testify against the RNC. In many cases they get a threat and back off. Sometimes their past is brought up. The RNC keeps records to destroy their credibility. Some do persist but they never get to present evidence, partly because their bodies are never found. Look, your investigation puts you basically at war with a good chunk of the LDPD. I think you should consider dropping it."

"I cannot. I have orders from the captain."

Chelsea sucked on a bit of lobster meat and wiped her chin. I fought back a chuckle at her feminine delicacy. "Yeah, so you have to ask yourself what's his agenda."

"You think he has an agenda?"

"Of course he does. You don't get to his position without being an agenda ninja. He's an ass, but he's not stupid. I see three possibilities here."

"Three?"

"Uh-huh. First, the least likely. He's an honest cop, knows you are an honest cop and you are the best tool to take down the corruption."

"You don't buy that at all."

"Nope. Second. He's as corrupt as they are, knows you are honest, and he's setting you up to fail. He will be able to show there was an investigation, but no evidence of wrongdoing."

"The third?"

"He is far more corrupt than we think and he's using you. He'll take your investigation to the public and there will be a lot of media involved when they announce that there was corruption in the department but will make Macklin the fall guy, and likely you too."

I felt my face slip into a snarl at the name of the former head of vice, who escaped after the riot at the convention.

"I am serious about you being cast as the other patsy. Del, I honestly believe if you pursue any real investigation into the RNC, you'll either wind up in prison, or dead."

I felt cold. Was I up to fighting half the department? I love this city. I've only lived here for six years after growing up in Haiti and then Florida, but something in the air here sang to me. The ground beneath my feet seemed more stable than anywhere else. I was supposed to be one of the city's protectors.

"Look, Del. The smart move is to generate a lot of noise, then beat Cappy to the punch and put the blame squarely on Macklin. He is a villain, after all. You feed bullshit to Cappy, he'll have nothing to pin on you."

"And the rest?"

"Back to business as usual."

I grimaced and she leaned forward, those immaculately lined eyes intense and serious. "Look. I would *love* nothing more than to shut the RNC down wholesale, but I can't. And I never will. They have all the money, and the power. That's the cold, hard truth. All I can do is focus on retail and pick up the pieces they leave bleeding in the ditches of Los Diablos, one Laura at a time." She took a bite of lobster and winced. "All this talk of those rotten bastards is ruining my food. After desert, give me an hour to show you what we're up against."

Chapter Ten

Chelsea would say no more about our proposed after-dinner activities, but what she did divulge said "stake out" to me, so I decided to head back to the station and swap my personal car out for one from the department motor pool. Call me paranoid, but I learned early on that the best way not to be followed home is to not let the perps ever see your real ride. I parked the grey Ford sedan just beyond the crest of a hill. From our vantage point I was confidant the only thing they could see of us was the top of the windshield and the roof. Crouching forward and peering over the pavement we could see a cheap motel. The owners did not put too much investment in the lighting, making it difficult to determine exactly how run down the place was, but what I could make out looked pretty shabby. It was two stories, and the ground floor units opened directly to the parking lot with spaces marked in front of the doors. Mostly empty spaces. I saw a dark alcove illuminated only by a dilapidated vending machine, and two stairwells.

Chelsea held up a pair of high-powered night-vision binoculars. She studied the place then handed the glasses to me.

"The RNC has five rooms on the bottom floor," she pointed out. "If you look carefully, you can see the lookouts in the stairwell by the vending machines. I don't see any of the enforcers, but the muscle is there somewhere, maybe also in the stairwells. The designated pimp is in the front office."

"The designated...?"

"The guy the clients go to and pay. Girls never get near the money. The frickin' pimp gives the johns a room key and they 'visit' the girls." The quotes were evident from the disgust in her voice.

"Why has no one else tried to shut this down?"

"Hard to prove anything. The girls don't have any money, they're scared, and they need their drugs too much to talk. The pimp is just collecting money. Anyone official would get nowhere. Anyone unofficial would need to contend with the muscle."

A figure moved from the office to Room 105. He used the keycard to go in. I felt repulsed. That man had to know the woman he was about to, uh, "visit" was a prisoner. I handed the binoculars back.

Chelsea saw the look in my eye and put a steadying hand on my shoulder. "Hey. There's nothing you can do about it. Bust into that room you will find a guy having consensual sex, at least that is what they will claim. With no money around, and unless the girl wants to testify, there is nothing to be done."

"And you say that those who do, tend to disappear. Why have I not I heard of these people before?"

"No magic being used. Not your department."

"This goes beyond my department—"

"Quiet," Chelsea snapped, and brought up the binoculars. "There's a black van pulling up."

"*Oui.*? Is that important?"

"That van is how they transport the women. Don't usually see it this early, unless…" She adjusted the glasses. "They're bringing in a new girl. Hi, honey girl," she said with a crack in her voice. "This is how I first meet a lot of the girls I work with."

One man pulled the woman out of the van but did not let go once she was out. He held a tight grip on her forearm, as if concerned she might try to escape. She appeared completely submissive in her simple, calf-length tunic. Even at the distance I could see she was shrunken in on herself. Her blonde hair shone like silver in the parking lot light, hiding her face.

Even distraught, she was stacked and jacked. The baggy tunic did little to conceal her curves, and the light material. implied there was nothing under the garment except a tight, toned body like a very busty gymnast.

The woman winced.

Without the binoculars I could only see her in the yellow glare of the sodium parking lot lights. Another man, very young, clambered out of the van. He wore glasses and was thin enough a strong breeze would take him away. He carried a bundle, maybe a blanket, and moved with awkward motions as if the blanket was unusually cumbersome.

"Oh, my god!" Chelsea exclaimed, and she passed the binoculars back to me. "You see what he is carrying?"

I studied the man. "Feathers?" I watched the woman turn back to him and saw lines in her face that spoke of loss, and a fatalistic resolution. I was mistaken in my earlier estimation that she was pretty. She was far beyond merely pretty. Even under stress her face was astonishing. Imagine the Venus di Milo, but more beautiful, oh, and with arms.

"That's a goddamn cloak of swan feathers, which means that woman is a swan maiden."

"A what?"

Chelsea wrinkled her nose at me. "Ya know, you're kinda ignorant for a magical crimes expert. She's a rare type of shapeshifter. She can turn into a swan at will, but only as long as she has her cloak. If a man steals her cloak, she will be subservient to his will." She gave a frustrated cough. "I guess this is your area, after all. Except she's not the first, Del. Hell, she's not even the first swan maiden I've seen 'em pick up, and swan maidens are literally one in a billion. You don't know about this because very powerful, dangerous men don't want you to know— hey what are you doing?"

I tossed her the binoculars. "That lady looks cold, and that rude fellow has her coat. I am going to help him return it to her." Chelsea convinced me that arresting the men would be a waste of time. Proving magical coercion is very difficult and most times when encountered it is best to just try to stop it before it goes too far.

"You wanna get killed? You and the swan?"

I turned to look at her. "I cannot just let her—"

"Yes, you can." Chelsea's voice was angry but determined. "How do I have to spell it out to you that they are protected?" She rubbed her fingers together to imply cash. "There're at least three armed men. You could call for back up, but once you give the address the call will be ignored. Any backup that arrives, and they'll probably be from vice, will work to, uh, dissuade you from any action."

I studied the trio walking slowly to Room 109. The man in the back held out the cloak to the girl, taunting her with it.

"I wish I knew what they were saying."

Chelsea held up the glasses. "I can't see the guy with the cloak; he's facing the wrong way. The girl is promising to do whatever they want, if they will keep the cloak safe. She has to know they will never willingly give it back."

"You are reading lips?"

"Of course." She gave me a quick side-eyed glance. "Can't you?" She didn't wait for an answer. "The first guy, he said something that frightened the girl. Cloakboy's turned a bit, and I can see him pouting. He is demanding to be the one to 'break her in,'—gross—since he took

65

the cloak. Oof. Big guy said something that pissed Cloaky off. He's hopping around yelling now."

Indeed, the man's voice carried to us up the hill. I had to act. The two men looked ready for a fight, one Cloakboy would lose. My concern was the innocent woman. If the men moved to violence, she could be the one hurt.

"Del, you can't go down there! They'll recognize you; we lose any chance of taking them down. One of their inside people will ensure it." Chelsea grabbed my arm as I pushed the car door more open.

"No. I, a member of this corrupt police organization, cannot, but a random passer-by with a gun? Well. It is America, after all." I pulled a bag from inside the front console. Standard supplies: latex gloves, minimalist crime scene kit, and, what I needed, a balaclava. I pulled it over my head as I stepped out of the car. Chelsea was right behind me.

"I don't have a second mask," I said in regret.

"Don't need one." She snapped her fingers. She was suddenly in her usual pretty-but-bland cosmetic magic, but this time her skin and hair were black. Not like me, or an African-American, but matte black. Her features blended into one another, like looking at a black-on-black design in dim light. "Besides," she continued. "They know who I am, what I do. They also know the insurance I've put together if anything happens to me."

The road was at the edge of a residential area, tree-lined and shrouded in shadows. I ran down the hill in a slow jog. The two men were arguing now, and a third man was coming out of the front office. His head was shaved, and he was a big body-builder type, obvious enforcer.

No weapons in sight, but I knew they were all armed. I drew my weapon and then frowned as, from the corner of my eye, I saw Chelsea draw. *Merde*, I thought. *This could go so sideways so bad.*

I circled around to put the van between me and the group; Chelsea circled the other way. I heard them arguing and I peeked around the van.

"I get her first!" Cloakboy was saying. "You told me if I could steal her cloak, I get her first."

"Look, dweeb," the first man said, still holding the woman with a domineering grip. "She's a real swan maiden. Do you have any idea how much her virginity is worth? Not for you, jerkwad."

"I have the cloak!" the little guy shouted.

The first guy roughly shoved the woman aside and paced over to Cloakboy. The third man stopped and grinned at the spectacle. The first man grabbed the slight man by the front of his shirt and dragged him up so they were face to face, the larger man staring down. "You think just because you're so pathetic the swan bitch let you get close enough to steal her cloak, you deserve some credit?" He smirked. "Listen, twit, you don't just look harmless, you *are* harmless." He shoved the guy away and snatched at the cloak.

"No!" the swan maiden screamed as a feather floated free.

New lights blazed from hotel windows. The first guy punched Cloakboy in the face. Blood flowed from his nose as he let go of the cloak and the first man pulled it away. The woman wailed and clutched her hair as more feathers drifted away.

The way they were manhandling her coat of feathers, she was going to die a virgin.

It was go time. I came around the van, my weapon trained on the first guy. I calculated that Cloakboy was unarmed. "Stop!" I commanded using my best attempt at an American accent. "Give the woman her cloak."

The first guy jerked his surprised gaze at me.

The guy with the shaved head changed his expression from amused to angry as he reached for a gun in his waistband. No holster. Stupid.

"Don't do it.," Chelsea rasped in guttural voice so raw and low I wondered if she could magically change her voice with her appearance.

"Drop the cloak," I demanded.

The first man stared at me, his face twisted in hatred and frustration. It is a fallacy that just because you have a gun a person will do what you tell them to do. This only actually works if they believe you will shoot. The man must have seen something in my eyes that gave him the impression I was reluctant to fire. Which was true. But I knew when I drew my weapon it might come to that. The weak man, deprived of the cloak, darted into the night.

"Put the goddamn cloak on the ground," Chelsea demanded., "Or I will blow your balls off."

Her tone left no doubt that was exactly what she would do,

The man dropped the cloak.

"Get ten feet away.," Chelsea barked.

The captive woman swooped at it with a speed and grace I could barely comprehend and snatched up the cloak. The man grabbed at her, his fingers clutching her arm in a cruel grip. He jerked at her, using his superior size to his advantage.

But with the cloak in her possession, she was not going without a fight. She waved her arm in a circle to dislodge the grip even as she spun and kicked him in the groin so hard that even Chelsea flinched.

He went down. The swan lady gathered up the wayward feathers in silent consternation

"Go," I shouted at the magical maiden. "Go now!"

The woman recovered her feathers, nodded, and ran toward the hill where we were parked.

"Partner," Chelsea called, avoiding using our names. We should have thought of that before. "We're out of here." She darted off as more people came out of the motel. I hesitated for a moment then turned to run.

It is said that you are most likely to be bitten by the dog you do not see. I failed to understand why the two men's angry looks faded into amusement right as a guy tackled me. It was my own fault for hesitating. I really thought we could get out of or this without hurting anyone. As I hit the ground it looked like I was the one who was going to get hurt.

Chapter Eleven

Wrestling a suspect while holding as loaded gun was dangerous and stupid, and I cursed myself for allowing it. My attacker was strong, but I had a background in the Brazilian art of capoeira and spun as he grabbed me, wrenching his body around. He released his grip, and I tried to bring my weapon to bear but the thug smacked my gun hand and threw himself into a clinch, his arms wrapped around mine. I struggled but my weapon was locked, pointed at the ground. The large man smelled of garlic breath and reeked of too much cologne, which added extra motivation to get him off me.

He lifted me off the ground. I kicked at his legs, but to no effect. So, I headbutted him.

The intention was to drive my forehead directly into his nose. This was a movement I practiced but never actually used. In the movies, people headbutt each other with little ill effect. In reality, my blow to his head was also a blow to mine. I pulled back, dazed, but aware enough that I could see blood fountain from his broken nose as my feet touched the ground. In seconds his eyes would swell and tear up. I feinted a knee to his groin, and he twisted his lower half out of the way. His dodge gave me enough slack to twist out of his grasp.

I brought my weapon up again and he seized my gun hand and tried to wrench it from me. The man had an iron grip, his fingers crushing mine. In desperation I clubbed him on the side of his head with a series of left hooks that left my knuckles sore, but he didn't seem to notice. He wrenched my gun hand behind my back, nearly dislocating my shoulder. Pain knifed through me as I countered the move to no avail. He kicked me and jerked at my weapon. I felt my grip waver; my right hand weak from his bone crushing clench.

A blood curling scream like a young girl being murdered echoed in the night. The young man who ran off earlier, was now running toward us, letting out another shriek. He was answered by a strange trumpeting sound.

Suddenly, swan.

The bird was a whirl of flapping wings, her voice blaring in righteous vengeance. The boy was a vision of terror, clutching his arm in such an awkward position that I was certain it was broken. The swan saw my predicament, discounted the boy, and rushed at us, trumpeting her charge.

She was a vision of white feathered fury as she came at us. My opponent looked up at the creature and jerked in disbelieving shock. I shook my hand free and rolled away.

69

The man swung a series of ineffectual punches as the bird danced around him and got her beak around his muscular arm and wrenched him off his feet, turning her head with a sharp twist. I heard the bone snap.

The man bellowed and tried to jerk his arm free. The swan was having none of it and pulled at the broken limb without remorse.

I jumped up.

The other thug still stood with his arms raised, but if looks could kill... It wasn't just his harsh glare, but the smarmy smile that played on his lips as he imagined what he would do to me. The swan strutted way from her downed opponent. She paused, taking in the enforcer, her blue eyes, more human than bird, narrowed at the other man, as her long slender neck inclined to acknowledge the standing man's raised hands.

"Come on!" I yelled at the swan and ran up the hill, the swan followed using her wings to push her faster. Ahead, Chelsea broke cover and sprinted to the car. We must have been a sight, a man and woman brandishing firearms with a swan in hot pursuit. I grabbed at the door handle and the autolock responded to my touch. A second touch freed all the doors and Chelsea sailed into the passenger seat as I collapsed into the driver's side. The swan took off and circled overhead, watching for signs of pursuit.

Sirens sounded in the distance and I holstered my weapon.

Chelsea placed her hand on the dash, and I could see she was trying to conjure something up.

Nothing happened as she snarled, "Frickin' cold iron."

"Plate under the seat." Basic anti-magic. Can't have the hexkiddies screwing with cop cars.

"This will be harder." She opened the door and leaned out, so her hand touched the ground. She slammed the door. "I couldn't disguise the car, but I've got an illusion ready to go. Make a U-turn." Suddenly a red Ferrari appeared to occupy the same space as us. It pulled out onto the street and sped down toward the hotel. It made a sharp turn, and I saw the black van give chase.

"Nice illusion. Maybe we should wait for the other police," I said.

"No," Chelsea barked with a tone not to be argued with. Her voice and face betrayed the strain of the illusion. "Get us out of here."

"Heard that." I started the engine, but before I could get it into gear the swan swooped down right in front of us. As she landed, she shimmered. The air around her flickered as a blue-white globe. Feathers merged together into a short cloak wrapped around the striking woman. There was no denying her effect on me, up close.

Freed, she was smiling with real joy. Her silver hair and bright blue eyes just led my gaze to the fine boned beauty of her face. The cloak reached only to mid-thigh and revealed long, tan legs. The front opening where the feathers met allowed tantalizing glimpses of smooth tanned skin, a curvaceous figure and impressive cleavage. Her rich, wide mouth changed as her lips twisted in consternation.

The swan maiden tapped her knuckles on Chelsea's window. Chelsea lowered it. The swan maiden bent over to peer in, gave an embarrassed smile and sighed, "Can I get a ride?"

"Get in," Chelsea commanded. "Del, drive."

The swan maiden wasted no time sliding into the rear seat.

I blinked at her. "Can't you just fly?"

"I could fly home," the swan said with irritation, "if I knew where I was, I don't have GPS. Look, I wasn't from around here. I only know Swan Lake."

"Seriously?" I asked.

Chelsea cut in. "She means Echo Park Lake. That's where the swans are."

"I thought the only swans there were the swan pedal boats," I said.

"We have a small bevy. A few of us maidens and maybe a half dozen swans. I need to get back there," the swan pleaded.

I made the U-turn running dark. I was two blocks away before I flicked on the headlights.

"So, Echo Park?" I asked.

"That's it, my home and also the place where I drowned," the swan maiden answered, leaning forward in the rear seat so her head was nearly parallel to ours in the front and I could see her clearly in the rear-view mirror.

"I'm so sorry," Chelsea said with real sympathy. "What happened?"

"I'd been in the city less than a day. I was going to the park but ended up blindly site seeing. Finally found the lake and sat on a bench just as the sun was setting. A man assaulted me. He grabbed my head from behind and jerked me of the bench. I told him I didn't have any money but what he wanted wasn't about money."

Chelsea sighed. A world-weary sound that conveyed the idea she knew this story all too well.

"I kicked him, but that only pissed him off enough to pull out a knife and, well..." She looked down the dangerous neckline of her cloak. A quick glance in the rearview showed me something I didn't see before.

A scar.

"He stabbed me in the chest. A lot. Then he threw my body in the lake, to hide it, I guess," the swan maiden finished.

"Oh my god," Chelsea said in a low voice.

"Oh, don't worry. Dying wasn't really that bad. And I didn't stay dead. That's when the swans showed up. They were ganging for this guy and beat the crap out of him. One of the last things I remember was them plucking his eyeballs out. After that I don't know what happened."

I could see her frown out of the corner of my eye. She took a deep breath, but I heard something catch in her throat as she regained control.

I saw the swans weeping as the world faded."

We sat in silence for a moment, me driving toward Echo Park in an emotional state of suspended animation, somewhere between the day this young woman was brutally murdered and tonight, the night I and Chelsea interceded on her behalf.

"But something must have happened next. You're here," Chelsea prompted in a gentle voice. I wondered if that was her courtroom voice.

The maiden shivered. "I remember sinking in this state of...acceptance, I guess you'd call it. It was strange, after I knew I was dying, it was the most peaceful I've ever felt. Like, it was OK. Then I saw the swans swimming down to me, trying to drag me back to the surface, shedding feathers, and the feathers floating all around me. Next thing I knew, I woke up a swan."

"Wait. Just like that?" Chelsea spun in her seat to look at the maiden.

"You have no idea how peaceful those first few days as a swan were. I would have stayed that way forever."

"I thought swan maidens were incredibly rare," Chelsea said.

"We are indistinguishable from other swans, and we find that it is much better to live as one of them."

"But you were forced to change back?" Chelsea asked.

"It's part of the rules. Monthly we have to revert to human form and bathe. It's the only time we are separated from our cloaks. The biggest rule, though, is first you must be, and stay, a virgin."

I could imagine I heard Chelsea roll her eyes. "Is that all?" she asked dryly.

"We're also not quasi-immortal like some other shapeshifters. Once we change, we get roughly fifty years to live, but we stay young until we die."

"As long as you avoid sex," Chelsea mumbled.

The swan grinned. "There are loopholes."

"So, you were separated from your cloak and that's how that kid got you," Chelsea said.

"I thought he was just a particularly awkward birdwatcher. That's what we call the poor dears that can't help but look while we're bathing. I get it, I mean. I'm way hotter now as a dead swan girl than I was as a living human. In our human form we are unnaturally attractive."

I could attest to that.

"I don't mind the birdwatchers if they are polite and respectful but when I saw him, he turned so red I had to laugh, which he took the wrong way. I felt bad."

She chuckled. "So, this month I let him get an eyeful. I had no idea he was going for my cloak. Bastard." She wrinkled her nose. "He made me get in that black van and they took me to the hotel. I guess they were meeting my buyer there."

"He sold you?" I asked.

The maiden grimaced. "The guy in the van told me in explicit terms what he was going to do. What I was going to be forced to do. He already had a buyer for my virginity. I couldn't believe it! I thought at first maybe they were going to try and sell me to Baba. I mean, that wouldn't be so bad. I could do the kinda sex work that lets me keep my cloak. And she would have paid for me, at least as a hostage. Baba be that way."

"Baba's?"

Chelsea answered, "Baba runs a supernatural brothel where they respect the needs of the workers. I do business with them, security. I'll take you by sometime." Chelsea turned to the swan. "If you lost your swan ability, would they still be able to control you?"

"I don't think so, but I got the impression they were gonna try."

"Likely with drugs or threats."

"Enslaving swan girls and swiping magical, mind-controlling amulets." I sighed. "What is the RNC up to?"

"The same old tricks. If they have an object of power that can control their women, then that would be much cheaper, and more reliable than drugs. God, can you imagine? The pimp has the money, and the girl thinks that she is acting of her own free will."

"Let's get the swan lady—"

The swan maiden interrupted me. "Hildegarde," she said.

"We'll get Hildegarde," she I amended, "back to her swan lake."

"Excuse me," Hildegarde said, "but are you a couple?"

Chelsea froze and I felt her gaze on me as she spoke in a tentative voice. "Maybe, it's complicated."

"Too bad." She leaned forward, her head between the seats. "You rescuing me is extremely hot and you're way cute. I'd love to take you down to my bower and show you my loopholes." Her voice was on the cusp of alluring and teasing.

I could feel the tips of my ears turning red. "Thank you, but—"

"I wasn't talking to *you*," Hildegarde laughed. She batted her blue eyes at Chelsea. "I can show you some very nice loopholes."

Chelsea smiled but I could sense her embarrassment. "Thanks for the thought. I'm flattered, but..." Chelsea placed her hand on my thigh.

I fought not to flinch in surprise.

"We are a couple, even if it is super complicated," she said with a decisive tone.

"Super complicated" was an understatement.

"Oh well..." Hildegarde said, disappointed, but without any rancor. "If you ever break up with him, just come down to the lake at sunset and call my name."

I turned into the park lane at the north end of the lake. Chelsea gripped my thigh in tight surprise. Two squad cars waited for us.

I pulled up to the cars with their lights blinking, making red and blue splashes over the water. The water was bout thirty meters away. It was a small, man-made lake and I couldn't imagine where a swan maiden would have enough privacy to bathe. I motioned for Chelsea to wait in the car, then opened my door and beckoned Hildegarde to join me.

There were two cars, four uniformed police, and a haggard looking man lying on the ground in handcuffs. The police were arguing with a woman whose black skin shone under the flashlight beam trained on her. She wore a black version of Hildegarde's tunic and was the most muscular woman I had ever seen, but somehow that made her more feminine. A warrior goddess. Her hair fell in thick cornrow braids over her covering of black feathers. Where Hildegarde was friendly, even sexy, this black swan was just as beautiful, but angry and not afraid of the officers.

"What's going on here?" I demanded, displaying my credentials.

A cop turned to me, and I saw the single white stripe on his sleeve that identified him as a licensed magician, junior grade. "Just trying to arrest this guy, but this woman is interfering. I'm about ready to cuff her and charge her with obstruction."

"You can try," the black swan snapped. Her accent was very British upper class.

"What did he do?" I asked.

"Oh, he's a mental case. Made a false report of an abduction. Said a girl named Hildegarde was snatched. But it turns out Hildegarde is his

74

favorite wild swan. I tried to explain that abducting a swan was not in our jurisdiction. That's when he got animated."

"Oh, Klaus," Hildegarde sighed.

I turned to her. "You know this guy?"

"He's a birdwatcher, one of the sweet ones." She turned to the cop. "*I'm* Hildegarde. This man saw *me* abducted. There was no false report."

"I took care of the abductors," I lied. "Uncuff him."

"He's still going down for attacking me." The junior cop's body language shifted to aggressive. Great. I needed some trouble from Los Diablos' finest tonight. I didn't have enough in my "Trouble from my Co-workers" collection.

I adopted a tactic many police use: blatantly disregarding any injury they've caused, or any injuries they don't want to deal with, and addressing real harm with a condescending sarcasm. I channeled the worst of that tactic and said with a smirk, "You don't *look* hurt."

"He came at me."

"Oooh. He came at you." I hit the sarcasm hard. "He looks like he got the worst of it. I found the girl, just uncuff him. It doesn't do anyone any good to haul him off."

"But—"

"Uncuff him or I will. I mean, you can spend the night locked in the interview room with a nut bag yelling about swans if you *really* want to." I stepped toward the guy, hands on my hips. "I can make all that paperwork happen. For you." I looked up to see the black swan eyeing me. She gave me the tiniest nod of approval.

The magic-using cop gave a long-suffering sigh as he produced the handcuff key and bent over."

"What about the girl?" the other officer asked.

"Part of an ongoing case. I will be responsible for her. I'll take care of everything." I turned to the magic user. "Your body camera light is off. Is the camera operational?"

"I guess I forgot to turn it on." He stomped off.

The black swan waited until he was out of ear shot to address me, all the while studying me with big, dark, unknowable, incredible eyes. "I am Nandi. This is my bevy. Threaten them at your own peril." The words were careful, her voice a regal alto.

I bowed my head in respect. "Noted," I said seriously. "Pleased to meet you."

Nandi replied with the tiniest of nods.

Chelsea tugged at my shoulder. "Don't you have a cat to feed?"

Chapter Twelve

Pakhet was not happy. Cocopuff missed her evening feeding and was threatening to cast her out. Which put Vlad on do-not-stop-petting-this-cat-for-any-reason-lest-the-ire-Cocopuff-be-known duty.

That meant Vlad was idly petting the cat as he perused the reports I left. She twisted away from him as I entered. Now the vampire was more tolerated than me.

"Come on, we have a big day tomorrow." I reached to pick her up. She jumped away.

"I'll walk, thank you." Her voice was icy.

I didn't argue and she followed me out to the car where she basically sulked the entire ride home, then ate her diner in quiet disdain.

Next morning, I met with Lenore and drove to the gothic mansion in the West Adams neighborhood in Southern LD. This was the "Chapter House" of the Nogs, the largest magical quasi-religious group in the world. There was no parking lot, but I knew from experience there was a carriage house converted to a spacious garage out back. Thirty monks and a cook lived in the house. How they survived in LD without more than two cars is beyond me.

I settled for street parking. A low wall topped with a wrought iron fence protected the red brick Romanesque building. Each joint of the wrought iron was cast with a different, protective sigil. The fence gave off the scent of iron but with a trace of something sweeter in the background. A garden scent, the smell of clean dirt.

We walked from the car and Pakhet followed us, moving warily. The tiny, shaved patch on her chest, about the size of a postage stamp, seemed to cause her unwarranted discomfort. There were consequences from the effort on my part. Even as she promised to cooperate.

The front gate stood open, and I pushed through to walk the short driveway to the front door. Lenore clicked her tongue at the ornate patterns of the façade. I always thought they were random decoration, but her expression hinted they must be magical. I took in a deep breath, more of the garden smell.

On the right of the limestone steps a stone turret stood out, the top crenelated like a castle, and below that the turret had multiple pointed arched windows.

I heard a faint buzzing noise and turned to find a large quadcopter drone with a camera staring at us.

"Boys and their toys," Lenore muttered.

The drone rose straight up and out of sight.

Cat Scan

The front door opened, and Archabbot Kaufman waited for us in his simple brown wool hooded robe, the cowl thrown back to reveal his smiling face and black hair with only a few strands of silver. In his hands he held the controller for the flying spy. He was clean shaven and smelled of lemon. "Come in."

"Nice drone," I remarked.

"Yes, it's partly for security but I'm also researching its flight characteristics. You see by studying the movement we hope to create a reliable magic alternative. One that can be controlled by a wand or crystal." He wrinkled his nose and jerked his head toward the front of the great room. "The others are already here.?"

"Others?" I stepped inside and followed Kaufman to the great room to find Modeste and Minors waiting for us.

In the presence of the archabbot Modeste was relaxed and an almost cheerful smile played on her lips. For a moment I remembered why I'd fallen in love with her. And that made me think of the ring. I needed to get rid of the platinum band. I had no intention to recycle. Maybe I should have hocked it for the money to buy gold and left the Nogs out of this.

Her eyes went to me and her smile became professional, cordial. "Delacroix," she addressed me politely.

"Ms. Modeste. I did not expect you here until eleven. When we are scheduled to move the amulet."

"Yes, well. Dr. Kaufman let us know about this little attempt to free the clown. Mr. Minors said he wanted to see the ritual." I deduced that she was here to limit Minors' access to the amulet.

I stared at an ornate chest in the center of the room covered in multiple engraved brass plaques. I recognized some of the sigils. That was some serious containment.

I looked at Kaufman, who raised one eyebrow. "Yes, the original amulet is in there. I told Ms. Modeste we would attempt to create an alternate amulet and draw the clown out." He gave me a tight smile.

"And I came to say, of course, that it's too dangerous," Modeste said. "There is something evil in there and you don't want it loose."

"Yes," Kaufman said with a sigh. "Nergal."

Modeste blanched as he said the name.

"Nergle? That's its name?" Minors said with a surprised half chortle.

"Nuhr-gal," Kaufman intoned. "An incarnation of a god of violence and death."

"Really?" Minors said, still amused. "It sounds more like the god of getting beat up and its lunch money taken."

Kaufman snorted. "Well, you saw what he started when he got just a little bit loose."

"A little bit?" I asked.

"The power you saw was but a tiny percent of what is there."

I'd been worried, now I was terrified.

"Wait," Pakhet said. From guarded facial expressions, I could tell that Lenore and Kaufman also heard. "I don't want to be in there with Westley."

Kaufman stooped down. "Come here, little one." He held up a finger. Pakhet sauntered up and touched her nose to the finger. She let Kaufman pick her up and carry her to the far side of the room.

The others stared at him as he talked to the cat in quiet, soothing tones. He looked up. "Just calming the cat. Poor thing is not happy you shaved her chest." He made it sound like it was my idea. He set Pakhet down and whatever he told her had calmed her. He turned to Modeste and Minors. "I'll need to prepare for the ritual; can you give me a moment please?"

I stood to leave.

"Not you. I need to talk to you about accepting you into our order."

Modeste and Minors headed for the door. Lenore looked like she was not going anywhere. Once the departing pair were out of the room, the door closed by itself.

Lenore grinned at Kaufman. "Show off."

The monk ignored her and carried Pakhet to his desk. He set her down and from a drawer he produced two tiny gold amulets in the form of a scarab. He petted and whispered something to Pakhet, and the cat rolled onto her back, displaying the shaved patch on her chest. I could have used him when I had the razor out. Hercules fighting a lion has nothing on shaving an unsedated cat. I explained it was necessary and Pakhet sullenly agreed, but when I started the process Cocopuff kicked Pakhet back and expressed extreme disapproval. Fortunately, I wore a leather motorcycle jacket.

It was a shame. I liked that jacket.

He tapped the first amulet with his finger. "We are going to try to free the clown, but I doubt Nergal will let him go that easily. Westley is his only current form of entertainment, after all." He hunched over Pakhet, undid the clasp on the brass and glass copy of the original, and let the ornate collar fall to the floor. He picked up one of the scarabs and held it against the shaved patch. Pakhet lay still as Kaufman produced a strip of self-adhesive bandage to hold it in place. He picked up the cat and set it beside the containment box. From a hidden pocket he produced white cotton gloves and donned them before he opened the containment box. He removed the original amulet, restored to the Usekh collar with its golden winged Isis and fastened it to Pakhet, concealing the scarab. "There you go, little one."

Pakhet rolled, stood, stretched and struggled with the weight of the collar and amulet.

"It's just for a short while, little one. Kaufman picked up the duplicate amulet and then from the box produced another Usekh. It would take great powers of observation to see which one was the original

Kaufman picked up the ersatz amulet and deftly fasten it to the collar. "Alright." He clapped his hands together and grinned. "Showtime." He escorted us to the ceremony.

The ritual space was a modest, twenty-foot circular room lit only by candlelight; the walls and ceiling covered with symbols. Four doors entered from the cardinal directions. Beside each door sat an ornate chair, practically a throne. Ten feet off the floor there was a railing, and more chairs arranged like a nineteenth century operating theater. Some of the sigils I recognized, but most were signs I never saw before. Which was good. My profession made sure I was mostly familiar with the evil ones.

We observers were arranged in the chairs, one of us by each door. The floor at first appeared black, but once I was in the room I could see it was an extremely dark charcoal gray, with a ten-foot diameter circle of silver. Ten monks, including Kaufman, were staging items around the room. To me it appeared to be random accent furniture, small tables and ottomans.

The monks were all dressed in identical brown robes, and all wore white cotton gloves as they arranged themselves outside the circle and chanted in a language unknown to me. I was expecting Latin, which the Catholic school part of me would understand.

Instead, all I could make out was an odd combination of a hum with sharp guttural highlights.

"This is the original." Kaufman placed the amulet supposedly recovered from the clown in the precise center of the silver circle.

I caught myself before I gave a start of surprise at the lie. The original collar, now won Pakhet, made of real gold and Lapis lazuli. The cheap duplicate Kaufman held was just as pretty but made of brass and artificial jewels. I gave a glance to see if Modeste or Minors noticed, but that detail was apparently lost in the dim light. Kaufman was being a sneaky boy, indeed.

He out the second golden scarab and placed it on the larger

amulet. "This is our proposed receptacle for the imprisoned man Westley."

No one objected as he then placed Pakhet inside the circle. She appeared asleep.

High Magick is arduous to perform but extremely dull to watch. Everything must be repeated over and over. The two naked dancing girls were interesting, although I am not sure how they fitted into the ritual.

I was nearly napping when the room shook. I started up but Lenore caught my eye and her glare held me down.

It is hard to describe what happened next. Something tried to ignite the middle of the circle like before, but what I saw was a ghost of fire, a mere shade of the flame the entity summoned before. This was like the shimmer you see over hot pavement, forming into a small ball in the center, pulsing. Tendrils of the ghost flame wafted over to Pakhet, who shivered mas shimmer embraced her in a translucent bubble.

The monks chanted in the same strange language, but now with more intensity.

The pulsing almost-fire vanished. I felt a weight I hadn't noticed fall off me. A steam-like haze gathered over the items in the center of the circle.

Pakhet jumped up and spun around as if seeing everything for the first time. I stood, intending to walk to her, but Lenore rushed to restrain me. Pakhet turned to me, arched her back and hissed.

Kaufman ignored the center of the circle and walked around it to pick up the cat, who calmed at his touch. He scratched the cat behind the ears. "Pakhet."

"Yes," she replied in her usual voice, but she sounded exhausted.

"Alright," Kaufman said as he sat the cat back on the floor. He rubbed his palms together. "Well, that's something."

"So, where's the clown?" Minors demanded.

Kaufman clucked at Minors and shrugged. "I am afraid we were unsuccessful. Two problems. He is now the unwilling guardian of Nergal, but worse, even though he doesn't want to be there, he is terrified to leave."

"So, he is still trapped," Modeste said.

Neither of the other two observers asked why the cat was in the circle. But that is one thing about High Magick. If you don't know what is necessary, you best be out of the way and let the magicians work.

"Are we done here?" Minors said in an impatient tone.

"Just one thing." Kaufman stooped low. He brushed Pakhet's back and deftly unfastened the elaborate Egyptian Usekh collar and laid it beside the other amulet. As he bent over and turned, the full skirt of his robe hid the pieces. I only noticed the sleight of hand because I was watching for it. He stood up and held the genuine amulet aloft with his gloved hands. Another monk appeared and set the containment box beside him. He carefully settled the amulet.

"Come and get your cat." He picked up the copy collar and held it out.

Pakhet crouched by his feet, her body limp.

"We need the scarab, as well," Kaufman said. I approached cautiously. When she didn't hiss, I picked her up. She was not happy. I would say her mood was sullen, angry and depressed.

"Are you okay?" I whispered in her ear.

Pakhet turned her face to me, raised her nose and turned away. She twitched; not comfortable and making sure I knew it.

"OK. We're done here," Minors announced. "I've signaled my team, and they're on their way with a proper level three containment device." He sneered at the wooden chest.

Modeste silently fumed. I think she wanted something more to happen, something to prevent Minors from taking possession of the amulet.

The team arrived in the magical version of hazmat suits carrying a steel box that looked like the bastard child of a dumpster and a parking meter. They jingled with amulets and charms. The silk robes swished as they moved the amulet from the wooden chest to the magical mechanical marvel they brought. They paid no attention to me holding the cat with the obvious bandage; they just marched out. Modeste and Minors followed.

Once they were gone, Kaufman handed the ornate brass collar to another monk. Then he unfastened the bandage from Pakhet and handed the tiny scarab over as well. "Fashion that with a strong chain, then figure a way to affix it to the collar, but so it can be removed and worn by itself."

The monk bowed and left.

I petted the cat. "It is okay, they will return the new amulet to you."

"I can still feel its magic," Pakhet said, her voice a depressed sigh.

"That's good, right?"

The cat gave world weary mental shrug. "I need that amulet," she said. "I don't think I want it, though."

"What's wrong?"

"Nothing." She sighed again. "Let it go."

"If there is a problem—"

"Let it go." Pahhet's angry tone was enough to make all who could hear it jump, which was pretty much everyone in the room.

Kauffman held the empty second scarab in his gloved hand, peering at it with all the detached confusion of a foiled academic. "I really thought we could pull off a two-for. Get a room for Pakhet and poor Westley the Clown at the same time. Huh."

"I want to get away from here," Pakhet hissed.

"Okay, little one."

The monk returned with the Usekh, now augmented with the scarab.

Pakhet was still acting sullen, although she preened a bit when Kaufman but her collar back on her.

"Dancing girls?" Lenore said in a mocking tone.

"You know my third rule of life."

Lenore rolled her eyes hard. "There is no situation that cannot be improved by swordplay or dancing girls. Or both."

I eyed the amused look on the archabbot's face. I wondered what the first two rules were.

"Fun as always, Bobby," Lenore said. "But we got to go."

"Come back any time," Kaufman said with mock salute.

"I may take you up on that."

"Well, my dear. When you drop by be sure to bring your saber."

"Oh, with the swordplay again." Lenore nudged me in the ribs with her elbow. "Maybe I'll change things up a bit and bring a falcata."

"What?" I asked.

"A falcata. An ancient sword that straddled the bronze age and iron age. Popular in Greece, Türkiye and Bulgaria. I think you could find one for me."

I had no idea where she was going with the name play.

Lenore strode out and I followed, carefully cradling Pakhet. Since everything appeared to be in order, Lenore and I went back to the office to do the paperwork.

Funny thing about the *appearance* of everything being in order.

Chapter Thirteen

The day went by fast. I opened the apartment door and Pakhet rushed inside. For the last week she was aloof, but as soon as she got the amulet, she became downright hostile. I followed her in.

She promptly disappeared. My apartment is not that big; one bedroom, one bath, a small living room and a kitchen that could be a walk-in closet. That did not leave many places to hide. But I was going to let her be, for now. She would eventually come out from hiding and let me know what was troubling her. Or not.

I took off my jacket, loosened my tie and was deciding which would be the better evening; watch an old favorite movie, or try something new? Or laundry?

There was a tentative knock at my door, and I looked out the peephole.

Chelsea Falcata stood there in a club dress cut down low and displaying very nice legs. She wore makeup; actual make-up, not cosmetic glamour, and her hair had an artistic, tousled look.

She stood rigid, her hands clasped in front of her. It was the first time I ever saw her dressed like this and I imagined this is what she looked like when she was an escort.

I had also never seen such a mixture of fear and embarrassment on her face. Her carefully shaded eyes were downcast, her crimson lips clenched in determination.

I opened the door. She changed her expression to an alluring smile and looked at me with bedroom eyes.

"Chelsea, something happen?"

She pushed past me and strode into my apartment. Her smile flickered as she took in my secondhand furniture. The green and gold couch had seen better days. The only expensive item I owned was my bed. There are somethings you cannot scrimp on.

She turned to me, her bearing going from sexy to professional, as if she reevaluated the situation. "Del, we need to talk." She didn't wait but walked over to my tiny table and sat in one of the two chairs.

I wished the place looked better; or at least more organized. Over three years, only Vlad had seen my place. I did not expect to have a female visitor.

I took a deep breath in through my nose and tried to ease the butterflies in my stomach. I really had no clue why she was here. The chair scraped on the tile floor as I settled at the table.

She was trying to be attractive, even sexy. I mean she looked good, real good, but I preferred her usual look, without glamour or the cosmetics.

Chelsea sat rigid with her hands still clasped in front of her, her thumbs rubbing together.

"You are worrying me. Something bad happen?"

That look of embarrassment flickered on her face again, just for a second, before she said, "Not yet, but the night is still young." She leaned toward me. "Last night I told Hildegarde we were a couple."

"Don't worry about that, you were humoring the swan."

Her face resumed the embarrassed look. Her forced smile looked fragile, and her eyes were wide with fright. She was terrified. "Del, when I said we were a couple, I meant it. A couple of what, I don't know. Look. I'm going to be straight forward with you."

"You have never been anything else."

"I'm not in love with you or falling in love with you."

"Okay." My tone was neutral but there was a hint of disappointment in my mind.

"But," she continued. "I've been obsessed with you since I pulled you out of that hotel room and pretended you were my fiancé." She took a deep breath to steady herself. "A decade ago, I made a very serious decision. I will not fall in love. I will not get married. I will not have children. I don't have time for the drama. Also, I am incapable of compromise."

I saw a flicker in the corner of my eye and Pakhet was out of hiding and now calmly licking her paws.

"I believe you have some feeling for me, and I know how absurdly complicated the whole thing is. But I am here to get over my obsession. So, I need you to tell me to leave, and you are not interested or…" She left that hanging.

Pakhet jumped up on the table, her tail swishing. "We need to talk."

Chelsea rocked back in her chair as she stared at the cat.

"You heard her?" I asked in surprise.

"The cat?"

"It is not the cat," I explained., "but an entity that occupies her for the moment."

"Detective Delacroix," Pakhet addressed me formally. "I told you the first time we met Ms. Falcata I should be with her. I stayed with you because I needed your assistance to get the amulet, but now that is done with." She turned to Chelsea and from the look on her face, I could tell the cat was talking to her. She did not include me in the exchange.

"I see," Chelsea said slowly. "I don't have time to take care of a cat."

"I'm pretty self-sufficient," Pakhet countered, this time letting me in on the conversation. "I tried to get along with the detective, but we don't really belong together."

I thought back to the first week we were at my place. She was far more playful and affectionate. What did I do to alienate her?

"I guess the cat can go with me. But the reason I came—"

"Was for clarity, I assume," I said. "I am attracted to you, but I have conflicting feelings. For us to even consider seeing each other would be beyond merely complicated. Everything would require a lot of effort."

"I understand," Chelsea said in her most professional manner. "Sorry to bother you, I will leave."

"*Non*, you do not understand." I reached across the table and took her hands. "Anything worth having is worth working for. I am not afraid of the effort. I am concerned that your crusade is dangerous, and being involved with me could make it more so." I looked her right in the eyes, but she didn't meet mine.

Chelsea seemed surprised by my hands on hers. She looked up at me and let her feelings show. She was still frightened and embarrassed. "Dangerous. That is my prerogative. You're more likely to be the one in greater danger." She let out a long, slow breath. "One more reason I should leave. There are too many people gunning for me as it is. I don't want you in the crossfire."

"Ah, but isn't that *my* prerogative?" I smiled, but a part of my brain thought Grand-mère would not be happy with no great grandchildren.

She looked down at her hands. Her eyes glistened with unshed tears.

"My mother was so sick that Laura practically raised me. After she died, after she was murdered, my life was destroyed. I thought I would die, too. I couldn't cook, I was a child, couldn't work. I barely knew how to get from my house to the school. Laura had always walked me, every day, and I held her hand and let her lead me without ever taking a second look around."

She sighed. Her body seemed to collapse with the weight of built-up sorrow and she pushed my hands away. "And then, she was just gone." Her lips clenched and a glint of anger flitted across her eyes. "So, I told myself, never again." She glared at me, her face an iron mask. "I would never be so reliant on someone that I might die if they were just gone one day. I wanted to die when Laura was gone, but I had to take care of my mother. She fought her cancer for two more years and I was there for her. I learned to cook, I fed her, and I cleaned her up. The worst days..." Chelsea paused and got a distant look in her tear-brimmed eyes, "...were the long ones, when I was gone for a long time and she was just lying there, in her own refuse, thirsting because I couldn't afford a nurse, and didn't know who to ask for help. And that's when I added another condition to my rules: Never would I be so indispensable to someone that they might die if I was the one gone one day."

"At twelve?"

"When she died, the body wasn't even cold before I was in the system. My new foster parents wouldn't even let me go to the funeral." The anger was back in her eyes. "Said it was better to have a clean break, forget my previous life, to create a new attachment. They believed if I was given time to grieve it would slow my attachment to them." She dropped her head and bit her lower lip.

A hard silence hung in the air. I felt I should say something, but my brain could not settle on what.

She raised her head and assumed an expression of grim determination. "That's when I understood exactly what it was to be *powerless*." She pronounced the word as if it was the most loathsome word in the world. And maybe she had a point. "I swore never to be powerless again. No one will ever have power over me as long as I live." She thrust a finger at me. "Not you." She turned to the cat and spoke to her, but more playfully. "Not you either, little one." She drew her gaze back to me. "Foster care taught me more about life than I wanted. As a prostitute, I learned even more. I told you before why I did it, but not my secret."

"Secret?"

She hung her head, and her eyes glinted with denied tears. "I was hoping the man who killed her would come for me." Her voice turned icy. "I fantasized about doing to him what he did to Laura. Explicitly detailed fantasies." She half chuckled. "I think they scared my therapist but I could never really do it. I would just kill him cleanly. Not for him, but because there would be someone else; a mother, sister, brother who would have to live with the images of what I did."

I reached for her hands again. Anger shone in her eyes, and she must have seen a flash of fear in my eyes as I pulled my hands back.

"I'm sorry. I'm not angry with you, I won't hurt you." She took my hands. "Not intentionally," She amended. "No, I never found him, and I haven't killed anyone."

"Ahem," Pakhet cleared her throat. "I am so sorry for your loss. I can taste your misery, but had no idea of the details. I would like to learn more about your sister, but I think we should depart and leave the detective to make up his mind."

I rubbed my thumbs across her clasped hands in mine, then gave them a firm squeeze. "I've made my decision." I stood and pulled her to her feet. Our eyes locked as I drew her to me.

"Please," Pakhet interrupted, annoyed. "Could you wait until I'm out of here before you do that?"

I put my hands on Chelsea's shoulders. "I've been thinking about you a lot." I was going to kiss her but felt Pakhet's angry glare, so I released her. But our eyes locked with all the intimacy of the aborted kiss.

Chelsea hung her head. When she looked up at me, she had a sincere, if sad, smile. But there was something in her eyes. Hope? Relief?

"I don't even have a litter box…"

"I'm a person and I know how a toilet works," Pakhet interrupted. "Take me to a pet store and I will point out the food I need," she said with sense of irrevocable conviction.

"There is fish in the fridge." I took a moment and gathered a few cat toys and put them in a box with half a bag of cat food and a dozen fish fillets, including a piece of bluefin tuna that cost more than my rent.

Chelsea took them silently and headed for the door. I followed.

We both froze at the sound of three knocks.

Chelsea glanced at me with a raised eyebrow. "You expecting someone?"

"*Non*," I said, trying to think who it might be. I looked out the peephole. A startled chuckle escaped as I identified the caller. "It's Leslie Modeste. She was working with the amulet. She does not know at all about Pakhet. She's also an ex of mine. Do you want to hide in the bedroom?"

"Not really," Chelsea answered. She gave me her best deadpan stare, but there was definitely a hint of mischievousness in her voice. Like she'd love seeing the other woman nettled.

I shrugged. "*D'accord.*" Leslie hurt me more than almost anyone in my life I am not ashamed to say I wept as I gathered my things from the storage unit, except that is not true. I did not just weep. I gibbered like an idiot as I threw my things into a rented van. I berated myself for allowing her to be so important to me that her absence may well kill me. I made such a fuss that two young women working in another storage unit came to ask if I was all right. I wiped away the tears streaming down my face and used every bit of self-control I had to swallow my feelings and pretend I was well. They left, unconvinced.

I was in the mood to give Leslie a tweak as I opened the door and, like Chelsea before, Leslie barged in. "Delacroix. What did you and that Nog snake oil salesman do with the amulet? And here I thought I could trust Bobby!" She froze at the sight of Chelsea in her sexy dress. She sniffed and her face reddened.

"It's not what you think," I said, and the cliché line felt amusing.

Chelsea laughed. "I'm just here to pick up the cat." Her voice was light and dripping sarcasm, implying that the situation was exactly as Leslie must imagine.

Leslie must practice that stare in the mirror, I thought. *Judgmental, angry and offended simultaneously. So familiar.*

"Pardon my interruption," she said, matching Chelsea's sarcasm but adding a dismissive smirk. She focused on Pakhet and the collar with the amulet.

She strode to Pakhet like she was going to seize the collar. Pakhet sat calmly, looking like a semi-feral statue. Leslie stopped and scrutinized the collar from beyond Pakhet's swipe range.

"That's a fake too," Leslie snorted. "But there is something…"

"Protective wards," I told her.

"Whatever. I'll have you know I figured out the amulet you two sent to the museum is a fake. A better fake than that poor cat's. But, why, Del? If you two weren't using the cat to steal the real amulet, why was the cat even there?"

Pakhet raised her head. I feared she was about to say something, but she must have thought better of it and sat down, licking her paws.

"What makes you think the one at the museum is fake?" I asked.

"They won't let me get close enough to study it. It's in a level three containment area. But there is zero residual magic energy."

"But that is the point of level three," I argued.

"She's right, Del," Chelsea interrupted.

The tight frown from Leslie showed how much she liked Chelsea agreeing with her.

Chelsea continued, "You'd still detect residual magic *if* you're sensitive enough." She raised an eyebrow at Leslie.

"Oh, I'm sensitive enough." She furrowed her brow and wrinkled her nose at Chelsea again and crossed her arms. Then she looked at me. "What's *really* going on here, Delacroix?"

"She's just picking up her cat." I pointed to the box of supplies. "She let me borrow the little one for the ceremony," I lied, surprised by how easy it was.

Leslie waved her hand at me. "I mean with the cat and the fake amulets, Delacroix, quit giving me the runaround. Save that for her. You give her that same puppy dog look you had when you told me about the Trinidad girl."

I did not rise to the jibe and gave Leslie a defensive shrug. "It was Kaufman's direction. If Kaufman could free the clown's spirit, he needed a place to keep it."

"So. You don't have it. You don't know who does." She glared at me as I shrugged again. "Magical crimes, Detective Delacroix. That's your area. God help us if that amulet gets into the wrong hands." She gave one curt dismissive nod to me and a sneer to Chelsea, then stomped out, slamming the door behind her.

There was moment of silence and Chelsea spoke, "That went well."

I laughed in spite of myself.

Chelsea picked up the box of cat stuff. "At least we got the awkward ex encounter over. I didn't think it was going to be *that* quick, but." She gave a little grimace that said, "Oh well."

I shrugged. "I'm sorry but considering how she left me I could not resist rubbing her nose in the fact that I've moved on. Sorry about what she thinks about you."

"I have a thick skin."

I looked at her cheeks, at her smooth, tan skin. *Not that thick,* I thought.

"As much fun as this is," Chelsea said with that sad smile, "I'd better be going."

I opened the door for her and Pakhet and she paused halfway through. Realizing there was something between us, a box of cat things, she set the box down and addressed me one more time "What now?"

"I can honestly say I don't know." I took her hands. "I want to get to know you better. Sorry about my ex."

She snorted and looked down at her dress. "This is not the way I expected the night to go. I honestly thought you'd be horrified at the thought of a relationship, especially if I played the whore. Your rejection would motivate me to stop obsessing. Either that, or I'd have let you have sex with me, and get you out of my system and pretend you were just another cop I paid off with my body, or the johns I hooked up with. But dammit, you are kind. I don't know how to process that." She gave me a peck on the cheek. "You're also kinduv oblivious."

My face warmed at the touch of her lips. I pulled her in close. I took in her scent; just a touch of perfume and felt… not lust, but something more refined, something that filled the many cracks in my heart. That hug was more emotionally intimate than the sex would have been.

"Dinner tomorrow?" I whispered in her ear.

"Tomorrow, but after dinner. I have something to show you."

Then she broke the embrace and strode down the hall, her hips giving just a hint of sway in her tight dress.

I closed my door before either of us changed our minds, and the look in her eyes burned into my mind. Her eyes were so bright when she pulled away from me. Tears?

Chapter Fourteen

The next morning, I was eager to get started on my last day shift, but my anticipation faltered when I saw Lenore waiting at my desk.

She had an aggrieved sneer on her face. "You have a visitor. That Modeste lady says she *urgently*, her word, needs to talk to you."

I sighed. "*Merde*, she stopped by my place last night. She is convinced that the amulet displayed at the museum's level three is a fake." The method of containment at the museum was designed to allow the item to be displayed, but no one could get within ten feet without a keyed charm.

"Most likely," Lenore said with a sharp nod.

"You agree?"

"Well, with the way my mind works, that's what I would do. Display a fake while I examine the real thing. Nothing nefarious, they're probably just playing it close to the vest."

"And if it is nefarious?"

Lenore spread her hands. "That is the question. Speaking of questions. Ms. Modeste was at *your* place? What's going on between you two? I know it's something. The frumpy look with the aggressive hairstyle doesn't seem to be your type. I thought you were into the sex worker vigilante sort."

I shrugged. "It is nothing, at least not now. We were involved back in Florida. Living together."

"Oh, Del," Lenore said with too much delight. "I didn't think you had it in you." Her smile begged for gossip. "What happened?"

"I bought a ring and was preparing to ask her to marry me."

Lenore's eye grew wide, and she impatiently waved her hand for me to continue. "And?"

I moved past Lenore and started unceremoniously shuffling files without really looking at them. "I honestly have no idea. My aunt died. I remember lying in bed and telling Leslie that I had to go to the funeral, in Haiti. She was crying because she could not go to Haiti with me. There was no way I could not go. After my mother died, Aunt Mirlande and my *grand-mére* took care of me. Mirlande supplied financial support for me all the way through college."

"Okay, then what?"

I sighed as I recalled all the hurt and confusion. "I don't know. It took two days before I could get to Haiti, and I immediately was put to work. Did you know the body must be protected for nine days, and there are also wakes and family gatherings? On day four I called Leslie to let her know I arrived and was safe, and the phone was disconnected. I called several times over the next five days, after all she'd likely forgotten to pay the bill. She'd done that before. No internet in my aunt's village, Fond des Blancs. I was frantic to get back and ensure Leslie was okay until she called, right as I returned from the funeral. All she said was 'It's not you, it's me. I'm leaving and please do not try to find me. I boarded out the horses and put your stuff in storage. My parents have a letter for you. Good-bye.'" I sighed. "I never saw her again until the other day."

Lenore looked angry. "And she never had to explain herself? Nothing in the letter she left you?"

"*Non*, just instruction to locate the storage unit. She talked about moving to San Francisco to complete her Ph.D." I shrugged. "I guess that is want what she did."

"That *bitch*," Lenore hissed. "You do not deserve that treatment." She grimaced. "And you didn't try to find her?"

"I got a lot of sympathy, but no one would tell me anything. Her father said she had commitment issues."

"Jesus, Del. You sure know how to pick 'em." She treated me to a wicked smile. "How are things going with Falcata?"

"*Rein.*"

Lenore smoothed her hair back. "It's not nothing. Del, I can read you like a book. One with the extra-large print."

"It's complicated. She came over last night."

"I thought *Modeste* came over last night." She saw the look in my eye. "OOOOH, I bet that was awkward."

I gave her a smirk. "You have no idea. Leslie thinks Chelsea is a working prostitute. Chelsea and I had a talk about expectations of a relationship."

"Look at you, so clinical, so unromantic. What happened? I bet they both left unsatisfied."

"We talked, Leslie interrupted, we talked some more. Chelsea took Pakhet."

"What?" Lenore had her back to me, leaning over something on my desk, but she turned to face me. "Is that safe? We don't really know what that entity is. There could be serious complications. They're both empaths." Her tone seemed to assume I knew what she meant.

"It was the cat's idea. Apparently, I did something, and she couldn't stand to be around me." I set the files I had been shuffling down. "There is no indication that the entity is malicious."

"God, you are so oblivious." She snickered. "I don't know how you made detective and are still so naive. No, I take that back. I have an acquaintance, Carmen, who, like you, thinks of me as a friend. She's asexual. As a teen she thought she was broken and set out to study human sexuality. Now she has two Ph.Ds., and still doesn't get it, because there's nothing to get. She just doesn't feel sexual attraction. You can smell magic but have no talent, which is great for your job. You are an expert in the *Voudon*, and malicious magical items, but interacting with entities, dealing with an evil magician? You know the how, but not the why."

I had no idea what her point was.

She smiled and changed the subject. "Let's go see your ex."

I barely opened the door to the interview room before Leslie snapped at me. "What are you going to do about the amulet?"

I blinked. "I don't know that I can do anything. We gave it to the museum. They took it to San Francisco. You were there."

"I've been thinking since I met your…" she made air quotes, "'friend.' I realized I don't know you anymore, if I ever did. You and Bobby did something with the real amulet. It was on a cat, for crying out loud! Don't bother to deny it, the good brother is not all *that* skilled in sleight of hand. And I could feel the way the energy flowed—"

"I swear, on my mother's grave, we gave the real amulet to Minors.

Lenore cut in. "What makes you think the one in San Francisco is fake?"

"I just know it is!" Leslie snipped and addressed me. "It is amazing how little you actually know about magic theory with what you do." She paused for breath. "No matter the containment, magic that powerful would leave some trace."

Lenore placed her hand affectionately on my upper arm. "Del, she's right. Especially if she previously handled it. Part of her is attuned to it. See, you are just like Carmen." She gave my arm an affectionate squeeze and bestowed a sultry smile.

I glanced at Leslie. Her face betrayed nothing, but I knew she was fuming. She glanced at Lenore and sniffed. "We don't have time for whatever it is you're doing. And I don't care who you spend your time, or money, with."

Lenore sighed. "It's probably nothing, but maybe we should check it out. We should pick up Bobby and drive up immediately."

"You do mean fly, right?" Leslie said with a note of confused contempt.

"You know the archabbot doesn't fly. At least not in an airplane," Lenore said, a little smug.

"Why do we need the archabbot?" Leslie demanded.

"Duh," Lenore continued, clearly enjoying Leslie's discomfort. "You think they'd let anyone below mage level examine it? Or let me in by myself? If they refuse Bobby that would be indication someone is screwing around."

"Well, I'm not riding in a car for six hours with…" Leslie let that trail off. "You can meet me at the museum."

"I'll talk to the captain." I figured he'd want me to go, but I should check in.

He was standing outside his office, an unlit cigar held firm between his teeth. It almost seemed like he was waiting for me. Before I could say anything, he barked, "Delacroix, my office, now." He jerked a thumb at the door.

I glanced at his window; all the shades were drawn. I nodded, and as he waved me past him, I stepped into the office. We were not alone.

A man who needed no introduction sat in a leather chair across from the desk. He was Hispanic and had no hair, not even eyebrows. I knew that if I looked closely enough, I would see tiny silver traces of scar tissue that spiderwebbed his entire body. The result of physically wrestling a fire elemental, a Chinese salamander, early in his career. He rose and gave me his best crooked grin.

"*El Jefe.*" I addressed Luis Rivera, the director and founder of the Magical Weapons and Tactics division, or "MWAT."

"Please, just *Jefe.*"

Rivera was considered the boss of all magical units. He looked like a well put together forty, but I knew he was over ninety. You can calculate a mage's age kind of like a dog, in reverse. Take whatever they look like and multiply by two. Mage age. He could expect another fifty birthdays.

The captain closed the door. "We would like to have a few words with you." He pointed at a small conference table in the corner of the office and landed heavy in one of the leather chairs. Rivera and I followed suit. I gave each man a quick glance. Something big was going on here. I clasped my hands on the table.

The captain went straight to the point but spoke with more empathy than I'd ever heard from him. "What, exactly, is your relationship with Ms. Chelsea Falcata?" The fact that his question was delivered in such a manner made me more nervous than his usual bluster.

"To be determined."

"But you are friends," Rivera cut in. "And maybe more."

I looked at him sideways. He was also playing nice. "Maybe, it is complicated."

Rivera sighed. "Do you know that she is a person of interest in over seventy-five open investigations?"

"How many from vice?"

Rivera grinned wolfishly. "All of them." He pulled two items from his pocket: an electronic signal jammer and a "cone of silence" charm. He activated them. He changed the subject. "What is my reputation in the department? In the community?"

I blinked. "Consensus is you are a good cop."

"No," Rivera smiled. "I am a *great* cop."

I nodded.

"But no one cares how pretty or sweet a flower is, if it is growing out of a stinking, festering corpse. My reputation is growing out of the most corrupt police department imaginable." His eyes swept over me as if passing judgement. "First question, and I mean you need to answer honestly. Do you trust Chelsea Falcata?"

I was not sure what they were fishing for, but I decided to be blunt. "Yes, I do. More than some on the force."

The captain glared at me. It was a weird expression, like he was trying to hide an approving smile.

"Good," Rivera said with a grin. "I've trusted her for some time. She has served as a confidential informant to me. Keeping me apprised of specific incidents of police corruption. Some of us are doing something about it. But because vice is the epicenter of corruption and all Internal Affairs officers come from the vice division it is a vicious circle. However, it is time to collapse the circle. Do you want to join us? I suspect you know how dangerous this could be."

I looked at the devices on the table. They wanted to ensure no one ever heard anything from this meeting. Was that to bring me in? Or find out what I knew before eliminating me? I glanced at both men. Truth is, I had never liked the captain, but professionally I trusted him.

I considered Rivera's reputation. "How many officers are involved?"

Rivera waggled his head. "More that you would suspect. Because IA is so rotten, we are conducting a special investigation."

"Outside regular channels?"

"I like to think of it as *parallel* to official channels." Rivera grinned. "We need to bring down the top. Commander Cooper."

"What about the IG? The FBI?" I grimaced internally. First mistake was mentioning the FBI. Going federal would bolster the "blue wall" of silence.

"We have no evidence on Cooper," Rivera said. "Either he's remarkably bright, or mostly innocent. Can't get his financials without a warrant, but he lives within his means. No evidence of expensive cars, houses, jewelry. No mistress. He and his wife live in a very modest neighborhood. No children. His only outrageous expense is twice in the last decade he went big game hunting in Africa. He killed two lions and a gazelle. Had the heads mounted."

"Trophy hunter."

The captain grunted and I realized my second error. "Trophy Hunter" was the name the press gave to a serial killer. The case that killed the captain's partner.

The captain leaned his elbows on the table, like he was going to flick imaginary ash from his well-chewed cigar. "But even if he's not pocketing cash, he's still turning a blind eye to corruption. He is likely not the actual boss, but that doesn't absolve him. It's a shame. He was one of the better vice officers." The captain pursed his lips. "You know how he got is first big promotion?"

I shook my head.

"Being corrupt is the best way to get promoted in that division but along came The Blood Red Rose murder. Because she was a prostitute, half the vice squad was working with homicide. And everything was screwed up. And covered in the press."

"Cooper was part of that investigation?" I asked.

"No. When things went to hell, they suspended all the cops on the task force and fired the captain of vice division. Cooper was the most senior man not involved in the case, so they promoted him." Rivera glared at me; his lips fixed in a snarl. "This corruption must end. I want my legacy cleansed."

"Who else is assisting?" I asked.

"For right now, for safety and security, we are organized in small cells. You only know those in your cell, and me."

I glanced at the captain.

"Cell leader," he growled.

"Who else is in our cell?"

The captain and Rivera exchanged glances. Rivera spoke quietly. "That is one of the most important secrets of our investigation." He leaned over the table, his fists resting on its surface, as if ready to fight. "Tell me candidly, are you with us?"

I already felt that vice had a target on my back. Maybe I had ignored the corruption too much. There is always a "go along to get along" mentality in the force. If another's corruption doesn't affect you, ignore it. But these two men made me feel embarrassed by my lack of action. "I am in."

The pair exchanged glances. Rivera pursed his lips Then Rivera looked at me, his eyes cold. "This is your point of no return. Right now, you can just leave. Forget this ever happened."

"*Non*, I'm in. And I know how dangerous this is."

"IA has destroyed careers, or worse, to maintain the status quo." He glanced back to the captain, who gave a barely perceptible nod. "The other member of your cell is our highest placed informant. Ted Gruber."

"Gruber from vice!" I blared. "Now you are jerking my chain. He is as corrupt as they come and—" I bit off what I was about to say as Rivera grinned at me.

His tone was friendly. "And he tried to sabotage your evening with Falcata. He did that on my orders. I wanted to see how that affected you, sort of the final test. Gruber is undercover, sort of. He is using his real identity, but we recruited him out of the academy. We coached him on the behaviors that brought vice's attention to him. So far, he's been with them, skirting breaking the law himself, while gathering intel on the rest."

"I would have a hard time trusting Gruber."

"Exactly. That is how good he is at undercover."

I chewed over Rivera's words. "What if I bring my partner into the fold?"

"Welles? God, no." Rivera sounded almost frightened.

"Not her, I understand the problematic issue with her, but I meant my regular partner, Vlad."

"The vamp?" Rivera said in amusement. "Can a vamp keep a secret?"

"I believe he can. I also trust his honesty and commitment."

"It's pretty damn hard for me to trust a vamp," the captain said. "The fastest way to spread information. Telephone, telegraph, tell a vamp."

Rivera turned and spoke directly to the captain. "Here is the thing.

We're bringing Delacroix in because we trust him, so and we must trust his judgment. If he is going to trust us, we need to trust him." He turned to me and leveled his gaze at my eyes. "If you trust Vlad, then bring him in. I just ask you do not reveal Gruber's involvement, for now."

"Yes, sir, of course. But in the meantime, I need to get to San Francisco. Ms. Modeste is insisting."

"That's one insistent woman," the captain muttered.

"Yes. I would like to go with Mage Welles and Archabbot Kaufman." I frowned. "We have to drive, he doesn't fly."

"Not today. I hear you gotta hot date tonight. Keep it. Tomorrow, start out early, I want you back the same day."

"How did you—" I looked at both the men, who sat grinning back at me quite conspiratorially. "Yes sir. I will make arrangements." I was speaking with more confidence than I felt. What was I getting myself into?

Chapter Fifteen

"You show me the most interesting sights," I said to Chelsea. It was late evening, just dark enough to distort the view. We sat in the front of my unmarked car staking out a small apartment building, maybe twenty units.

In front by the entrance was a fantastic sight. "The hut," I asked, "are those chicken legs mechanical?"

Outside the main entrance was a simple hut supported by a pair of six-foot-tall chicken's legs, their claws crammed into stiletto heels. A disco ball hung in front of the open door.

Chelsea smiled like we were at the playground and she showing me her favorite slide. "Magically mechanical, like a homunculus. All the parts are organic. The legs started out as chicken bones at some point."

I fought away a grimace. I knew too much about homunculi. I unmasked the former vice captain, Macklin, as one while he tried to rip my arms off. My right elbow ached at the thought.

I was dressed in a loose-fitting black suit, shirt, and tie. A remnant of my strict catholic school education, I didn't feel I was working without a tie. Ms. Falcata was dressed down, a far cry from the previous evening. Worn blue jeans and a charcoal gray hoodie made up her ensemble. No makeup or glamour.

In other words, exquisite. Her enchantment was stronger than any vamp serving cocktails.

"So, Baba is Baba Yaga?"

"One incarnation of Grandmother Chicken. Like Dracula, several people have become the object. Baba is perfect for this role. She is fiercely loyal and demands gold coins to get past her."

"So, you pay her, and she directs you to a girl? I don't see this as any different than the hotel."

"Well, for starters the inside is actually nice. It's set up like apartments and the girls can live there if they choose. The thing is, they are free to leave at any time and say no to any customer."

"And that makes this more ethical?"

"Every woman here, is here by choice. I mean, there are circumstances, but no one forces them. No drugs. They get their rightful money, and Baba provides assistance to get out of the life when they're ready. And everyone is ready, eventually. Baba welcomes change. She welcomes growth."

I took the binoculars and studied Baba Yaga. She appeared ancient; her wispy white hair pulled back in a colorful kerchief, her skin weather-beaten and her face plowed with age lines, not laugh lines. Her face had that crumpled appearance indicating no teeth. No one is that ugly by chance, she had to work at it. And yet, there was some feeling of a grand archetype. A living institution.

She sat in a rocking chair in front of her hut, arms crossed over her ample bosom, wary and protective. Even as I watched, a man in a gray hoodie stepped up to the hut. The chicken legs shuffled, and Baba Yaga held out her hand for coins. Or, in this case, banknotes. I could see the old witch grin and nod. The visitor passed by her.

"So, she is the pimp, collecting the money."

Chelsea gave me a knowing smile. "No. That's an admission fee. Plus, Baba Yaga has ways of determining if you intend to cause problems, or even if you are an unintentional problem. Inside the complex the girls set their own fees, working hours, and client set up."

I lowered the glasses and frowned.

"Del, are we going to talk about last night?"

The question came out of nowhere, but on some level, I expected it. Anticipated? Dreaded? "I didn't think you wanted to."

"I don't but…" Her voice faded off. "Mental health is very important to me. Many women I meet professionally have some sort of issue and I try to steer them into treatment, even though I feel embarrassed about my own treatment."

"You think you need treatment?"

She shrugged. "Everyone needs help at some point. My only diagnose is PTSD, since my sister was killed, but…" She furrowed her brow and I could almost hear the wheels turning in her head, trying to get something out.

"I have been struggling with depression and anxiety for years. In many ways I'm comfortable with them, but something has changed over the last year or so. I'm thinking I need to go back. I get these urges to act irrationally, like last night."

"Urges? You are not hearing voices or anything?"

Chelsea gave me a small, knowing smile. "No, not like that. I haven't discussed this with anyone, but you should know. I haven't been diagnosed with bi-polar disorder, but my therapist and I have discussed it in the past. Every so often I get this idea fixed into my brain that I have to take some drastic action, and it has to be now, demanding immediate satisfaction. I get so much energy from these thoughts that I feel compelled to go through with them, but I usually don't. I have a very strong 'sleep on it' procedure to calm things down. In the morning, I see how foolish my actions would have been. But there have been a few times I acted on these impulses."

"Last night."

Chelsea nodded; her lips pressed tight in embarrassment. "I was wrong to try and force something. It was our mutual indecision that prompted me. It won't happen again."

"That's too bad," I said as I tentatively rested my hand on her knee.

She jerked her head around to face me then her tense lips relaxed.

"Like you said," I continued. "We are a pair. Now we need to see what kind of pair we are."

"Even with my past?" she said with more than a little contempt.

I accepted her rancor in stride. I'd earned it, in a way. "Because of your past. It shaped you into a remarkable woman. You have gone from victim to survivor to protector. That is one hell of an evolution. I talked to Captain Riviera today, by the way. You have been speaking to him behind my back?"

Chelsea frowned, making the corners of her eyes droop. "It's not like that. I had to protect both you and him."

"He has high praise for you."

Chelsea snorted. "Not in public."

"*Non*, but where it counts."

Chelsea's phone chirped and she pulled it out. Her face melted into one of patient indulgence. "It's just a text from Pakhet. Asking me to bring some cream."

I whipped my head around to stare at her. "Pakhet can text?"

"I set her up with a keyboard and track pad. She needs to wear a little rubber bootie to use it. Cocopuff hates that. But Pakhet picked it up very fast. She can even use it to change TV stations."

I hit my fist on my forehead. I should have thought of that. "I miss *ce petit coquina*. I wish I knew what I did to offend her."

"God, you really are oblivious." Chelsea sighed. "Halima and I have become very good friends."

"Halima?"

"Yeah. Her real name. Turns out after the ceremony, a whole lot of her memories started flooding back. Which is part of the reason she was probably extra hateful. To you." Chelsea looked at me with wide eyes."

Pakhet, or Halima, might be able to project her thoughts, but Chelsea's were lost on me. "Oh."

Chelsea blinked and looked away from me with the same expression of patient indulgence she gave the cat texts. "OK, I give up. She didn't want me to tell you any of this, but you should know. She is embarrassed, but I assured her you were non-judgmental and kind." Chelsea paused, evidently choosing her words carefully. "It seems she's remembered her name, and other things. But as long as she's in the cat she prefers you to call her Pakhet. Because she believes you only see her as a cat and, under the circumstances, you should treat her like one. But Del, she's a *woman*."

"Okay."

Chelsea snickered. "OMG. You still don't get it. When the clown put her in the cat it was the first physical form she'd had control of in over four thousand years. At first, she thought she *was* a cat. She felt like a cat and even liked being a cat. Then you took her home. You talked to her and were good to her. Then you showed affection and that confused the hell out of her. You petted her like a cat, but she wanted you to pet her like a woman and was super humiliated to say anything."

"But—"

"She was hanging on until your Nog friends did some ritual with her that pulled her buried memories out. She was one confused, frustrated, and angry woman/feline. She understands that you and she cannot have the relationship she craves; so, socializing with you is too hard. She likes me and has explained that she is envious, not jealous."

"I'm not sure I understand the difference."

"Neither did I. She explained she wants two things I have, a full female human body and your affection. But she doesn't hate me for it. She wants you and me to get together because she believes that will make us happy and that is important to her. So, if you do see her again in cat form; treat her like a cat. That is the only way she can be comfortable around you. You show her human affection; she might lose it. Emotions are still new to her and in certain areas she is hanging by a thread."

Talk about being confused. I cared for the spirit inside the cat, and

I intellectually knew she was human; but I could not emotionally separate her spiritual nature from her physical form.

"She was only eighteen when she was selected to guard the demon. She's had over forty years riding along with Mrs. Childress, so she knows about our time, our society, and she wants to be part of it. So, I had to let someone else in on Halima's secret. Her therapist."

My eyes opened wide and I sat up straight. "*Her* therapist?"

"Same one I see off and on. I took her this morning, and she's scheduled for twice a week. I think it will help."

I picked up the binoculars just to have a moment to think and saw Baba Yaga lighting a pipe.

"She's relaxed," Chelsea said. "This is a good time." She cracked open the car door.

I slipped out and took a few tenuous steps; sitting too long made my muscles bunch up.

Chelsea was already halfway to the hut when I caught up with her.

We approached and Baba Yaga regarded us with professional distrust. "You two together?"

"Yes," Chelsea replied.

Grandmother Chicken squinted at me with one big, heavy eye, then addressed Chelsea again. "Ehhhh...didn't expect to see you in bed with a cop."

"Not here to cause any trouble for you or yours," I said.

The old woman's eyes burrowed into me. "I'll be the judge of that." Baba Yaga didn't really have feathers, that I could see, under all those layers of knitted skirts, but still she seemed to make a ruffling motion at me. "Oh, yer not gonna cause any trouble 'cause I won't letcha. Anyhow, I was only askin' to determine the rate. Couples get a special rate, two for one and a half."

"We're not here to visit the girls," Chelsea said. "Actually, we came to see you, Mama."

Baba Yaga broke into a spell of raucous laughter that ended in several sputtering coughs that could also be described as clucks. "Sorry, baby. It's just been a minute since I heard *that*, is the truth! I assume you want *information,* not this finely aged frame." She hefted her bosom at me and I respectfully stared a hole in the dirt before my feet all the way to China. "Well, that's fine, but there's still a fee." She glared at me as she waved a feathered fan over her suddenly ruddy features. I think she was expecting me to brandish my badge and make demands. Instead, I got out my wallet.

Baba Yaga leaned over her porch and plucked the money from my hand with a wide, toothless grin. "Well, a sweetie pie cop, heehee, next there'll be unicorns at my doorstep!" she said, leaning closer to me. I smelled chicken coup smells and maintained a neutral expression. I hoped. Her magic had a strong *odeur de* free-range, but there a lot of it springing from her. She might be old and funny, but she was also terrifyingly powerful.

"What we are looking for is your take on the RNC," Chelsea said. "And to show my friend here what makes your establishment different."

"Hmm? Different from what?" Baba's gaze jumped from me to Chelsea.

Chelsea knelt at Baba's side and took the old chicken mother's hand. "I love you, Grandma. Please. You need to speak plainly, and *obviously*." Her eyes snaked to me, crinkled by mischief.

That had an effect on Baba, and she petted Chelsea's head. "Oh, goodness, child. You get younger every time I see you. You were not born with an old soul, but it aged too damn fast, but I feel it is lightened some." Her eyes were slits as she appraised me. "Well, then. You ask about the RNC?" Baba Yaga spat off the side of her porch. "Sadistic bastards. I've had a few girls that escaped them. But I didn't put them back to work. They were too skittish, traumatized. Waren't no fun in it fer 'em no more, and if'n it ain't fun, what's the point? So, I found them other employment. Only one of the girls ended up working here, bless her heart."

"May we talk to her?"

Baba Yaga gave a sweeping gesture to the door. "You paid your entrance fee. But remember, the girls are free to set their own fees and terms, even for information. You're still taking something from them you can't put back. The girl you want is Coquette. Unit number eleven."

We headed to the indicated unit. "She didn't seem too concerned I might try and bust her."

Chelsea quirked an eyebrow. "She's all paid up with vice. You try to arrest someone or cause trouble, she knows vice will take care of you."

I sighed in frustration. We found the apartment on the first floor. The hall was unexpectedly spacious and clean. There was a slight sour smell of disinfectant.

Chelsea knocked on the door.

It opened to reveal a petite African American woman with a carefully trimmed short afro covered her ears, but not her six hoop earrings. She wore low rise cutoff jeans, a white crop top and stiletto heels. It was evident she wasn't wearing a bra. I had to admit she was extremely attractive, and I sniffed, wondering if there was a very subtle glamour. There was none. And then a stiff ache formed in my gut. She reminded me of someone else. A woman I had once known from Trinidad, a long, long time ago.

"OOOH, a couple. I likes couples." She meant to sound excited, but there was no sincerity in her voice. She batted her eyes at me, then at Chelsea and added sexy pout.

"We're not here for—" I exclaimed.

She laughed, a far more sincere sound. "I'm just busting your chops, baby. Baba called me and said you'd be fun to mess with. My standard fee is $100 an hour, double for a couple, that includes information."

Chelsea took out her wallet. "That's fair. The information we're looking for is big. We just want to ask you about the RNC."

"Those fricken clowns?" Her nostrils flared and she suddenly took up a lot more space in her doorway. "What's your deal with the Clowns?"

"We're gonna shut them down," Chelsea answered, the money in her extended hand.

Coquette gave us both a hard stare. "That's a suicide mission." She cocked her head to one side. "You serious?"

Chelsea nodded.

"Put your money up. And get in. You're in for a wild ride, honey." She stepped aside and firmly closed the door behind us. "You'll never do it," she said matter-of-factly as she walked into her kitchenette and popped herself a bottle of cheap beer. She toasted us before drinking. "But I respect the hell out of you for wantin' to try."

Chelsea plopped down on the couch, and I chose to stand. I didn't know where Miss Coquette usually transacted her business deals, and I didn't know how to ask.

Chelsea clearly didn't care. "Can you help us understand what we're up against? And can I have one of those? C'mon, booze me up a little, babe. I might tip." Chelsea's tone had an easy familiarity to it, almost like she was coaching the other woman.

Coquette gave Chelsea a mean smile while she opened her fridge. "Bey, a hundred percent tip off ah nothin' is nothin'. Here you go, sweet stuff. You, too, or—" She jerked the bottle away from me as I reached to accept it. "Are you on the clock, Detective?"

"I am not on the clock, but I am also fine, thank you."

"Sure you are," she said with a sly side-eye as she sat on the couch, facing the door, by Chelsea and propped her stiletto boot heels on the glass coffee table. "Your biggest problem is that they are a national, hell international, outfit. It's like a hydra, cut off one head and two grow back to replace it."

"How do they recruit girls?" I asked.

"They're not above abducting young girls and trafficking them, but mostly they seek out people like me."

"Go on."

She raised her eyes and spoke plainly without embarrassment or shame. "Women with a broken and/or abusive home. Already runaways and disappeared, desperate enough women. I was terrified, unwanted, unloved." Her lips formed a half smile like she recalled a bittersweet memory. "Then I met a man who treated me good. Now I know he was the first line, a so called 'Romeo' pimp. Made me feel important, loved even. He wined, dined me and then seduced me. I thought he wanted to marry me." She shook her head and clenched her eyes shut. "What a fool. Then he asked me to do a few 'favors' for some men. I thought the first time was sort of an adventure. The coke definitely helped with that. And there was a lot of it. Next thing I know, I'm on shit that's worse than coke, begging for a bump, a hit, this and that, and the men in those days are just...an unpleasant blur in my memory."

"So how did you get out?" I asked.

"I was aging out of their demographic, turning twenty-five. Most women my age they just abandon and let them try to exist on the streets. You know Opioid Annie? Hard to believe she's one of the lucky ones. Most girls either OD or get picked up by small time, local pimps. But with me, they made a mistake. They thought I'd cause 'em too much trouble if I got out. They planned a hotshot for me."

"An intentional overdose?" Chelsea asked, disgusted.

"They intended to murder you?" I held my hand out to Chelsea, and she handed me her beer. I took a swig, the feel of her lip gloss rubbing on my chapped lips more intoxicating than the cheap lager. A strange intimacy, sharing a drink. I handed it back to her and the interaction was over before Miss Coquette even spoke again.

"Yeah, the tippies and the hobos, they can be pretty careless with the shots. Some girls call them Overdose, Incorporated. I mean they kill girls they're not supposed to all the time on accident, but they didn't know I'd been weening myself off the drugs and I was more alert than they expected. I got away before they realized I hadn't shot my dose and managed to disappear. I'd heard that Baba would protect me, help me survive my addiction and she has." She looked at her watch. "Yeah, um...I'm about out of time. I don't usually stack clients like this, and you still have the rest of your hour, but I do have another appointment."

There must have been something in my face.

"Not that kind of appointment. He's an old dear friend, an author. He drops by to ask me questions about my work. And no, I don't think he gets off on it, it's not like that." She leaned forward with a girl-like giggle. "I'm afraid I'm going to appear in one of his books one of these days."

"Before we go," I asked. "Can you give us any names?"

"No real ones, just street names. But I can spirit paint their pictures."

"Spirit painting? That's a hell of a talent," Chelsea said.

"Doesn't pay near as much as my specials." She licked her lips. A surprisingly suggestive gesture.

She was still working on the pictures when there was knock at the door.

"Keep painting, I'll get it," Chelsea jumped up and ran to the door.

"Just tell Geoffrey to have a seat," Coquette called out.

Chelsea opened the door, and a man stepped in.

"You?" I said, shooting to my feet.

Chelsea gave me a stern look as she addressed the man. "Sorry. This is my friend's first time. He mistook you for someone else."

Coquette stood up and handed me five sheets of heavy paper.

"Thank you," I said. "We will be on our way."

Coquette waved at us with waggling, playful fingers. "Ta Ta."

I nodded to Geoffrey and followed Chelsea out. "That's the author we met at the convention," I said softly as we walked.

"Yes," Chelsea said, her voice with a note disapproval. "And we were under a glamour spell. We don't know what that guy's deal is and we don't have time to sort it out. Let me see those pictures."

I held up four pictures with the street names, Streak, Beef, Mac and Adolfo. There was one more picture. It was signed with the street name "Creeper", but I knew that face immediately.

We were staring right at Brad Minors.

Chapter Sixteen

We drove back to my place where Chelsea left her car. The drive was silent, but still companionable, although Chelsea found something very intriguing about looking out the passenger window. Or maybe she was hiding her expression.

I pulled into the parking garage in my usual spot. "I need to go with Ms. Modeste tomorrow. If Minors is really working with the RNC then she might be right about the amulet."

"Ms. Modeste? Not Leslie'?"

"That was a long time ago."

"And me? Am I Ms. Falcata?"

"At the station. Here you are Chelsea." I rested a hand on her knee and felt her twitch. "Let me walk you to your car." I pulled my hand back and got out.

Chelsea got out but did not move toward her car. Instead, she stood close to me. Intimately close. "Aren't you going to invite me up for coffee?"

"*Non*, no caffeine this time of night, not while I work days."

She grimaced. "Now I can't tell if you are truly that oblivious, or you find me repulsive."

My mind was in turmoil from the day's events. I abruptly realized what she meant, why she stood so close. I put my hands on her shoulders and she inched even closer, her lips not quite touching mine, and she waited. I felt her shoulders tense and knew she saw my pause as rejection. Nothing could be further from the truth. It was a moment I wanted to remember.

So, I kissed her. I intended our kiss to be light and sweet, but as our lips touched it was like an electric shock ran down my body, making all my parts tingle. The kiss intensified. Our lips moved hungrily, eagerly, tongues were involved. I wrapped my arms around her as her lithe body molded to mine.

Somehow, we made it to the elevator. The privacy was alluring, and our lips reunited as our hands wandered.

In my apartment our clothes evaporated, figuratively this time, and we were in my bed. I was embarrassed that I hadn't washed the sheets. I mean, after last night I should have expected something.

Chelsea did not notice. She was in a hurry, a frenzy almost. I worked to slow her down. I wanted this to last.

She pushed me back on the bed and mounted me, her hips thrusting in a greedy, hurried rhythm. I grabbed her and rolled her over, so I was on top. "Slow," I told her. "Let me set the tempo."

She complied. Soon our bodies moved together. Lost in the motion. I did not want this to end, but her heat, her nearness, the touch of her lips threw me over the edge. I lay there twitching. She was breathing raggedly, her face flushed. When she stopped moving under me, I rolled off. She immediately rolled away, her hands up to her face as she shook her head.

I tugged on her shoulder, but she resisted facing me. "I'm sorry," I said.

She turned to me, her face still flushed. Her eyes were red-rimmed and repressed tears glistened in her eyes. "I wanted this."

"Then?"

She stayed silent.

"Chelsea?"

She wiped away the moisture from her eyes. "I need to talk to my therapist." She shook her head violently as if trying to rearrange her emotions as she sat on the edge of the bed. "Part of me wanted it to be bad, or at least awkward. I don't do emotion. God, you have no idea how I hate the 'L' word,"

It took me a moment to guess what word. Lust? Oh. No, not lust. "...love?"

"Pitiful, isn't it? But I don't, well can't, love you. I'm not even sure I know what love is. I mean, I loved my sister, but when I think of that I just feel rage at her fate. My mother? There was a tiny part of me that was relieved when she finally died. She was at peace, and I was released. But when I remember that what I feel is all consuming guilt. Love has got to be more than rage and guilt, right? I am so pathetic."

"*Non.* You are definitely not pathetic. I believe we are creating something real."

"Real love?" she said with a sarcastic lilt. "But I will say this. You haven't won my heart, but you've won my trust. Given that you are a dude and a cop, that's pretty impressive."

I worked my way to sit next to her and tentatively placed my arm over her shoulders. She relaxed against me. "I have my own issues with saying what I feel. To me, love means loss. Everyone I have been romantically involved with has broken my heart. So, if I do not love I will not lose. I am still not certain where this is going, but I am willing to go slow because you are important to me."

She chuckled.

"What?"

"This is the point when I usually say, 'thank you', shake your hand, then leave and delete you from my contact list." She took a deep breath. "But I don't want to delete you. Besides, that rhythm thing you did, that was inspirational." She noticed my blush. "What?"

"Leslie, uh Ms. Modeste taught me that. She was an ardent horsewoman. She learned that various gaits produce different sensations."

"Leslie, she was your great loss?"

"*Non*, she was a rebound relationship that I took too far, if I am being honest with myself. My first great love was Renee. She was from Trinidad. We met in college. I was studying for an associate degree in criminal justice; she was studying for an MBA."

"What happened?"

"I asked her to marry me, and she said yes." I shrugged. "But when she told her parents they pulled her out of college and told her she was marrying an established businessman. There is a backstory to her family, not mine to tell, but she felt duty bound to marry as her father requested."

"Oh, Del, you just let her go?"

"Things are different in Haiti, Chelsea. She asked me to move to Point-à-Pierre and be her lover." I sighed. "But I couldn't do that. Six months later I met Ms. Modeste. *Ma grand-mére* told me that I was grabbing onto the first thing I could find. That such a relationship would be 'comfortable.' She says that is why it hurt so much when Leslie left. I'd given up passion for comfort and security. That woman…I don't know that I actually loved her, but I was committed to her. She left and I mourned all my losses. That is why I left Florida."

Chelsea shrugged my arm off her shoulders and stood. "I should go."

"Why? Please stay. I make a mean omelet."

She laughed again, a sound pleasant to my ears.

"What?"

"Old joke. Guys would ask how I like my eggs in the morning. I always said unfertilized."

"Oh," I said, alarmed. "We should have discussed that."

Chelsea quirked her eyebrow at me, hard. "Oh, honey. I had that conversation with a surgical gynecologist in Canada about four years ago. My tubes are tied up tighter than Penelope Pitstop on the railroad tracks. That's how far I had to go, by the way, to get it done at twenty-two without a note from my nonexistent husband."

"That's ridiculous," I said, but my voice was solemn; to give up on children would break *ma grand-mére's* heart.

"Yeah, the doctor *still* told me he made sure it was reversible. But is it safer and more reliable than the pill."

I reached for her and something in my touch made Chelsea turn to face me then, and her blue eyes searched my face. For the truth? For a lie? No telling, but apparently she found it, for she gave me a benighted smile. "You really want kids, don't you?"

"That is complicated. I want you in my life."

"And in your bed?"

"I consider that a perk."

She laughed, that sweet ringing sound, turned to me and pushed me back down onto the bed. I snuggled up to her, spooning. She twitched as a specific part of me touched her.

"Is that?"

"*Oui.*"

"Then we should take care of that."

We didn't sleep.

* * *

The alarm was painful. I unwrapped myself from the most enticing embrace I could remember and dutifully got up. I made strong coffee for her, a triple espresso for me and the promised omelet.

I called to her to come and eat and she appeared, draped in one of my shirts. She used a glamour to hide her bedhead and puffy eyes.

"*Non, s'il vous plait,* I worked hard to mess up that lovely hair of yours. Please." I held my hand to my chest. "Allow me to bask in the fruits of my hard labors. I long to sit at breakfast with the real you, Chelsea Falcata." I spread my arms. "For you are glorious."

She stared at me, her mouth slightly open, alarm in her eyes.

I raised an eyebrow and allowed the corners of my mouth to rise.

Chelsea laughed, unrestrained, unrefined, shameless laughter. A full, deep throated sound of pure merriment. My poetic speech had its intended effect, and I soaked up the music of her happiness.

She launched herself at me. I barely had time to brace for the impact and staggered as she jumped at me, her arms around my shoulders and her shapely legs around my hips. Her cheek pressed against mine and she still laughed. Tears wet my cheeks and she made no move to wipe them away. It was as if I gave her permission to be happy. The thing she denied herself most.

I patted her backside to get her to release, and her dismount would have made a gymnast proud. She stood before me, still giggling, the glamour gone. Somehow, seeing her hair tousled, the shirt clinging to her breasts and the shirttail barely covering her was the sexiest thing I'd ever seen.

Later we ate warmed over omelets and took coffee to go.

* * *

The drive to San Francisco was even longer than I anticipated. I picked up Lenore first and asked her to drive while I slid into the rear seat. She was dressed almost casually in red leather pumps and a floaty summer dress she carefully tucked under her thighs as she settled in the driver's seat. She adjusted the rearview mirror and stared at me, an impish smile playing on her lips. She sniffed at me and broke out in uncontrollable giggles.

She looked directly at me, still driving down the road.

"Did you know," she said teasingly, "I can identify recent intimate partners by their smell? It's one of my powers."

I leaned back in the bench seat, and the warm light hitting me through the window threatened to lull me immediately into a nap. "If that were true, Lenore, vice would be out of a job."

"Ah, ha! So you *were* with a lady last night," Lenore pressed, eyeing me in the rearview.

"I neither confirm nor deny."

I still felt those eerie wizard eyes on me in the mirror. "That's functionally the same as confirming."

"Look," Lenore said as her eyes turned opalescent white and rolled up into her head. Her eyebrows twitched as she spoke in a deep, eerie voice. she used her second sight to find Kaufman. "You know I could read your thoughts if I wanted to. And I have no problem doing it, if necessary, but Del, I respect you and won't do it. But I don't have to be a mind reader. You're practically glowing and you smell of feminine perfume."

"You *know*, you could maybe just call the archabbot to see if he's ready rather than using your second sight while you're driving. I am certain that is a traffic violation," I said as I tried to surreptitiously sniff myself.

"Don't worry. No one who isn't familiar with your scent will

112

notice." The car stopped with a jar and Lenore's eyes popped back down to wink at me.

I should have taken the time to shower. "Kaufman, do you think he will smell it?"

Lenore grinned. "Don't kid yourself. The archabbot has less compunction about reading your mind than I do."

I hoped she was wrong.

We picked up the archabbot and I dozed.

My phone pinged to indicate a text and I woke up to read it.

"What?" Lenore said. She took her eyes off the road and looked over her shoulder at me. The fact that she didn't need to see the road to be safe was unnerving. Kaufman didn't seem to notice.

"From Ms. Modeste. She left the airport and will meet us at the museum."

"Oh, I thought it might be from Ms. Falcata."

I didn't rise to the bait. I looked up, relieved to see the museum.

"Could you drop me at the front door, please?" Kaufman asked. "The parking here is horrendous."

Lenore obediently pulled up. Kaufman got out and looked at me. I didn't move. "I'll go with Lenore. I need a few minutes."

He gave me a look like a jovial hunter eying his mark. "Alright. Just remember you have an appointment when we get back."

The damn tattoo. I wondered why I'd agreed.

Kaufman walked away.

About half an hour and several horrendous parking experiences later, including Lenore levitating a car *just enough* to get it out of the way, we reached the front to find a very puzzled Kaufman staring at the door.

"Problem?" I asked.

"It's locked," Kaufman replied, his tone peeved and puzzled.

I glanced at the posted hours. The museum should have opened hours ago. "Perhaps it is closed because of preparations for our visit?"

"Could be," the archabbot replied, unconvinced.

"Have you tried knocking?" Lenore asked with in the same sardonic lilt she used on me earlier.

Kaufman glared at her.

"We have an appointment," Lenore continued. She produced a cell phone and dialed the museum's number. She put it on speaker. There was no answer, not even voicemail.

"I find this very suspicious," Kaufman said slowly.

"Ya think?" Lenore retorted with a wry look. "I think it's just fine. I'm sure they didn't screw around with an ancient, powerful amulet and find out."

Her statement made Kaufman look more worried. "We have to find a way in."

"Obviously," Lenore replied.

"Obviously *not*," I rebuked them. "You're discussing a criminal act."

Lenore poked herself in the sternum. "Del, we're the cops. And we have probable cause that something is wrong."

"You are stretching… It would be best to find someone who can let us in."

Both Kaufman and Lenore snorted.

"You have two mages here," Lenore said, as if I'd insulted her.

"It will take both of us," Kaufman said. "It has a pretty strong ward on it. Leni, you get the ward, and I'll get the lock."

I started. No one used a nickname for Lenore. I stood back to let them work.

Lenore produced a wand and mumbled under her breath as her brow creased, twisting the flexible wood stick as if untying a knot. "Are you going to attempt to blast the lock, or use telekinesis to open it?"

"Neither." He pulled a set of mundane lockpicks from his robe.

I stifled a laugh, but he was very proficient. It took ten seconds, and we were in.

"Christ," Kaufman swore.

I pushed past him to see Minors' body lying in a pool of blood, a gaping knife wound in his chest just below the gold and lapis lazuli amulet around his neck. In his right hand he clasped a small bronze statue.

I heard a groan and Ms. Modeste pushed herself to her feet. She had a wicked looking knife in her right hand and a bleeding lump on the side of her head.

"It's not what it looks like," was all she could say.

Chapter Seventeen

Leslie stared at me with big, scared eyes as they cuffed her and led her away, as if any moment I was going to magically make this all OK. But I cannot do magic, and they tucked her in the back of a squad car as the San Francisco coroners bagged and tagged Minors. The ME techs looked like they could have been the same guys working for LD; down to the unphased looks on their faces.

Before the murder, someone ransacked the museum and broke several showcases. We were dragged away as the evidence recovery team sifted through shards of glass and possible magic items scattered on the floor.

We were escorted to the station house to give our statements. Now we sat before a fellow who looked like every detective in LDPD; down to the unimpressed look on his face as Kaufman demanded to see Leslie.

"Jurisdiction," said the homicide detective, as if that were any sort of answer. He was a burly man with slicked back hair and every word he spoke sounded thoroughly chewed before he spat them at us. A north Midwest transplant who didn't bother to rise to greet us. Not the manners I would expect.

Kaufman took a deep a breath and continued his request. "This case started in Los Diablos. Detective Delacroix here knows what is going on and is prepared for the magical elements."

Before I could speak, slick boy talked over me.

"But the crime was committed here," the detective replied, looking at me as if daring me to try and interject. "We have magical cops too, don't cha know."

Kaufman dropped his head and sighed. "May Delacroix at least question Ms. Modeste?"

"Above my pay grade," the detective replied with indifference. "Besides, she's lawyered up. So, what cha gonna do?"

"This is very serious." Lenore pointed out as she leaned over the detective's desk. "Your men took no precautions with the amulet,"

The detective altered his voice to a long-suffering patient tone. "Because there was no magical energy detected."

My lip twisted as I recalled the last time I encountered a dangerous artifact that was supposed to be "non-magical."

Lenore stood straighter and crossed her arms. "You know, detective…" She paused pointedly.

"Baldwin. Horace Baldwin."

I saw him take in her flirty dress and dismiss her.

"Detective Baldwin, you're right." Lenore spoke with a smile that didn't extend past her lips. I knew that smile. It was deadly. "This is *way* above your pay grade. So far, I'm not impressed by your team of keystone cops at *all*."

Baldwin shoved a finger at Lenore's face. "Listen here little lady—" his voice cut off sharply and I worried Lenore had done something to him.

She locked eyes on him, her face still wearing that cold, deadly smile. "I believe the commissioner's office is just up the stairs?" she said, like a cat talking to a mouse about where the traps are in the house.

"You can't just…"

"Watch me." Lenore spun away from him and addressed me and Kaufman. "Come on. We need to talk to someone who is actually in charge and knows to take this seriously." She practically pranced out the door, her shiny red pumps giving terrifying little clicks as she went.

Kaufman shoved my shoulder. "We need to stay with her."

"She can take care of herself," I said with a shrug.

"It's not her I'm worried about."

We raced up the stairs in Lenore's wake as she plowed through two assistants and a secretary before she stormed into the commissioner's office.

The room was smaller than I expected, and not a corner space.

The commissioner sat behind a very old desk leaning forward, his fingers propping up his head as he spoke into a phone and only looked up to glare at the intrusion.

"Hey, Billy," Lenore said with a casual mischief.

I only knew Bill Cruz professionally. He was a short, compact man who spoke with a mild Spanish accent. His skin was a shade darker than mine, but his teeth were far whiter.

Cruz winced at Lenore's greeting. "We'll finish this later," he sighed and hung up the phone. He looked at Lenore and brought his palm up to cover his face. "Magister Welles. It is nice to see you again."

Ah, so Commissioner Cruz was also fluent in sarcasm.

"I knew you would be up here as soon as I heard you were involved. I assume you want to examine the body, the amulet, and question the suspect. Raise the corpse, question him, open the Book of Secrets, read the names of those involved, jump over the sun, oh and throw in some super-secret cult stuff with knives and dildoes with this guy, and case closed, happy hour's at five amiright?" He said with a flat look as he pointed at Kaufman. "Thank god you're here, Mage Welles. I didn't know what to do."

"You're so dramatic," Lenore said with an icy smile. "I *only* want the jurisdiction moved to Los Diablos with the body, all the physical evidence, and the suspect."

Cruz looked like Lenore had just said "jump the sun *twice* and extra dildoes for the secret ceremony." He gave her an even stare. "And if I said that's not going to happen, would you turn me into a newt?"

Lenore gave him a smile that said she was picturing how cute he'd be as a tiny lizard.

"You know, Lenore, you could just work with me."

"I could, but where is the fun in that?" She jerked a thumb at Kaufman. "I know you recognize the archabbot here. This is Detective Delacroix. The best nonmagical, magical investigator there is."

"High praise," Cruz said grudgingly. "Look. I can't just waive jurisdiction, but I was just talking to your precinct captain and my mayor. We're gonna form a task force. I understand that you're worried about the amulet, even though my boys found nada. So, I'm gonna let you and Dr. Kaufman put it into containment and take it back to Los Diablos. And, as a professional courtesy, we'll transport the suspect back to LD, too. Frankly, she's lawyered up, so she's just wasting valuable space in my jail. But our ME will perform the postmortem and our forensic team will need to process the physical evidence. The murder happened *here*," Cruz stabbed a forefinger on the desk. "Lenore. I can't change that. But we will share all the information we gather with you. And, Magister Welles, you will share all your information with my people. *Comprendé?*"

Lenore smiled. "Oh Billy, you are so cute when you're decisive."

Cruz held two fingers to his forehead and clenched his lips. I think he was suppressing a chuckle.

"May we talk to the suspect?" I asked.

"Would you like to read her statement?" Cruz said, exasperated.

"*Non*, I want to gauge her reactions without preconceptions."

"I'll read it," Lenore said. "Gives me something to do while he prattles with his ex. I don't want to talk to her, yet."

Cruz turned a sharp gaze my way.

"Long time ago," I said in defense. "I can be professional, objective."

Lenore nodded. "He can be professional." She sat on the edge of the San Fran commissioner's desk and gave him a wicked grin. "Just like you and me."

It was my turn to give a sharp look at Cruz. I suspected that if his skin was lighter, I'd see him blush.

Five minutes later I was led to the interview room where Leslie sat behind a very sturdy table with a stainless-steel top, her hands cuffed to a steel bar. There were red rims around her bloodshot eyes; her lips were pursed, and she wouldn't meet my gaze. Her head wound was bandaged, and I saw a concussion talisman stitched to it. She still wore her street cloths, but they were disheveled, and she didn't have the incentive to straighten them.

I turned to the guard. "Could you remove those, please?"

He shrugged, produced a key, and released her.

She sat there silently chafing her wrists.

Leslie, what have you done? I thought. I considered teasing her about how she was going to look in an orange jumpsuit. It was not her color. "You want to tell me what happened?"

She still couldn't look at me as the words spilled out of her. "He was dead when I got there. I got blood on me while I was checking his pulse."

"Please don't tell me you pulled the knife out."

Frustrated anger flashed in her eyes. "No, I'm not stupid. But that was when I got hit on the head. Next thing I knew I had the knife in my hand, and you were arresting me."

"Your right hand." I let my breath out in a long sigh and held out my hand. She took it with her left.

"Does that make any difference?" she asked in a small voice, still staring at the table, eyes rimmed in red. "Because I'm left-handed?"

I wanted so much to tell her it would help her case, but the reality was that defense would be smashed in an instant. "Not really. There are any number of reasons for you to use your off hand to attack him." Her eyes drooped. "Leslie, look at me. The police here believe you did it. You attacked him with a knife; he grabbed the closest thing he could reach and hit you with it as you stabbed him. They treated your head wound but there is no way to determine the order of events."

She groaned. "Have they told you about the voicemail?" Her gaze drooped and her face scrunched up.

"What voice mail?" I asked, my voice cold. I already knew I wasn't going to like this.

She paused and let out a slow breath. "I called him from the airport." Her voice was so low I could barely hear it. "When he didn't answer I got angry and left him a message that if he didn't produce the real amulet..." She sighed and shook her head. "I said I would kill him."

"*Merde*, Leslie, you didn't." It was like a pit opened beneath my feet. So much for keeping it professional.

"It was hyperbole, Del." She snapped in frustration. "You know me! I couldn't stab anyone."

Stab someone? I wouldn't have thought so. I saw how she behaved after having to put down a lame horse.

I paused. This could not get personal. I had to step back, way back. I didn't want her to be guilty, but if she was, I had to prove it. "You may address me as Detective Delacroix, *s'il vous plais*." My tone was sharp. "Ms. Modeste. I believe you, but that is not relevant. Only the evidence is relevant and right now it weighs heavily against you. I noticed you had some hostility toward the victim. You were found at the scene, the bloody knife in your hand. You threatened him."

She buried her face in her hands and spoke slowly, her voice full of fear and anguish. "I'm going to go to jail, aren't I?"

"For now," I said stoically. "There will be a bail hearing, but they usually do not allow bail for first degree murder."

"First degree?"

"You threatened him. I will do what I can, but for now you are going to have to look good in orange." I immediately felt bad about the dig.

Tears streamed from her eyes and she blinked in an angry attempt to deny them. "Del, uh, Detective Delacroix, I can't do this." She buried her face in her hands, and I heard a restrained sob.

"You can," I said without emotion. "They are going to transport you back to Los Diablos."

Tears streamed down her face, dripping from her fingers. Something in me twinged and my determination to keep my distance faltered. "I will look out for you."

She pulled her hands from her face, wiping away some tears. She looked at me as her lips formed the saddest smile I'd ever seen. "I thought you would want me to rot in a black hole. Look, I'm sorry about what happened. I didn't learn until later I called you right after the funeral. I owed you more consideration than that."

I stood. "I have to go." I turned away from her as mixed emotions swept through me. I never expect any sort of apology, but it affected me far more than it should.

The guard stepped forward to reapply the handcuffs.

More tears streamed down her face. "Del... I can't..."

I did not turn back. "You are going to have to follow through with this. I will do what I can," I said, then I walked away without looking back.

"Del, I'm so sorry," she called after me, sputtering on tears she could not wipe away with the handcuffs reapplied. "I trust you!"

I left, a trembling pile of conflicting emotions.

The drive back home was very excruciating. Emotions that atrophied long ago bombarded my brain. I couldn't play music as Kaufman and Lenore were dozing. So, I was trapped in the car with only my memories of Leslie, whom my emotional ju-jitsu had somehow separated from the incarcerated Ms. Modeste.

I did not love Leslie anymore but mourned the memory of loving her.

It was near to 2 a.m. when I dropped the others off.

Kaufman looked at me, bleary eyed. "You're still gonna get the tattoo, right?"

I nodded agreement. In Haitian culture tattoos are not just decoration, but powerful symbols, not to be applied without consideration. But I was accepting the idea of being a lay brother; just had to discuss with *ma grand- mère*. I left and returned to my place.

I opened the door to find Chelsea lying on my couch. She was wearing my shirt again. She stirred as I entered and rubbed her eyes. I had not given her a key, but she wouldn't worry about a minor detail like that.

"Where is, what did you say her real name is? Halima?"

"Yes, but maybe you should call her Pakhet, especially when she can hear you." She reached for the coffee table and picked up a fine gold chain with the tiny scarab amulet. A small, metal box sat next to the amulet.

"Oh."

"Don't worry, she's asleep right now. She was getting restive, so I let her do a ride along with me today. I know it seems sudden, but we've gotten close."

"Do you think it's a good idea?"

"Mrs. Childress did it for forty years, so Halima told me. But for our privacy…" She opened the metal box and carefully set the amulet inside. "She can't hear us in there. Dinner is in the fridge; it will just take a minute in the microwave."

Her words made my stomach rumble. I had not thought about food since we got to the museum. I found a plate of lasagna and told Chelsea what happened as I ate.

"Your ex," Cheslea smirked, the corners of her mouth turned up in an impish grin. "She's not very bright, is she?"

"She is brilliant in her work." My words were more defensive than I intended.

"I'm sure she is. What is her job title, frumpy sensitive?"

I gave in with a half-smile. "Something like that."

Chelsea awarded me a quizzical look.

I finished the lasagna and washed it down with a beer. Chelsea came over and sat in my lap. "I suppose you want to sleep?" She stroked my hairline as if trying to smooth the tiny, c\curled strands into place. She nuzzled my ear. I noted two things simultaneously; a blush spread across her face, and the shirt was the only thing she was wearing.

"*Non*, not yet. I have not really adjusted to the day shift." My voice had an unusual huskiness to it.

"Good." She sat up straight and sensuously unbuttoned the shirt. "I've been thinking about that rhythm thing. I need another riding lesson."

Chapter Eighteen

I left Chelsea to sleep in and made it to work on time, running exclusively on caffeine. Not just my usual espresso, but one of the energy drinks that advertise so much. Wings? I'd settle for consciousness. I barely made it through the door when Lenore appeared as an astral projection. A bright light formed an image of her face as her words projected into my mind, "Hey Del, captain's office right now."

I passed the desk sergeant and encountered the physical Ms. Welles waiting in the hall. She looked collected, as if she'd slept far more than seemed likely. Her customary lab coat was freshly pressed. Or it could all be a glamour and she was as run down as I. I sniffed delicately in at her direction and only detected the sharp ginger scent of her background magic.

"You're awfully early. I had the projection set up because I thought you'd be in late."

"Too much going on."

Her face was impassive while her gaze swept up and down my body, her eyes reflecting a playful attention to detail. A sly smile lit up her eyes as she focused on my tie. "You look rough," she said, still appraising me. "Falcata keep you up late? Or get you up early?"

I patted the haphazard Windsor knot. *"Non,"* I answered, not completely truthful. "She is still on a nighttime schedule, and she is worrying me, but my manner is because Ms. Modeste is in jail. We are not together, but I still worry about her. Then there is the amulet. I've seen that thing that resides in there."

"Oh? What's worrying you about Falcata? Are you afraid the hooker with a heart of gold thing is a myth? Generally, it is...or is it the fact that she's a vigilante working against the police that's got yer dander up?" Lenore approached me, arms crossed and for a split second I got a creepy feeling that I knew what a rabbit in the jaws of a wolf feels like. She narrowed her eyes and gave me a little pout. "Or are you really scared that vice will snap her up any chance they get? Or maybe she's using you to thwart vice?"

"*Oui et non*. Well, those are concerns..."

Suddenly, Lenore swung her right fist around and landed a hard thump on my upper arm. "Del, get over yourself! Chelsea's good people. And she's smart. My nature doesn't allow me to be an empath, but I don't need magic to see she cares about you. Trust her to take care of herself."

I nodded. "But...Pakhet."

"The cat?"

"Rather, *Halima,* the woman who has been inhabiting the cat." I sighed and rubbed my temple. "She did not want to stay with me, so she went with Chelsea."

Lenore's eyes opened wide. "Oh, Del, you *didn't*."

"It seemed for the best and it was what Halima wanted. They have become close and last night Chelsea told me she was wearing the amulet, allowing Halima to accompany her."

Lenore held her hands to her face. "It's moments like this I'm glad I don't care about anyone else. Just a warning, be prepared for heartbreak. Pakhet, er Halima, is a powerful empath, as is Falcata."

I spread my hands to show my lack of understanding.

Oh, boy, Carmen moment incoming. Look, when two compatible empaths meet, which is truly pretty rare, they bond very quickly. Within days, that is the primary relationship. Del, by the end of the week you will be superfluous, a fifth wheel. Two's company, but three's a crowd."

"You think they are that compatible?"

"Del, they're sharing a *body* already."

"Mrs. Childress did that for forty years without a problem."

"Yes, but Del! Think about it! Falcata has *Talent*. Look, if you liked someone, and knew at the most visceral level they liked you, and both of you *knew* you could trust each other, what do you think would happen? Look, I don't need to read your mind to know you care for Falcata, but she could just be using you, another tool in her crusade."

I rubbed my hands together. "I don't know what to think."

Lenore put a hand on my arm. "Honestly? In my opinion, maybe you should let this love triangle play out. I'm just warning you to be on guard. Being hurt by an empath, let alone two empaths, is dangerous.

They feel your pain, and though they don't intend to, they multiply it. Tell you what, I have a ring. It will temper your feelings."

"*Non.*" I straightened my shoulders and took a deep breath. "I will see this through."

She stared at me while I tried to grasp the emotions warring inside. Just the thought of a potential breakup affected me far more than it should.

"Del," Lenore said with a sad smile. "Let me give you the ring. The longer you wait, the less it can help you. You can decide when/if you need to wear it. But don't wait too long. Wear it at the first symptom of heartache."

"Lenore, why are you trying to help me if you don't care?"

Lenore blew out her lips in a mirthful flutter. "Well, we are partners, for now. I can't have you distracted while I'm trying to get what I want, and I need you for that. Just be glad I'm not compelling you to wear the ring."

I thought about my breakups with Renee and Leslie. It was true, just the echoes of those experiences threatened to overwhelm me.

If breaking up with an empath is worse... I let my chin drop to my chest. "*Oui*, I will take the ring."

Lenore sighed, like admitting a reluctant triumph. "I'll fetch it after our meeting with the captain."

"The captain," I repeated her last word, allowing my tone to show reluctance.

"What's up?"

I realized she wouldn't know about my meeting with Rivera. "I had a meeting with the captain yesterday and I used the term 'Trophy Hunter.'"

"That was the guy who cut off the faces of his victims and nailed them up in public places, right?"

"*Oui.* The captain's partner caught him nailing up a trophy. The perp shot him, cut off his face and mailed it to the station."

"Shit. I can see how that's a sensitive spot. Scumbag like that give us law-abiding sociopaths a bad name. So, don't mention the part about his ex-partner having his face shaved off and mailed to the station, again." Her eyes crinkled in humor. "Unless you wanna make him upset. Then definitely mention that, like, as much as you can. Work it into the conversation in weird places—"

"Lenore."

Lenore waved at me to follow her. "OK. Come on, Cappy has the report on the recovered amulet."

I trailed behind with unsteady footsteps. My stomach felt queasy.

What if I already needed the ring?

The door was ajar. Lenore knocked, then pushed it open without waiting for permission.

I raised my head, took in a deep breath through my nose, pushed all my churning emotions down, and entered the office.

I was greeted by an awkward tableau. Lenore stood with her impassive gaze trained on the people waiting. She crossed her arms tightly across her body and raised her chin. "Hello, *Jefe*," she said, her voice sour as she addressed Luis Rivera.

There was one more person in the room. Rosie the desk sergeant sat in a corner, her arms aggressively crossed.

Lenore turned to me with an appraising stare. "I see. *Et Tu Brute?*"

"See what?" Rivera said with faux innocence.

Lenore flicked a finger at the MWAT director. "You've dragged him into your little project." Her lip curled in a dismissive snarl. She waved at the office, a dismissive gesture. "I'll just step outside and let you boys have your little cabal meeting."

Rivera laughed. "Now Leni, don't be like that. I know you have ideas about what I am up to these days, but you don't *know*, and that's killing you. But that's not why I am here today, okay?"

Lenore's arms tightened and she frowned, her lower lip protruding in a pout. It was almost cute if she wasn't a terrifying sociopathic mage. "Why are you here?"

Rivera waived a hand at Lenore. "Leni, you know I have nothing but respect for you." His voice sounded sincere, maybe too sincere. I could read her body language, and she was also wary of his earnestness. "It is because of respect I am keeping you out of the loop, which is pretty damn difficult. If things go bad for me, it would be worse for you." He scratched his ear.

"Or maybe you just don't want the sociopath involved?"

Rivera raised his head, and Lenore bobbed her head toward me. "He knows."

"Come on Leni, we both know that is exaggerated and over simplified. If I believed that was completely true, I'd have had you out a long time ago."

Lenore's arms loosened slightly. "So, what *are* you doing here?"

"The amulet you recovered. My boys have examined it closely and it's clearly modern. No more that fifty years old, but more likely a week old. There are no natural impurities in the gold, but it is mixed with modern brass. Also, no magical resonance. And yes, we checked if it was capable of cancelling magic." He gestured at me, as if Lenore wasn't the only person present capable of telepathy.

"So, Ms. Modeste was right?" I asked.

"Yes. But the real one is still out there, and its resident is very dangerous. We believe it's in the hands of the RNC."

"Based on?" Lenore said.

The captain spoke up. "We've been doing a deep dive into the deceased Mr. Minors. We found his greasepaint backstory with the Giggle-O's and—surprise, surprise—turns out his position at the museum is funded by a series of shell corporations believed to be connected to the RNC."

"Believed," Lenore said. "No evidence?"

"If we could prove it, I'd have the whole damn museum staff in custody." He snapped open a cigar box on his desk and took one, rubbing it in his hands. I could see a clear longing in his eyes.

"But," he continued, "the security footage is clear. There were no employees on the grounds at the time of the murder."

The captain gripped his cigar, and I worried he was going to break it like a twig. "C'mon, Lenore. Get your head in the game. You know someone with Talent doesn't have to be present to be involved."

I nodded. "Ms. Falcata believes that they intend to use the amulet's mind control powers to keep their girls in line. Perhaps they used it on Ms. Modeste?"

"Chelsea is a smart woman, but has a very narrow focus," Rivera sighed. "The RNC is a national organization. So far, they've limited themselves to prostitution and magical protection racketeering. But now we believe that are getting into the filthiest racket of all."

"Drugs?" I asked.

"Politics," the captain snapped.

I saw Lenore tense and I felt a shiver down my own spine.

The captain sighed. "There is a local businessman, one Marlon Meadows. He's just announced that he is a candidate for Senator."

"What, for District Twenty-Four here in Los Diablos?"

"No, the Senate in DC."

I frowned in thought. "That election is four years away."

"Oh," Rosie spoke up, "You haven't heard." Her voice was smug, but also sounded...wrong. "The current junior senator just announced his resignation. He wants to spend more time with his family. It was on the news this morning." Her voice was oddly familiar and a poor attempt to imitate Rosie's smoker's rasp. I glanced at the actual mages in the room, but they seemed to ignore the discrepancies.

I turned to Rivera, watching the person who might be Rosie from the corner of my eye. "And you think the amulet had something to do with it?"

Rivera furrowed his brow. "The senator's been tested by three mage level experts and they say he shows no sign of intrusion."

"I don't think I could do that," Lenore said. "I don't think even the amulet could."

"*Oui*," I agreed. "We detected influence on the women the clown targeted. Very mild traces, but there."

Rivera pursed his lips. "The clown had Talent, but nowhere near mage level. Now, what if someone had that kind of precision? You don't think you *or* the amulet could do it, but what about you *and* the amulet?"

Lenore's forehead creased as she cocked her head to the left. "It's possible."

"Exactly what we think," Rivera said.

"*Très bien*," I said. "Influencing one senator to resign is bad…"

"But what if that's not the limit?" Lenore said quietly. "What if it can influence large groups? Political rallies that have no idea they've been manipulated?" She looked at me. "So, it stands to reason that they used your grumpy ex to kill Minors." She grinned and glanced at "Rosie."

I chewed that over, but several somethings didn't seem quite right. I couldn't even imagine the ramifications of such an act. "*Non.* I mean, if they can influence a senator without detection, they could influence her, but my observation of the amulet's function indicates that she would admit to the act, even be proud of it, if they convinced her it needed to be done. *Non*, I believe her version of events, but the proof will be difficult. Also, why would the RNC kill one of their own valued members? It doesn't make sense. Isn't that right, *Leslie*?" I used her first name pointedly.

"Rosie" nodded sharply, and the glamour spell dissipated, leaving Leslie Modeste, looking only slightly the worse for her recent incarceration experience.

The captain chomped at his cigar and spoke around it. "Ms. Modeste has been released but and she's being kind enough to pretend to still be locked up. We think that might make the real culprit overconfident."

I looked at Leslie. "I assume I was fortunately wrong about the evidence not clearing you."

"Normally you would've been spot on, but our man was stupid," Rivera said. "The killer cleaned the knife with bleach, *after* sticking it in Minors. He dribbled some on the corpse. But it was really her fingerprints that cleared her."

I raised an eyebrow. "They placed the weapon incorrectly in her grip?"

"A rookie mistake, really," Rivera said.

"And Ms. Modeste is a southpaw," Lenore said before I could.

"So, the killer put her hand on the knife in the easiest way, but that made the direction of thrust impossible."

"So, the killer thinks the San Francisco department is incompetent," I muttered.

"He knew no one would be fooled long," Rivera said. "But it gave him time to tie up any loose ends and destroy evidence."

The captain chewed on the end of his cigar. "Find the proof. Find the damn amulet. Go."

Lenore and I turned to leave.

"Not without me," Leslie said, back in her glamoured Rosie.

"*Absolument pas*," I said firmly, her words triggering memories, or rather the feelings associated with those memories.

My feelings.

Rivera stood. "We made an agreement with Ms. Modeste, here. In exchange for her cooperation, she gets to help look for the amulet."

"Fine." I walked out, Lenore behind me and Leslie again wearing Rosie's form scurrying to catch up. Out in the hallway, Lenore stopped me. "I'm gonna get with Bobby and set up a scrying for contained magic."

"Is that even possible?" Leslie asked.

"Don't know." Lenore shrugged.

I turned to my ex. "Any idea where the amulet might be?"

She shook her head. "I'm sorry. I wish I was more helpful."

"I'll call Bobby." Lenore gave a sideways glance at Leslie, then fixed her gaze at me as she spoke to the other woman. "Wait here. You," she said, her eyes boring into me, "follow me to my office."

I meekly walked behind her. In her office she selected a blue ring box from a dozen on the shelf. Each box was a different color and marked with a sigil.

"Here." She offered it to me. "As soon as you put it on it will immediately, and permanently, dampen your emotions for those on your mind. Even after removing it, those feelings will not come back."

I would have killed for this ring when Renee went home to marry another, or even the day Leslie called to discard me. But then again, I only knew I wanted the feelings gone when I was hurting and at that point it would be useless.

Was this pretty little thing my salvation, or was I just trying to dump Chelsea before she left me for a body-surfing, four-thousand-year-old spirit girl?

Chapter Nineteen

I sat in an ornate chair by the north door that looked better than it felt, watching an ancient ritual of finding unfold before me. A version of the catholic "Tony, Tony, come around" wherein I felt someone named Tony might actually answer. Leslie faced me, sitting in a matching chair by the south door in her glamour. I don't know why she bothered. I was the only person in the place who could not see through it.

Measured snare drumrolls ending in a sharp snap sounded as Lenore and Kaufman walked around the circle in opposite directions.

Brrrrrr bump, brrrrrr bump. The sound drilled into me.

Their slow steps were timed precisely so they met at the east and west edges of the circle every ninety seconds.

The only source of illumination in the chamber shimmered from a silver circle on the floor, pulsing with intense light. It took me a moment to realize the glow was not magic, but rather an embedded screen spanning almost the width of the room. A pyramidal frame stood over the ritual space and from its apex hung a glowing purple amethyst gemstone the length of my forefinger. The long stone was set in a fine silver filigree and swung from a faintly glowing silver chain. The stone's tip ended in a delicate taper that pointed straight down. That would be the mark, I figured.

The monitor on the floor shimmered and showed a bird's eye view of the city. The stone spun in slow, lazy circles an inch above the detailed view of Los Diablos. Four points of interest glowed purple; the home and office of the new candidate for the US Senate, Marlon Meadows, as well the home and office of the outgoing Senator Joe Letterman. The picture changed, cycling through closeups of each of the spaces.

"You know, Bobby," Lenore said, about a quarter of the circle away from him, "there's no *real* reason to suspect the amulet is anywhere near those locations."

"It's a place to start," Kaufman responded, his tone a touch defensive. He was dressed in his customary brown robe, but added a set of glasses, the lenses made of ruby. "If we're lucky, though, we'll find the frequency of a magical trail."

"Residual energy from use? Good luck. We've already looked for that. Nothing," Lenore said with a frustrated air as she passed him. "Unless the user left an unbroken sympathetic bond. The people we're dealing with are not that stupid."

They were not actually arguing, more like testing ideas against each other. I tuned their voices out and fought to ignore the incessant snare drum. I focused my thoughts and slipped my hand into my pocket to touch the ring. I ran my finger over the red garnet, feeling for impressions of the microscopic symbols I knew were etched there. A product of High Magick. The thin, silver band would barely fit over my pinky, but it weighed on me like a ton of lead.

The problem was that I was rapidly falling in love with Chelsea and wanted to hold on to that feeling even as I wanted to push her away. *Merde*, I even had some affection for Halima that I did not want to dampen.

"It's not working," Lenore said in a taunting sing-song voice as they passed each other for what felt like the hundredth time.

Kaufman held up his hand. "I'm stopping here, you continue to the far side. We're going to need more power."

"You and I constitute the highest degree of magical energy in the state," Lenore said, not bothering to look over her shoulder. "We should be together."

Kaufman returned a rueful chuckle. "Oh, Leni, you only want me for my magic."

"Is there anything wrong with that?" she called out as she came to a stop. They now stood facing each other; Kaufman at the easternmost point, Lenore to the west.

Kaufman pulled out a cell phone. "I'm signaling for more power."

"From a cell tower maybe?" Lenore taunted.

"No," Kaufman replied with a chuckle. "The usual."

"Oh damn," Lenore muttered.

The drum stopped and a palpable silence descended.

All four doors burst open simultaneously and through each stepped a black man in evening clothes and a top hat. Their brows and noses were painted a stark white to give their faces a ghastly, skeletal look I knew so well. They were all greybeards and carried broadswords before them, the tips pointed up, the quillons centered at their chests.

I gripped the armrests so hard my knuckles blanched. Kaufman's *usual* was MMA, or mixed magical arts. While proven effective, the practice was extremely risky and required permits. Surely, Kaufman had the documentation, but still… One early experiment triggered the Loma Prieta earthquake in the middle of the 1989 World Series and nearly leveled the city. Not only did the quake register 7.1 on the Richter scale, but the resultant magical fallout traveled in a cloud over the ocean before fading near Hawaii. That was just dumb luck. A change of winds to the east would have hurt thousands of sensitives.

The newcomers were undoubtably *Voudon* practitioners like me, made up to invoke the lord of the dead, the Baron Samedi. These men reeked of magical power, the cloying rotten smell of Samedi spilled from them, but their swords were crafted for the purpose of High Magick.

To be blunt, I wanted to be anywhere but here. I could tell my eyes were wide with panic, they burned. But the only other person present who seemed adequately afraid was Leslie. She sat rigid with her back pressed to her chair as if trying to disappear into it; staring with her mouth agape, like she wanted to scream something like, "Can these people not feel the magical forces whipping through the chamber?"

In perfect unison, the four swordsmen pointed their weapons at the center of the room. I knew the swords were ceremonial, and not as heavy as combat-ready weapons, but still. How long could these elder practitioners hold them up? Any instability could disrupt the potent forces raging around us and make the 1989 earthquake look like a rumble.

Four shapes appeared in the open doorways, and the four doors slammed shut at with one thunderous clap. I detected the pungent tang of cinnamon and cloves.

Kaufman had added the final, most powerful element to any High Magick.

The dancing girls. There were only four this time and they were dressed, but they were no less potent. The women spun and weaved through the air in expensive formal gowns that would not have been out of place at the Met Gala. They were adorned with silver jewelry, necklaces, rings and bracelets. Oh, and they also held tiny daggers. Athames. This mishmash of magic boggled my brain as waves of terror washed over me. This could go bad. Very bad. I fought the urge to run. It would be useless, anyway. If something went wrong now, there would be no getting way.

Even Lenore watched the dancers with a wary eye. She must feel the unbridled forces assembled, the potent scent—strong and spicy— threatened to overwhelm me. I watched her, hoping to see some kind of sense manifest in her features, but all I saw in her wary look toward the dancers was an even more frightening emotion.

Envy. She felt the power swirling about us, and she wanted it.

The dancers approached the circle, each winding and spinning toward a cardinal point as Lenore and Kaufman retreated. I jumped as a loud thump of a bass drum echoed in the chamber and the snares fell silent.

The deep rhythm of the drum continued its eerie thump, perfectly measuring the seconds. The women stepped sideways in a silent but coordinated pace. Two steps to the left, then one to the right; progressing widdershins. Another magical tradition layered on.

An icy chill shot up my spine. The air tingled with power, like static electricity; that charged feeling just before a thunderstorm when the hair rises on your forearms. This was magic anyone could feel.

Pressure built in my skull. I fought not to cry out, fearing any sound might distract the participants enough for disaster.

Just when a terrified sound threatened to spill out against my will, the drum stopped. Everyone, including the dancers froze in the unnerving silence.

No one dared to breathe.

In that thunderous silence a collective gasp sounded. The pendulum stopped, pointing forty-five degrees from vertical. The floor map now had one tiny pinpoint of green light; nowhere near the marked spots.

"Of course." Kaufman smirked and pointed at the marker. "I wasn't thinking clearly."

"Neither was I," Lenore echoed. "Too obvious." Her brow furrowed in concentration. "Way too obvious."

There were no street names showing at that resolution, but I knew exactly where it was; the storage unit where I first encountered the clown. The one spot where the malignant energy of the amulet had come closest to freedom.

"But it's been a month," I protested. "No magic leaves a residual that long."

Their heads turned to me as if unaware I was present the whole time.

"It's not residual magic," Lenore replied, her voice thoughtful and somewhat distracted. "It's contained."

"Gotcha!" Kaufman shouted.

The dancers remained frozen, like rigidly posed wax statues.

Suddenly, Kaufman clapped and all the High Magick practitioners seemed to deflate. The dancers relaxed and the Samedi houngans dipped their swords. It was as if a room full of pungent incense was suddenly vacuumed out. I took a long inhale and blew it out. My knuckles ached from gripping the armchair.

"We'll need a high-powered team to reclaim the amulet," Kaufman explained. "Different power than we use, aggressive. We need to coordinate this with MWAT."

Lenore smiled at me and raised an eyebrow. "I think Del has *Jefe* on speed dial."

I bristled at her presumption, but the fact was, I did. I called and he answered on the first ring.

"You have something? You better, I'm getting statewide reports of wild magic. That cocky bastard was using MMA, right?"

I explained the situation, confirming the use of MMA.

"That son of a bitch is licensed, but I don't want to be around when he screws up." There was no hostility in Rivera's voice. Even in personal jabs he kept a sort of friendly warmth. Like what I just witnessed was a cute prank.

Rivera continued, "I'll alert fifty squad."

"We need the best," I said and regretted it. Of course, Rivera would only send the best.

"Fifty squad has two combat demonologists, and a top quantum mechanic from Berkeley."

I paused, two? Combat demonologists are a rare breed of powerful exorcists who can enter the spiritual world at will and physically wrestle with demons. Two on the same coast felt incredible. Having two on the same team seemed, well, excessive.

I also had reservations about the quantum mechanic. I generally respected quantum mechanics, but didn't trust how they attempted to manipulate magic with their bulky toolboxes. They are too focused on manipulating magic through theoretical subatomic particles they call magicons and paracons, which they claim they can detect and manipulate by their conspicuous absence.

True demonic possession is rare, and I had never heard of one that required that kind of firepower. "You think it will come to that? Why didn't they just possess Minors?"

"Whoever has it," Rivera answered, "knows what it is and is ready to kill to keep it. They won't move the entity into an inferior vessel. They're gonna get someone who's a powerful Talent, and a strong combatant."

I gave a side-eye to Lenore. "Their own combat demonologist."

"*Amigo*, I gotta bad feelin' it's way, way worse than that. Meet me downtown to plan the raid in person. We're gonna need maximum containment spells. I hate to say it, but we're probably gonna have to get the Feds involved."

"FEEBLE?" I said in disbelief. The Federal Emergency Exorcism Bureau for Limited Exposure was supposed to contain fallout from out-of-control magic. They do not have a great track record. "After what happened in New Orleans, do we really want to inflict them on Los Diablos?"

"Look, *ese,* it chafes my ass, too. But MWAT just doesn't have the manpower. I'll call the regional director and have him meet us."

I hung up.

All we needed was to find a way to get vice involved and this manpower nightmare would be complete.

Chapter Twenty

Kaufman joined us on the ride back to the station, sitting in the back with Leslie. Rivera was waiting for us in the tactical prep room. With him were twelve tough looking magic combat specialists in a combination of Kevlar and warded amulets. Two, a man and woman, wore a red patch with a crossed olive branch and a sword. Around the insignia ran the words, "Peace to the possessed, destruction to the demon."

The quantum mechanic was also easy to pick out: worn jeans with a heavy work shirt and instead of a weapon or wand, he carried a steel toolbox. He was heavier than the well-conditioned combat officers but looked like he could take care of himself. He wore a trucker's cap and sprouted a thick beard, haphazardly trimmed.

Two black MRAP vehicles pulled up— Mine-Resistant Ambush Protected. Designed to counter IEDs in the gulf wars many ended up with police forces. They barely stopped before two more squads poured out of the vehicles. Two men in sergeant's stripes jogged ran toward us. Rivera stood, glaring at the intruders.

"What is the meaning of this?" he demanded.

"Sir, we have orders to provide back up."

"We have a plan and are ready to go, we don't need back up." But even as he spoke, Rivera rubbed his chin. "Who sent you?"

"Orders came from the commissioner's office."

Rivera bit his lip and eyed the extra men. The three squads combined constituted the main body of MWAT. "Okay, here's the plan. Fifty squad will take the lead. You get your men to form an outer perimeter, just inside the FEEBLE containment."

"Yes, sir!" the two sergeants said, practically in unison, and spun off back to their squads.

Rivera looked at me and frowned. "If this is as big as we fear, more men can't hurt." It was sound logic, but he sounded dubious.

A strong scent of magic invaded the air that reminded me of dollar store incense. Then a skinny man with thick glasses perched on a beaky nose clambered down from the first SUV and approached us. His entire body had a shimmery quality to it and I realized immediately I was looking at an astral projection. He wore a perfectly pressed suit that accentuated his awkward bearing. His thick black hair was slicked and gelled into place.

Rivera nodded to him. "This is Orville Milke, regional director of FEEBLE."

Of course that was the reason for his hairstyle. Couldn't have a stray sympathetic bond screwing up containment. Likely he was too vain to just shave his skull. Even though I knew he was a projection, I had to fight the urge to proffer my hand to shake. "It is a pleasure to meet you."

Milke pressed his lips together and vigorously bobbed his head.

Rivera smiled to hide his apprehension. "Director Milke has graciously allotted fifty Talents and two mages to create a magic containment field around the site."

"The best in our region. Heck, the best on the west coast." Milke twitched nervously. "You are certain that we're dealing with a manifestation of Nergal?"

"*Oui*," I responded.

Milke regarded me and he wrinkled his nose. "What makes you qualified to identify a demon?"

"He's qualified," Rivera stated in a firm voice.

Kaufman and Lenore nodded.

"I'm just saying," Milke griped. "If it's not at the level you suggest, then my people could cause more damage than containment. The agency doesn't need more bad press."

"It's that level," Rivera said grimly.

"Okay," the nervous man nodded and vanished.

Rivera turned to me. "His people are cordoning off a five-block radius from the identified site. They will be evacuating civilians and setting up their containment barrier."

"What do you think we are up against?"

Rivera grimaced. "My fear is they've already possessed something and have it under control."

"Something, you mean someone?" Possession can take time if the target is intelligent and fighting it. But it is very fast if the target is stupid or willing.

Rivera gritted his teeth. "If it were me, I'd use a vessel that pushes the physical boundaries in strength and endurance, but mentally controllable. I'd use a homunculus."

"Macklin," I muttered.

* * *

We stood on the safe side of a well-situated steel barricade, both a physical and psychic barrier cordoning the area off around the storage facility. No repairs were evident from my struggle with the clown. All around us MWAT personnel checked their gear pre-raid with the measured motions of people who knew their life could depend upon their tools. Leslie stood on my other side. I didn't like that she was here, but she was the only person who could positively identify the amulet.

Los Diablos weather is screwy, but consistently screwy. October was still generally warm, but the temperature had dropped down to the mid-sixties. In the north that would be considered summer, but here it was sweater weather. I grew up warmer climes, so I wore a long, black wool coat.

"Don't worry, Del," Lenore said. "If that is a manifestation of Nergal you'll be plenty warm soon enough."

I gave her a side-eye. "If? I thought you were sure."

She stared over the barrier, frowning. "I got a bad feeling about this," she finally said. "Finding it was too easy."

"What? Kaufman pulled out all the stops."

"Yes, but like he said, he did his usual. And got a result he half expected. Too obvious," Lenore muttered. "Maybe I'm paranoid, but there is something not quite right."

"Pretty straight forward," a voice said behind me. I turned to see the quantum mechanic standing with his beefy arms confidently crossed over his chest and his steel toolbox on the ground by his feet. "Ms. Welles, Detective Delacroix, we haven't been introduced. I'm Jason Mangel." He still wore jeans and a work shirt, but now also wore a tactical helmet that appeared to be covered in aluminum foil. He extended a hand to me and nodded at Lenore, knowing better than to try and shake hands with a sorcerer.

The man smiled as he attempted a bone crushing grip. I matched his grasp and he let go. Intimidation is one of the tools practical mechanics seem to enjoy using.

He waved an unconcerned hand at the space beyond the barrier. "We got this all under control. I've set up three particle detectors to triangulate any magical sources. Your storage unit shows a complete absence of magicons, which you would expect from a containment, but there is a significant absence of paracons."

"Absence?" I said.

"Well, you know. We can't directly measure where the paracons are. We have to use their current absence to surmise a likely location. Think of it as a vector thing. We don't know where they are, but by their absence, we know where they were."

"That sort of logic is why I am wary of you mechanics."

Mangel surprised me with a rueful chuckle that ended in a sigh of resignation. "Yeah, I get that a lot. But don't worry too much about my mumbo-jumbo, it's those two you need to be concerned about." He nodded at the pair of demonologists. "Shiela isn't too bad, although she's constantly seeing signs of demons where maybe there ain't, you know? Not exactly paranoid, but extremely cautious. Our first and only date started with an exorcism." He shrugged. "Makes for an awkward night, ya know? But her boss, Damien Blutshtälern, I don't know who's scarier sometimes, the demon or the demon hunter? What I'm saying is: he's good at what he does, just stay out of his way."

"Good to know." I waved at the storage center. "You detect any life signs?"

"None," Mangel stated confidently.

"They could be veiled," Lenore pointed out.

"Nope, our detectors would show the absence of particles from the veil spell."

"Even so," Rivera said as he approached. He was dressed in full tactical gear, and I could smell the number of protection wards. Gummy bears. Green apple is what they smelled like. "We're going in like there's an army in there, possibly superior."

"*Jefe*," Lenore said. "I think I should go in alone and reconnoiter."

Rivera treated her with a grin. "Nice try. Wouldn't be a good idea to put you alone with the amulet." His tone made it ambiguous whether he was scared for her, or of her. "We have a drone flying in for the recon. Still no life signs, but we spotted ten prepared positions. Heavily protected. We have to assume they have a tactical purpose." He turned to Lenore. "We'll call you and the detective in when we've isolated the amulet. Until then…" He fastened the chinstrap on his helmet and flicked a confident two fingered salute at Lenore.

In minutes, a column of MWAT combatants lined up behind Rivera and marched to the storage unit at a measured pace, each one armed with either a carbine or wand in their right hand, and their left hand on the shoulder of the guy in front of him.

Cat Scan

My phone chirped and I silenced it. All I needed right then was someone talking about how I needed an extended warranty on something.

The column closed on the building and broke into two squads, moving to encircle. And then they breached. First, wands flared like tiny sparklers, and wards flickered in and fizzled out. Simultaneously explosive charges were placed around the door and, once the magic faded, they blew.

My phone chirped again, and I froze in dread. Police phones have a failsafe enchantment. Even if you turn the thing off, a message that could save you or someone else's life goes through.

Something just came through.

Lenore gave me a nervous look. "Ya gonna answer that?"

The transcript said, "INCOMING T. GRUBER: Don't let them go in there, it's a trap."

Stupidly I stared at it as Lenore read over my shoulder and said some of the choiciest foul words I've heard in English. "It's a trap!" she screamed both with her voice and a powerful psychic wave. Standing so close to her, my head throbbed as the penetrating alert hit me like a physical force.

I saw the flash of physical bombs reacting to the breaching charges. I grabbed Leslie and threw her to the ground, covering her with my body as the shock wave knocked everyone else down. I smelled magic, dark magic, a stench of putrefaction and things recently dead and decayed. It wasn't like Samedi's smell of decomposition, which was both foul and oddly comforting, like *Grand-mère's* bathroom filled with tobacco smoke, *non*. This was old and foul, like something you should never, ever smell. Like a sick room. A death room.

Like contagion.

A wave of malignant magic spilled from the storage center, originating at the unit where I fought the clown. It was formed in the darkest manner, full of negative energy. I felt myself falling into a morass of depression, anxiety, and anger. I felt Leslie squirm and buried feelings flooded through me. I focused my pain and anger her. My hands ached to wrap around her throat and make her pay. Fantasies about what to do to her corpse flooded through me. I felt myself yielding to a sick compulsion.

I reached for the ring in my pocket. Lenore said that it would not have an effect after emotions set in, but I had to try. I touched the metal band and felt the despair slowly draining away from me. I slipped it on and concentrated on what I felt. The sensation abated enough for me to stand. I was the only one not on the ground. I heard someone groan and looked toward the door. Mangel had rolled onto his back.

I sucked in my breath. "Oh, no!" I gasped and staggered forward.

Lenore lay on the ground, bleeding from her eyes, nose and ears.

Help, we need help, I thought vaguely as I stumbled to the MWAT van and grabbed a radio. "Officers down. Multiple injured. Send medical immediately." I fought to form each syllable, and they left my mouth in slow motion. I wondered if this was what having a stroke felt like.

I dropped the radio mic and slumped against the van, slowly siding down until I was sitting on the ground. Sirens wailed in the distance and I stared blankly at Lenore's unmoving body.

Chapter Twenty-One

It was after midnight before I was released from the hospital. I wanted to stay and find out what the hell happened, but the captain ordered me to go home.

I pushed my door open hoping to see one Chelsea curled up napping on my couch. What I got was Pakhet dozing there. "Oh," I said, hoping the cat was a good omen. "Hello, little one." She ignored me and kept dozing, so I threw off my coat and shoes and proceeded to the bedroom.

"Ah, *cheri mwen!*"

There she was, stretched out under my thin flat sheet. I could tell from the way the sheet fell on her curves that she was naked.

"*Mon kè, mwen te manke ou.*" The old words, the forbidden words, tumbled from my mouth as I shrugged from my shirt. It felt dirty to say them out loud, but perfect to such a creature *enchanteresse.*

She sat up, wide awake. "I was waiting for you, Del. I saw on the news. How bad is it?"

I slid onto the bed next to Chelsea and her hand found mine as I spoke. "*Mon kè,* I have struggled this night. Bad night. We were set up. Thirty MWAT officers in the hospital, *Jefe* and Lenore are in a coma. Five FEEBLE agents who may not make it." I stopped speaking, my words cut off. I wanted to tell her that for about a mile all people with Talent were reporting migraines and symptoms of brain burn, how the FEEBLE containment barely worked, and how they were all also in the hospital, but my words ended at "Lenore in a coma." I felt Chelsea run her hands into my hair and shush me, though I was already silent. I felt her lips brush my temple, but I could no longer comprehend. "You know," I finally managed through the trauma seizing me, "you think you'll never get caught. That when things happen, you'll be tough and impersonal. Detached. But Lenore. *Lenore.*" I pressed my fingers into my eyes, too embarrassed to cry in front of a woman I wanted to bed. "I don't care what she says about herself not having feelings or friends. I am her friend, and I saw her, Chelsea, I saw her on the ground, covered in blood. She was invincible, Chelsea. Some part of me thought she couldn't be hurt—"

"Oh, Del," Chelsea said in a soft, worried voice as she ruffled my coarse hair. "You really did hit your head."

"*Mon ami?*"

She gave me an apologetic smile and touched her nose to mine. "You just used a contraction," she murmured.

"I didn't mean to/"

After an awkward beat of silence, we both burst into giggles. As our laughter died, I smoothed Chelsea's ruffled hair. "I'm tired, *mon kè.* I had hoped that I left the day behind in the hospital, but it has found its way home with me. Can we sleep?"

Chelsea butted her head up against my shoulder. "Get naked, *mon ceur.* Pants are for chumps." Her tongue stumbled over the French, and it made me smile as I stood.

I undressed and turned off the light. She turned on the bedside lamp as I slid into bed next to her. She molded her form to me. She was warm, almost feverish. I was used to the cinnamon sweet scent of her magic, but tonight there was another scent clinging about her. I wondered if she was wearing a strong perfume.

"Are you okay?" I asked, examining her flushed cheeks.

Her hands stroked down my stomach. "Never better." Her hand strayed further, but I caught it in mine and stopped her.

"I'm sorry, my darling. I need sleep."

Her hand came up and caressed my face. "You've had a bad day and I can help you relax. I'll do all the work."

I looked into her eyes and saw desire there, deep and irresistible. To be wanted like that. "Tempting, *mon kè,* but you know I enjoy the work."

She kissed me, her lips and tongue a promise, but I grew wary of her ardor. She was almost too eager and there was something that felt off about her. I smelled a strange magic. Enticing. Alluring. The scent should not be this strong; she was not even using a glamour spell. Her ministrations soon pushed concern from my mind and before I knew it, she was on top of me, grinding into me, trying to mimic the rhythms I used. Her breath came in gasps and sweet sweat dripped into my face and I grinned as her eyes rolled back into her head.

Then she screamed.

Not in passion, but fear.

She flung herself off me, rambling. "I'm sorry, I'm sorry, I'm sorry!" she sobbed. "I didn't mean to do that. I didn't think I could." She sat on the edge of the bed, her face buried in her hands.

I reached for her shoulder. At my touch, she jerked, but then the tension left her body. "It's alright," she said in soothing voice with more than a touch of embarrassment. "It's my fault, not yours."

"Fault?"

"I had no idea that would happen," Chelsea continued. "It's okay, no one blames you and I understand your anger."

I started to protest, but then something terrible began to dawn upon me.

"I'm not angry," Pakhet's, or rather Halima's, voice sounded in my head. "But I did tell you this was a bad idea."

"What's going on?" I demanded as a slow anger started to burn in my heart. Who had I just been in bed with? Who was it that just shared such intimacy with me?

With an embarrassed look, Chelsea turned and brought her left foot up. In the dim lamplight I saw that damn amulet around her ankle.

My cheeks burned with shame even as I raised a finger to point at her. I should have known. I should have detected that something was wrong. "That was—"

"No," Cheslea interrupted. "Only for a minute. I lost control. It is one hundred percent my fault."

"You're damn right it is," I snarled with hurt, anger, humiliation. "You did this without telling me?"

"I meant to, but it was late and..."

"That is not an excuse."

"No, but it is an apology. You're right, both of you. Del, I can see you kicking me out after this but please let me explain, first. The bond I have with Halima is so new and exciting, I wanted to share that with you before we inevitably implode."

"You expect us to...implode?"

"Del, you are so good. You make me so happy." She shrugged. "It can't last. Nothing good in my life has ever lasted. I screw it up. Maybe that was what I was doing tonight."

I sat beside her and put my arm around her. "What you did was disrespectful. A violation, to both me and Halima." I kissed her on the shoulder, a peck.

She mistook my gesture. "You're not mad?"

"Chelsea," I said, my voice cracking with the emotions warring inside me. Anger. Shame. Confusion. Guilt. Fear. Revulsion. Pity. Caring. Forgiveness. More anger.

So, I spoke. "If you went to bed with a man, and another man inserted himself into your lovemaking without your knowledge, but definitely without your consent, what would you call it?"

We sat in silence for a very long time, and I felt her tremble in the throes of her grief. Her lips moved silently, and I thought perhaps she was explaining the concept to Halima. Then she answered in a tiny, broken voice. One word. The devil of a word.

"Rape."

I felt her body tense like she was going to throw herself onto the floor and I pulled her against me, wrapped her in my arms as she cried. "Oh, God, I didn't mean to, Del, please believe me, neither of us would ever want to hurt you, we both care for you. I care for you, I—"

I kept my grip on her, like we were both lost in a storm on a moonless night.

"I was warned that Halima would be your primary relationship. And maybe this was your way of saying good-bye."

She gazed up at me through tear-stained eyes. "But I don't *want* to say good-bye. Yes, my bond with Halima is powerful, but I..." Her shoulders slumped. "I, uh, god it is so hard to say, especially right now, but I have to say it. I love you. I never meant to hurt you in any way. I just wanted Halima to feel our relationship. I never expected her to take control."

"I'm pretty sure you gave it to me," Halima's petulant voice spoke in my head again and my heart strings pulled for her. She was also scared and hurt. I just wanted both of them, all three of us, to be okay.

"Maybe," Chelsea admitted. "I wasn't in control. It was so exciting to have the two people I care about most with me at once that I...I don't know, I went somewhere. I was going to tell you. But it was late, and you were already so in need of comfort. I didn't want to pile more on you. I decided to tell you the next time. And after you accepted that I'd confess to this. Please say what you need to. Slap me around if you feel the need, it won't be the first time. Just please, don't hate me."

"If you think," I said through clenched teeth, "that I would ever 'slap you around' then you have no idea who I am. I do not hate you, but I have lost trust in you. I feel as if you made me violate a young woman who was not in a state to consent."

Chelsea blinked rapidly to hold back more tears.

"But," I said, fighting to keep my voice calm. "I think I can..." I paused, trying to organize my feelings. "...convince myself that you meant no harm. Such a betrayal smells more like stupidity than malice."

She flinched at the word stupidity as if I *had* slapped her.

Empath, I thought. She must have felt the hurt and anger in my words, despite my attempt to appear calm. "Trust is hard to rebuild."

She sat silently. Then, with a shy movement, she reached for my hand. I took hers and clasped it. She squeezed my hand like it was a lifeline.

"Can I rebuild your trust?"

I took her hand in both of mine. "It will be hard work."

She gave a rueful chuckle. "Wasn't it you who said that anything good requires hard work?"

"Something to that effect," I agreed.

"I promise to work hard, if you will let me."

"I am willing to work with you," I said. "But not now. I need some space. We will work this out later. But we will work it out."

Relief spilled out of her. "That's all I ask. I promise never to do that again. Or anything like that. I'll be good, I swear—"

I audibly took a breath through my nose. "Please do not. I…" I cocked my head to one side and took a moment to fully understand my feelings. "I do love you, but I must be able to trust you."

"And her. You will need to trust Halima. You should meet her."

"What?"

"I'll give her control and you can talk to her. She needs reassurance. She's…pretty upset and scared. I guess I hurt both of you," Chelsea said, teetering on the edge of tears again.

I was too tired, too emotional to deal with this. But the urge to fix everything, to make it right, won over. Halima was, perhaps, as much a victim in this as me. How could she say no, after all? She was trapped in a trinket, could she really hide deep enough in there to get away from our lovemaking? It made me think of the studio apartment I lived in when I was with Renee in Haiti. Our upstairs neighbors couldn't take their pants off without us hearing. *Non*, there was nowhere for Halima to hide from this episode, and I hated that. "Very well."

Chelsea made a pinching motion above her head, the invocation of a glamour spell. Her form was replaced by a dark-skinned woman with big amber eyes rimmed in kohl. This newcomer wore the familiar Usekh collar over a linen piece gathered on her right shoulder which hung to her knees beneath a wide, cotton sash cinched around her waist. The thin fabric covered only her right breast, leaving the left bare. I jerked my gaze away. Her hair was knotted into hundreds of tiny braids and somehow, I knew it was a representation of the wig she wore in her mortal life.

"So, you are Halima?"

She corrected my pronunciation. "Ha-li-ma, emphasis on the last syllable."

I heard Chelsea's voice in my head, letting me know she was still there. "Sorry, I never heard you say it before."

Halima clasped her hands before her and her chin tilted delicately forward as she spoke. "I'm so sorry." The glamour gave Halima's deep, lovely voice a British accent that lent her words a stately air.

British? Of course, she learned English through Mrs. Childress.

Her chin dropped to her chest, and she turned away from me.

"None of this is your fault," I said.

"Yes, it is. I could have locked myself in the amulet, but, please understand. I was curious." She chewed her lip and batted her eyes as she looked at me. She carried herself like a noble, but also like a child. "I am a four-thousand-year-old virgin. I have never known a man." Halima stopped, a confused look on her face. "I suppose I'm not a virgin anymore. I can't honestly tell. Anyway, Mrs. Childress was very careful to cast me out whenever she was affectionate with her husband. Chelsea gave me access and I wanted to see. I never expected her to lose control. Please believe me, I never intended to be *that* close to you."

"It is okay." I cupped my hand around her jaw and turned her gaze toward me. "Although that does some minor damage to my self-esteem. When you put it like that."

Halima looked up at me with plaintive eyes and I noticed my hand and her cheek...our skin was nearly the exact same tone. "Please do not be too harsh with Chills."

"Chills?"

"That's what her sister called her. Also, Jelly."

"I wish you hadn't told him that," Chelsea muttered psychically.

"She hates that. So, if you want to punish her..." Halima's eyes crinkled, and her face lit up with mischief. Like a loving sister. One that will tease you without mercy and also beat the balls off anyone who bothers you. My heart broke for Chelsea in that moment as I realized, in some strange way, this was Chelsea getting a sister back.

"I'll keep that in mind." I brushed my hand over the tiny braids, but the glamour was only visual. I felt Chelsea's hair. Marveling at the discrepancy, I stroked it a few more times.

Halima froze. "Are you? Are you *petting* me?" she asked, her voice a mixture of humor and disbelief.

I jerked my hand away. "*Non*, I mean *oui*. Petting, but not like a

146

cat. We humans like petting, too."

She chuckled. "I know. Do you remember that night we watched an old movie about a...a detective looking for a golden bird?"

"*The Maltese Falcon*. You were in the chair, cuddled up close and butting me with your head insisting I pet you."

"But when the movie ended..." Halima led me on.

"You rolled over and I tried to rub your tummy, but you bolted. Hid away for hours and after that you were aloof."

"I thought I was a cat. I really did. One who could communicate, but still just a cat. But that moment when you touched me. I realized how much I wanted your touch, and that I was not a cat. And as long I was in a cat's body you couldn't show the affection I desired. After the ceremony with the amulet, it was even worse. I had memories of being a woman. Feeling desire." She buried her face in her hands. "It's so overwhelming, these emotions. I have not felt anything like this in millennia." She sighed. "I should go back in the amulet. I like what you said. The way you said it. I need space."

"Will I see you again? I have so many questions."

"Yes," Chelsea replied in my mind, then Halima made the pinching gesture over her head, and Chelsea once again stood before me. "What do you think?"

"About?"

"About her, us?"

"I need to process this." I climbed out of bed. "Uh, I'll go sleep on the couch." I grabbed sweatpants and a T-shirt from the top dresser drawer. I had just got them on when there came a pounding on my door.

"Police," a voice called, "open up!"

I ran to the door, nearly stepping on Pakhet—err, Cocopuff—and looked through the peephole. I recognized the two cops, so I threw it open. "What's this about?" I demanded.

"Step aside," a female officer commanded, her service 9mm in her hand. I didn't know her well. Her surname was Standhill—I couldn't remember her first name—a rookie who had been on the force for only a few months. Behind her stood a male officer armed with a wand. I knew him better, James Desmond. He was working to be a detective and was alarmingly close to the men in vice.

"Where is Chelsea Falcata?" Desmond demanded.

"Here," Chelsea said from the bedroom door. "What's this about?" She had also donned sweatpants and a T-shirt.

Both trained their weapons on her.

Desmond gripped the wand like he was itching to use it. "We have

147

a warrant."

"This is ridiculous," I barked.

"Stay out of this, Delacroix," Desmond commanded. "If you know what's good for you."

That outburst earned a side-eye from Standhill. Perhaps a touch of disapproval. She seemed to be just doing her job, while Desmond enjoyed it.

Cocopuff yowled in outrage.

They ignored her.

Standhill holstered her weapon and pulled out a set of handcuffs. She marched to Chelsea, commanding, "Turn around."

Chelsea complied as the woman deftly snapped the cuffs on her.

"Chelsea Falcata," Standhill pronounced, "you are under arrest for the murder of vice detective Ted Gruber."

Chapter Twenty-Two

I rushed into the bedroom, any thought of rest obliterated. I couldn't go with the arresting officers, but I had to act. For that I needed to get dressed.

There on the bed, I saw it. The amulet.

I stared at it for what seemed an eternity as several facts clicked into place.

Chelsea and Halima were bonded empaths, therefore, Chelsea was increasingly resistant to the idea of parting from Halima at all, to the point that she had, quite foolishly, brought Halima along into our bed.

And yet, she had taken the amulet off and left it on the bed before coming to the living room, therefore...

She knew she was going to be taken and left the amulet behind. For me.

My hands felt clammy, sweat formed on my head and I felt the taste of metal in my mouth. Fear.

Not like at the storage unit, or maybe an echo of that. I knew what she expected me to do, but it took a powerful effort of will to walk to the bed. I touched the amulet it gingerly, expecting it to burn.

It didn't. Perhaps I was nowhere near sensitive enough?

I stared at the item in my hand. What to do?

I could put it on the cat and discuss plans with Halima, or...

I took a deep breath. The chain was so long Chelsea had to wrap it three times around her ankle. My lips clenched in trepidation as I lowered the chain around my neck. I do not know exactly what I feared. Someone inside my mind? Influencing me? Controlling me?

The amulet landed against my chest with a gentle *thump*. I felt nothing. I touched the amulet and tucked it under my T-shirt, practically rubbing it on my chest.

Still nothing. Was she gone, too?

"Halima, are you there?" I said aloud.

I did not feel anything for several seconds, then a frightened voice stirred in my head. Less invasive and more tenuous than my conversations with Pakhet.

"Are you there?" I repeated.

The thought message was tentative, frightened. "Delacroix? Is that you? What's happening? Chelsea threw me out into the amulet. She didn't explain, just threw me away," Halima wailed in fear and anger.

I explained about Chelsea's arrest as I changed my clothes.

"Oh," Halima replied, her initial anger turning to fear and concern. "Is she in prison?"

"What do you know of prisons? Human prisons are not like yours."

"I've seen movies and tales Mrs. Childress told me."

"One of the holding cells by the station, I am sure. It will take an hour or so to book her."

"She didn't do it," Halima stated emphatically. "She was with me the entire time."

I was relieved to hear that. I mean I believed Chelsea was innocent, but...also with their bond, would Halima lie for her? Would I know? No; the voice in my head was real and compelling.

"You're getting dressed. Where are you going?"

I paused. I meant to go down to the station, but they wouldn't let me talk to her, not tonight. Everyone who could help me was either asleep or in the hospital.

"Put me on the cat," Halima said with the same sort of dread I felt. She had a taste of real human existence and her reluctance to return showed.

"Are you sure?"

"No, I'm not," Halima said with a strong note of determination. "But I need a body of my own and you, well, you're male, and everything feels wrong."

"Maybe if we—"

"Delacroix," Halima's mental voice rang in my head. "For four thousand years I've recognized my duty and have never failed."

I walked out to the front room where Cocopuff was staring at me expectantly. "This is temporary," I promised.

"I hope so, but I will do my duty as I see it."

I took off the amulet and figured out how to attach h it to her collar.

She shook herself, stretched and yawned.

"Halima?"

"No," the mental voice said. "I have to accept that when I am in this body, I am a cat. Otherwise, it's too confusing, so for now, I am Pakhet."

I felt a familiar tingle. It burst through my body like light energy.

"Oh *non, non, non*. She must have a feeling that I am in trouble."

"Who?" Pakhet asked, confused.

I accepted the call. *Ma grand-mère* appeared in front of me as an astral projection. At least she'd understood the need to call ahead. Since the incident with a cute redhead... That was our first, and last, date. It seemed the only way to explain boundaries to *Grand-mère* was in the form of my odds of giving her great-grandchildren. That night she reduced them to zero, and has "buzzed" ahead ever since.

Now she stood in front of me with her arms crossed and looked me up and down. "You are injured."

"Just bruised. Too close to a bomb."

"But dat did not alarm you as much, I sense, as now." Before I could explain, she continued. "And who is dis woman in your apartment?"

"The cat, Pakhet. You've met her."

Grand-mére squinted at Pakhet, her nose scrunched. "No. Last you had a cat wit a spirit. Dis is no random entity. Dat is a woman." *Grande-mére* clicked her fingers and Halima replaced Pakhet, looking exactly as she had under Chelsea's charm. No, it was a glamour, not a transformation. I felt embarrassed in front of *ma grand-mére* with Halima's breast exposed.

"You are involved wit my grandson?"

Halima, shocked by her sudden unveiling, looked at me like we had just got dragged to the principal's office and *ma grand-mére* was the principal. "We are involved, but it is complicated."

Grand-mère sighed. "You were involved wit da confused werewolf and I was afraid you were going to have puppies. Now what? Are you going ta have kittens?"

Halima chuckled.

"It doesn't work like that," I muttered, embarrassed.

Grand-mére smiled. "Of course not. So, what has the two of you so upset?" She looked at Halima with narrowed eyes. "She is a pretty ting. Good blood, strong mind."

"*Grand-mére*, I don't have time for this. Chelsea is in trouble," I said, then explained about the arrest.

Halima frowned. "We have to go, it's urgent," she insisted.

"Den be gone," *Grand-mére* said. "But first you need to get dressed." Both women closed their eyes and suddenly Halima was wearing Chelsea's professional look. Black slacks, purple blouse and a black blazer. "Dis way she can go wit you."

"But—" I tried to object.

"I can maintain da glamour as long as I stay awake. Dey just started the Real Housewives of Florida Marathon, so you be all good, now git."

* * *

I could not see Chelsea until after she was booked, so I went to the hospital to check on Lenore and Rivera. I stood in the doorway of Lenore's room, surrounded by ominous beeps and blinking machines. A combat demonologist sat rigid, holding her right hand while the quantum mechanic fiddled with an apparatus on her left arm. I watched for a little while, then went to check on Rivera, relieved to see he was awake. I got the feeling he was expecting me.

"Is it common to have your girlfriends arrested for murder?" Rivera grunted as I entered the room, followed by Halima. He was conscious and alert, but he looked like a shrunken version of himself in the loose hospital gown. He raised his arm to show a quasi-legal vitality charm. "I mean two girlfriends in one week." He glared at Halima, and I could tell he was not fooled by *Grand-mére's* impressive glamour spell. "What's with the cat?"

I pulled one of the visitor chairs to the side of his bed. "I am glad you are awake."

"Yeah, one more round with the healers and maybe I can escape, you know? They tell me I was hit pretty hard, physically and psychically. Doctors are wringing their hands, but I think there's no permanent damage, except to my ego. Stupid. But tell, me, my friend, *quién es este gato secreto?*"

"A very old friend." I didn't explain four thousand years.

Rivera pursed his lips but didn't say anything else.

We all stayed silent a moment. Then Rivera lifted the blanket enough to show me he had his signal jammer and privacy charm on.

"What really happened, *Jefe?*" I asked.

"They used a physical containment that was blasted open by physical bombs," Rivera said.

"*Merde.* What was inside?"

Rivera gave a nonchalant tilt of his head. "How many Djinn are there in the world?"

I was taken aback by the change in topic. The Djinn were

imprisoned by Solomon and the queen of Sheba. Their release brought magic back into the world. "There were seven jars broken at Nag-Hamadi, so seven?"

"Seven," Halima said slowly. "Or eight."

Rivera tightened his lips and nodded. "You've heard the tales of Egyptian gods torn apart and later reformed? We think that the Djinn can do that. That is why there are only seven, but they seem to be everywhere simultaneously. Nergal was imprisoned before the rest, making him the eighth, or another piece of the seven we know about."

"Nergal is a piece," Halima asserted. "A diseased piece cast out of the greater whole."

Rivera cocked an eyebrow at the illusion. "You know a lot about demons, for a cat. But then, I did once own a calico, so I guess it tracks."

"Halima is sort of an expert on Nergal," I explained by way of non-explanation.

Halima leveled those big, beautiful eyes at Rivera and spoke with an even, dignified tone. "I lived with him for at least four millennia."

Rivera blinked hard in disbelief at Halima, then shot me a glance that said I had a lot of explaining to do. "Well, I'm glad we finally have someone on our side who sorta knows what's going on. Maybe you can shed some light on your former roommate and how they're keeping him from tearing everyone a new psychic ass."

Halima's gazed dropped, as though she were considering her next words very carefully, perhaps so that the modern men before her would comprehend. "I suspect they must be using some magical nullification, similar to the seal Solomon used. You must understand, they are entrapping a piece of a piece." Halima paused, as though she didn't have the words for what she was trying to explain to us. "It is true, that Djinn can be fragmented, but always the whole will be greater than the parts. No one wants to be just a limb, do you understand? The pieces of a Djinn will always seek each other out to rejoin. No matter *what*."

"To what purpose?" I asked.

"Someone in the commissioner's office ensured that all of our top Talent would be there. This appears to be a planned weapon of mass destruction. The goal was to wipe out all potential opposition to the RNC move into politics." Rivera looked at the door as if expecting someone. "You have a chance to look in at Lenore?"

"Still unconscious," I replied.

"And in terrible peril," Halima interjected, her voice strained and trembling. "*He is there, with her.*"

Rivera blew out his lips and gazed at me. "You *have* found an expert. You're absolutely right, Halima. I wish you weren't. At the last second, Lenore tried to absorb the malicious magic. The only thing that saved our asses."

"Makes an argument against that 'sociopath' thing. She was willing to risk her life to save us," I said.

Rivera grimaced as he tried to push himself up in the bed and failed. "No, she didn't. There was no altruism involved. Only arrogance. She really believed nothing could outmatch her. So, you're correct, Halima. The sliver of Nergal did not rejoin, it's somewhere even more dangerous. Trapped inside Lenore Welles, the greatest mage and craziest, most cold-hearted bitch I've ever met. We might be doomed."

All the ominous magical equipment and personnel dedicated to Lenore suddenly made sense. "So, if it remains trapped within her?"

"Welles can either wrestle control, which will make her far more powerful, or dangerous depending on how you look at it. Or, she will remain locked in combat with the entity, so basically in a coma."

"And if the demonologist and mechanic set it free?"

"It will make a beeline back to its greater self, annihilating all sensitives in its path."

"So, no good options."

"I will do combat with the demon Nergal, in any of his pieces or forms," Halima announced, her shoulders square. "It is my duty, I swore before *my* gods I would not fail. It is the purpose I was born for."

River chuckled. "No offense, miss. But at the moment, you *are* just a cat. What's Nergal going to do, stop to boop your nose and that's when you'll get him? I think our only real option is to find the original amulet, before Nergal is released."

"Great, we need Lenore to find the amulet, we need the amulet to get Lenore back."

Rivera reached out to pat my shoulder, but his IV was too short. "That's why we get paid the big bucks."

"What are we going to do about Chelsea?" Halima asked.

"She's being framed," Rivera sighed. "Two birds with one stone. Kill the mole in vice and frame someone they've been trying to shut down. Gruber took too much of a risk to warn us. Who actually arrested her? Do they have any evidence on her?"

"I know they have a video of her screaming she was going to kill him," I said. "No context and I am sure it is at least a year old. Report says there was no struggle, and no body.

"As for the arresting officers, Desmond was one."

"That makes sense."

"Assisted by that rookie Standhill."

"Anna?" Rivera sat up. "That doesn't make any kind of sense. I've had my eye on her. She's exactly the type of officer I'm trying to work with."

At that moment both of our phones alerted. I opened mine and read the words with confusion and horror.

COP KILLER CHELSEA FALCATA ESCAPED AND AT LARGE. CONSIDERED ARMED AND DANGEROUS. TAKE NO CHANCES.

"This is a shoot on sight order!" I cried out.

Rivera shut his eyes as he spoke in resignation. "Smart bastards. They've used the arrest as a pretense to nab her. They can't afford for her to go to trial. I'm sorry, Delacroix." Rivera shook his head. "I know she was important to you, but the odds are she's already dead."

"No," Halima said. "I would know."

"She and Chelsea are close," I explained. "Empathic bond. She's kind of an expert on Falcata."

"Oh?" Rivera stared at the cat, studying it for the first time. His eyes widened in understanding, then looked at me. "Oh! That *is* complicated."

Tell me about it, I thought

"Look, I know you want to keep hope alive, but this is not going to end well."

I didn't want to believe him. "Where would they take her?"

The silence was unbearable.

I took my phone out and called the captain on speaker phone.

"Delacroix?" the captain barked. "You need to get down here right now. This is turning into a real shit show."

"Chelsea is innocent, Captain."

"No one believes that. She shot Standhill to escape."

A lump lodged itself in my throat. There would be no going back for Chelsea, now. "*Non, impossible.* Standhill is dead?"

"Nah, the rookie's tough. She's in surgery."

"Thank god. When she gets out of surgery she will clear Chelsea."

Rivera stuck out his lower lip and scrunched his face. "They want Standhill out of the way. She's an honest cop. The only reason she's still alive is so she can testify that Falcata shot her."

"Get down here now," the captain fumed. "And tell Rivera to hurry the hell up and get better."

"Will do, boss." I ended the call.

"If we only had Lenore," Rivera said.

Halima looked pensive. "I might be able to help with that."

Chapter Twenty-Three

"Do you think that amulet is too small?" I asked as I indicated the glamour version of the tiny scarab around Halima's neck.

"The physical size has nothing to do with the capacity of a spirit trap," Rivera explained in a fatigued tone as he followed us to Lenore's room, wrapped in his hospital gown and robe, dragging an IV set behind him. He had also acquired another quasi-legal charm, a far more dangerous one, for stamina. The energy such charms gave wasn't magical itself, the magic simply ramped up your metabolism to use the deepest reserves. Highly habit forming, and users always felt amazing right up to the moment they dropped dead.

The two men were still in Lenore's room, reeking of defensive magic. Jason Mangel looked up at us, still dressed in a denim work shirt. He'd added a camping vest to his look this time, pockets stuffed with crystals and small vials.

The other, the senior demonologist Damien Blutshtälern, frowned and said with disdain, "I don't think you're supposed to have a cat in here."

"Look closer, asshole," Rivera said with the type of contempt reserved for long-time associates. "You're supposed to be an expert."

The demonologist narrowed his eyes, then blinked rapidly. "Well, you're definitely not supposed to have a *possessed* cat." His reply was peevish, defensive. "I'm a little distracted at the moment."

"She's a benevolent entity," Rivera snapped back.

The demonologist shook violently and released Lenore's hand. His tense grip left angry red marks on her flesh. He suddenly looked exhausted, and I realized that even while talking to us he'd actually been on the astral plane physically fighting. I couldn't guess how long, but it must have been grueling.

156

"I'm not making any progress," he said with a weary sigh. "I've never wrestled a demon this powerful before."

"So, it is a demon, then?" I asked.

The demonologist glowered and scratched his jaw, his nails scuffing the stubble. "Not a demon per se. That involves a specific belief system. But this *is* an intrusive entity. One that wants out, but the host is holding it tight."

"Because she wants the power, or she's afraid to let it loose?" Rivera asked as he eyed the stricken mage.

"No telling," the demonologist muttered. "A little ah column A, a little ah Column B."

"We have an amulet," Rivera explained. "And someone who knows the entity thoroughly, Halima."

The demonologist saw through the glamor and regarded the cat. "Her?"

"Yes," Halima said. "I was the one chosen by our highest priestess to block the escape of Nergal. Like a cork in a bottle, my presence assured his entrapment. My *sacrifice*. Gladly, I took this duty, but who of us could foresee four thousand years into the future? Nonetheless, it is I who have failed in protecting the world from its evil, and it is I who must put it back in its place. Locked away forever, his name never to be uttered among living men."

I sighed. It must be an awfully stuffy place if they talked that way at the temple.

The demonologist rubbed his forehead. "What do you think you can do?" The exasperation in his tone burned like acid.

"I think," Halima said, "I can inhabit the cat completely, leaving the trap in my amulet empty. Once the amulet is on Ms. Welles, the entity may think it's found a way out." Her glance shifted between the three mage-level operators in the room. "You will need to make Ms. Welles let go. As soon as Nergal's Shard goes for the amulet, I will block his escape, like a cork in a bottle of fouled wine. That task will take all my strength. I will not be able to leave the amulet or communicate."

"For how long?"

Halima shrugged, a fatalistic gesture. "Another four thousand years? I don't know."

I didn't like the sound of that. "Can't we just find the original amulet and get the piece to rejoin the entity and trap it for all time with the clown as the stopper?"

"Possibly," Halima said, doubtful. "But whoever did this—"

"The RNC," Rivera said. The demonologist scrunched up his face as if he wasn't so sure.

"Whoever," Halima continued, "will not let that happen. They are trying to put Nergal into a body they have some control over, but if pressed, I think they would destroy the amulet."

"The equivalent of a nuclear weapon going off," Mangel said.

"I am prepared to go," Halima said, her voice shaky. "But before I go, I want to speak with Detective Delacroix in private." "You are three mages? Can you make this illusion solid? A solid astral projection?" She turned to me, but her eyes were downcast.

Rivera grunted. "Two mages and maybe a half? I'm done in, and they are not much better."

"One and a half," Blutshtälern said haughtily. "I will not be party to giving an unknown entity any power."

Rivera glared at him. "Your participation's not a request. It's an order."

Blutshtälern bristled. "Then I will follow your order under protest."

"Noted," Rivera said, then turned to Halima. "Maybe the three of us can get you, uh, I don't know. Five minutes?"

Halima, her eyes still on the floor, took in a deep breath. "Please?"

"We can try for five minutes," Mangel said, "but I think that's optimistic, three minutes is more likely. But I have a widget..." He fished around in one of his pockets, "This might give us another minute, it's a magicon amplifier."

"It amplifies the absence of the particles?" I said rhetorically.

Mangel bobbed his head with unironic appreciation that I was been paying attention. "Absolutely."

The two mages approached Halima and with a wave removed the illusion. I could sense *ma grand-mére's* shock as the energy rebounded. Blutshtälern sullenly joined them.

The demonologist drew a chalk circle around the cat, and they all stepped inside and chanted over the animal. There was a shimmering of the air, and Halima returned. I was relieved to see she was still in Chelsea's clothes. The other outfit would be far too distracting.

Halima touched her chest just below the shoulders, assuring herself she was solid. "A moment alone?" She kept her head down, avoiding eye contact with everyone.

Rivera handed her the cone of silence charm, and she led me to the other side of the room and pulled the curtain closed.

She looked at me with that imperious gaze, like she was staring down at me even though I had several inches on her. "I'm not going without saying certain things. I love Chelsea. She knows that, but I would like her to know the second greatest regret of my life is leaving her. Please, tell her."

"I will."

"Do you want to know what my greatest regret is?" she asked and raised her chin in a delicate motion. So young, so old. So elegant, so naïve, so wise. "It's not having the chance to love you. I can feel that you think I'm just echoing Chelsea's feelings, but it doesn't work that way. We are joined, but we are not the same. I feel love, and desire, for you in my own right. You are the first man to show me true affection. Even if it *was* just petting a cat." Her body tensed. "I ask you one small favor. Kiss me farewell."

I stared at her, and maybe I have some little bit of an empath in me. I felt her fear, sorrow and longing. I touched her chin and moved forward to give her a sweet kiss, but just as I was about to make contact, I jerked back. "What?"

She was standing there with her tongue stuck out and her lips clamped tight.

"What are you doing?" I asked.

"I've seen this in the movies. Isn't this how you are supposed to kiss the one you love? The tongue is involved, no?"

Boy, the Childress' were freakier than any of us thought. "*Oui*, the tongue is involved, but the lips…" I touched hers. "The lips are committed. Relax these."

"I've never kissed anyone."

"I can tell. Just relax." I moved to her and pressed my lips to hers. I nudged at her lips with my tongue, and she met it. We kissed, a passionate, sad kiss.

I reluctantly broke contact. "I'm guessing this wasn't a common thing in Egypt?"

"No, not in my time. We do this." She came close enough to kiss me, but instead gently nudged her nose along the side of mine. Her face flushed and her breathing became irregular.

The touch was far more erotic than I would have thought, made so by her reaction. She was taking a great deal of pleasure, and her ardor warmed me.

I started to say, "I would like—" But she was gone. The cat looked up at me and I felt a sad smile. I crouched down close. "I would like the chance to learn to love you, too."

The cat's head rose abruptly, and her nose bumped mine. Her whiskers fluttered against my face and her cold nose surprised me. I laughed and I could feel Halima chuckle as well.

"Alright, I am ready," Halima/Pakhet said.

Changing names may be less confusing for her, but it was far too bewildering for me. I stood and opened the curtain.

"I'm ready," Pakhet announced, her psychic voice afraid, but determined. "Take the amulet." She stretched her neck out for easy access. I undid the clasp and pulled it from her fur.

"Give it to me," the mechanic said. The others nodded agreement. The three of them spent several minutes examining the amulet, Mangel holding it while the others waved their fingers over it. Blutshtälern grimaced the entire time.

My brain demanded I tell them to go faster, but I kept silent. As I said, High Magick is boring to watch, so I didn't. I just thought about Halima. I knew her, and didn't know her, but I knew I wanted the chance to know her better, and that was unlikely.

There are two woman I could love, and they may both be gone today.

Rivera picked up Pakhet and held her over Lenore's chest. The cat looked relaxed, but I could sense her tension as she watched Lenore's chest move with her breathing.

The demonologist took Lenore's hand and instantly fell into a trance. The mechanic carefully placed the chain around Lenore's neck, holding the amulet away from her skin as he produced a purple crystal. Only when he was sure everything was ready, did he allow the actual amulet to touch her body.

As it touched her skin, her neck arched, and her mouth opened in a silent scream. Her face went pale as death and her hands clutched convulsively at the covers. Her breath came in ragged wheezes and her head jerked in odd motions, left, right, forward, back, all the while trying to scream as Pakhet writhed to stay in place.

The demonologist, still in his trance, tensed.

"Now!" Pakhet shouted in our brains.

Rivera plopped the cat down on Lenore's heaving chest. Now she did scream.

"I command you, let go!" Blutshtälern shouted while Mangel touched the crystal to her forehead. There was a flash of light, and the energy pushed Mangel away.

Lenore's scream morphed onto a loud wail that faded into a weak cough. Then she blinked, and finally her vision focused on me. "Whoa." Her voice was hoarse.

"Lenore?" I asked.

"Yes, it is her," the demonologist proclaimed. "The entities are both locked in the amulet, together. Good riddance to both of them." He glared at me as if daring me to say something. When I did not, he said under his breath, "Demon lover."

Lenore raised a shaky hand to the amulet to remove it. The fine chain tangled in her short hair and she was too weak to fuss with it. She jerked at the chain and the chain came free, along with several of her silver hairs. "I believe this is yours?" she said in a hoarse whisper as she held the amulet out to me like it weighed a hundred kilos.

I took it in both hands, squeezing the amulet tight. "Halima?" I said aloud.

There was no reply.

Cocopuff meowed a long-suffering meow.

Chapter Twenty-Four

"We need to lock that up," the demonologist said.

I still held the tiny gold piece in my hands. It felt heavy, far heavier than it should. "*Non*," I said with a firm shake of my head. "This is mine, I will care for it."

"It's not yours," Blutshtälern replied, "if it has a malicious force inside. It is my responsibility that thing is locked away, so neither entity escapes."

"Blutshtälern, stand down," Rivera snapped, holding a rummaged cold pack to his face.

At that moment a doctor burst in, brandishing a medical chart. "What the hell is going on in here?" he demanded.

"An exorcism," the demonologist said with a sense of calm finality.

The doctor froze and examined the room, his eyes ending up on his now conscious patient. "Successful?" he asked as he glanced at the chart and then back at Lenore who gave him a week nod. "I wish you would have alerted us what you were doing. The whole floor's in a tizzy about the magical pulses from this room."

"Yeah, well, they're stable now," the demonologist said as if he did it all by himself. "I took care of it."

"I'll be the judge of that," the doctor said as he moved to Lenore.

The demonologist smirked at me. "Now, hand over the amulet."

I squared my shoulders and clutched the amulet to my chest. "*Non*."

"What? You and all your magical Talent are gonna keep it safe?"

"I am to be initiated in the Revealed Gnostic Elite. I am certain my brothers will render any assistance I need."

"You?" the demonologist said with surprise, and maybe a trace of envy, in his voice. "A Nog?"

Lenore coughed as the doctor placed a stethoscope on her chest. She weakly gestured in my direction. "He has the grandmaster on speed dial."

The demonologist reevaluated me. There was a reason the Nogs called themselves elite; out of hundreds of applicants a year, only one or two were chosen. I, on the other hand, was drafted.

The mechanic joined in. "He's right. His lack of Talent actually makes him the perfect guardian. Entities can't take advantage of Talent that ain't there."

Lenore looked at the demonologist. "Don't underestimate him. What he lacks in Talent he makes up for with knowledge, good sense and courage. Also, he has more experience with dangerous magical items than anyone I know of."

I wanted to sink into the floor. I was unfamiliar with that kind of exaggerated praise, especially coming from a mage.

"Now what do we do?" Lenore \.

"You are doing nothing," the doctor said. "You need rest. There is no magic or medicine that will make it safe for you to get out of this bed for at least a day. Maybe two."

"Well, we tried magic," I answered. "It got us here. I think it is time for mundane police work." I glanced at my watch; it was still early morning. If I paid attention, I could smell bacon and eggs being passed out to the patients down the hall. My stomach rumbled and my mouth watered at the thought of bacon.

"Your plan?" Lenore pressed.

"First, I'm going to get breakfast. Then head into the station and go over everything we know and have collected. There must be a clue or lead to follow up."

Lenore looked up at the doctor. "Yeah, am I gonna get a plate, doc? I need protein."

I stepped closer to Lenore's bed as she harassed the poor medical professional and started to take her hand. My deepest inclination was to smooth her ruffled hair and kiss her on the forehead. I was so glad to hear that sassy voice. I settled for a quick pat on the part of her arm not covered in IVs and wires. "I'll see you at the station, Lenore."

My stomach ached with hunger and I considered the hospital cafeteria, but I needed good food and powerful caffeine. I took the elevator down to the parking garage and headed for my car.

163

"Excuse me," said someone with a husky female voice.

I turned. A woman stood there, a stranger to me. She had dark skin, about the color of my own. She looked dowdy, carrying about twenty pounds too much, almost all of it spilling over the waistband of her baggy jeans. To top that she wore a man's plaid flannel shirt, untucked. Her hair was styled in a modest afro with red and gold highlights. Her face was unremarkable, but there was something odd about her nose…perhaps she had work done, poorly. She wore a lot of makeup, likely to hide the issue with her nose. I sniffed. No magic, no glamour, though the woman had some Talent.

"May I help you?"

She approached me, stopped and gestured for me to get closer.

I looked around the garage, very wary of her behavior, but I stepped into an intimate distance.

"It's not safe, we need to get into the car," she said, her words low, but now the husky quality was gone, and I recognized Chelsea's mezzo-soprano voice.

"Escape is not a good option for you. Let me take you in."

"I wouldn't survive a minute in police custody. I didn't escape, well, not exactly. Get in the car, I'll explain."

I hustled to the unmarked car and slid into the driver's seat. Chelsea climbed in next to me. "Let's get out of here. It isn't safe."

I drove slowly out of the parking lot. "You didn't escape?"

"No, the guy with the wand let me go. The bastard shot the female cop."

"Shot her and framed you. There is a shoot on sight announcement out on you."

"It seems they've got me in checkmate. They have one of my kompromat stashes."

"What?"

"The material that's to be released to the press if anything bad happens to me. That particular stash was supposed to be my nuclear option, released whenever I wanted to. There are three other stashes, but I don't have control of them. They will only be released if I am murdered or disappeared. I'm not sure that me being killed by a cop while resisting arrest will trigger the release. There is little actual evidence, mostly it's just enough to make some well-connected people uncomfortable, and enough information on vice to make them quietly squirm for a while."

We stopped at a red light, and I fumbled in my pocket to draw out the amulet. "You should hold onto this."

She grabbed it like a drowning man grabs a float. "She's in there?"

"*Oui.*"

She closed her eyes in concentration. "I can sense her, but there is something blocking her." Her voice trembled.

"We used the amulet to trap an entity, a fragment of the other," I explained. "She asked me to tell you her greatest regret was leaving you."

Chelsea held the amulet to her forehead and sighed relief. "She's there. Fighting. I can't hear her. Oh, god is she fighting. I think I can help her. Make her stronger, but it will take time." She looked at me and raised an eyebrow. "I know you lied to me, just now, by the way."

"Not a lie, a clarification. I felt what she meant,"

Chelsea's face grew hard, defensive and she turned to look out the window. I could not see, but I knew there were tears in her eyes. "Where are we going?" she asked.

"Nowhere right now. Just getting you away from the hospital and making sure I am not being followed," I sighed as all the adrenaline wore out, replaced by anxiety. But with Chelsea here, I had direction. "I will call Rivera; he can take you in and protect you."

"There is no protecting me right now," she said firmly, "and good luck with the 'not being followed' plan. This belongs to the motor pool. It has GPS and some sort of magical tracking. We need to ditch this car."

I shook my head. "*Non, non, non.* We cannot spend the rest of our lives on the run, that is what you are asking me, *non?*"

"*Oui,*" she said with the hint of a smile. "But what are your other viable options? Dump me here? Turn me in?"

"*Non,*" I countered. But damned if I could figure out what to do.

"Then we ditch the car and pick up one of mine."

"Your van?"

"No, I have two burner vehicles both with GPS disabled and licensed to a shell company. One's parked in long term storage at the airport; the other's in a private garage in Lincoln Heights."

"Lincoln Heights? The police do not go there with less than a squad."

"Which is why we are going there."

"And we will be safe?" I asked.

"I know a guy."

I turned at the next right and headed for third street, the fastest way to the worst side of town. I glanced at her sideways. "Nice disguise and no glamour?"

"Too many people looking for me can see through glamour."

"Skin tone?"

"Spray tan. I know a guy. It'll wash off in a week."

"Nose?"

"Latex, it's supposed to look like a bad nose job so that's what people remember. I have five identical ones in my bag. This look takes an hour of makeup."

I stopped at a light. The distance was less than ten miles, more like seven, I think; but the traffic was thick.

"Standhill survived. Last I heard she was in surgery."

"I'm glad of that, but, crap, it makes things worse for me."

"How so?"

"They were taking me to the lockup, hands manacled in front of me, leg chains connected. You know that everyone going in is strapped with a plate of cold iron so they can't work magic? That includes the police visitors and guards. But we turned a corner, Standhill in the lead, suddenly Desmond had a glamour, looking like me. He shoved me back, pulled a gun and screamed, 'You're not going to take me!' or some dumb shit like that. Standhill turned and he shot her in the chest. The last thing she saw was 'me' pulling the trigger. Bastard hauled me out of lock up and set me free. I think he planned to shoot me right then, but a bus showed up. Too many witnesses."

I furrowed my brow and clenched my lips. I made a decision and pulled into a market gas station. "Wait here," I told her. I ran in and bought two pay-as-you-go phones. I ran back to the car and tossed them to Chelsea. "Put each other's phone number in them."

Nose-job Chelsea gave me a crooked grin. "Ah, Del, I love your style but I'm way ahead of ya. I got four burners in my safe house."

"I'm not going to your safehouse," I explained, trying to keep the frustration out of my voice. "And I do not want to know where it is. I can't go on the run with you. I want to. I love you, but who is going to prove you innocent?"

Chelsea bit her upper lip but then nodded understanding.

"Tell me how to get to your car."

She gave directions as we moved though the heavy traffic. The route ended at a dilapidated building that might have been a used car lot at some point. A black guy in a white wife beater sat in a camping chair out front. He had a red bandana on his head, tied in front. He stood as we drove up. I did not see a weapon, but he had a predatory look. This was his territory, and he likely had the means to protect it. And we were obviously driving an unmarked cop car.

"I do not want to know what car you are driving." I eyed the gangbanger out front. "But I will walk you to the door."

"Hold up," she said, lightly resting her hand on my thigh. "I got this."

The man tensed when Chelsea got out. I followed her.

"Hey, Ramon!" she called and the man visibly relaxed as she ran into his arms for a friendly hug. He hugged her back but stared suspiciously at me. Up close I saw the gang tattoo on his neck, the number *5r*. The task force calls them the Fivers, I know they call themselves the restrictors, but not much else.

Chelsea stepped back as I caught up. "Gang member," I said with more accusation in my voice than I intended.

Ramon looked me up and down. "What's it to you, 5-0?"

"Easy, Ramon." Chelsea put her hand on his chest. "He's a friend." Her face twitched as she tried to keep a poker face. "More than just a friend." She turned to me. "Del, Ramon and his gang are good people. They don't traffic women."

"Just drugs, then?"

"No drugs, man. I mean some weed, but that's mostly legal now, anyhow. Lot of crime 'round here, we just make sure the neighborhood is safe. Homeowners and shop owners pay us a small fee. Would be a shame if sumpthin' should happen to our people."

"Protection racket?"

"Protection yes, racket, no. We charge a small fee, like any security company. The big difference between us and the cops, is if someone calls for help, we show up action."

"Breaking heads," I filled in.

"Something like that. And we don't start rousting people for no reason. Guess that's another difference 'tween you and me."

Given my knowledge of the vice division, I understood his scorn.

"It's okay, Del. I'm safe with Ramon and his people. You go back to Rivera." She came at me and wrapped herself into a hug that was beyond friendly. Her lips met mine, eliciting a smirk from Ramon. I ignored him and kissed her. I stepped back from her, and she reached for my hands.

"Um…" I paused to think my words through. "There is something I should tell you. Before she went back into the amulet, Halima asked me to kiss her farewell."

Chelsea gave me an expectant look. "And did you?"

I nodded; guilt written all over my face.

"Good," she said with a wide smile. "Del, I can't be jealous. I just don't have the time, and I love Halima like the sister I lost. So, kiss me farewell like you did her." She moved in and we kissed again, a sweet kiss full of love. She broke the embrace and stepped away from me and I caught a light scent of magic, sweet peaceful magic. "Leave."

I reached out to touch her one last time, but she moved out of reach. "You need to go before you lead other cops here." She held up one of the phones I bought. "*Au revoir*, Delacroix. Now I'm off like a dirty shirt!" she said before bouncing past Ramon and out of sight.

I headed back to the station, alone but for a thought and a memory.

I never made it.

Chapter Twenty-Five

Chelsea was in the wind, so her best routine would be no routine. No patterns, stay lost.

I didn't feel that was necessary for me, so I stopped at my usual coffee shop. I parked two spaces down from an idling van. The unmarked navy-blue van initially raised my hackles, but then I recognized the license as an MWAT transport unit.

I entered the café and looked around for some of Rivera's people. No one was in uniform and no one I recognized. I let it go and went for my coffee. The barista was a new girl, a year younger than Adrianna, the regular barista with whom I habitually flirted. I knew that we could never be a match, but we enjoyed the banter.

Plus, Adrianna spoke French. There is something innately attractive about women who speak French.

The petite blonde girl behind the counter looked like a child to me so I kept it polite.

"*Café au lait*," I ordered. "If you please."

"Coming right up." She gave me a tight smile.

I paid and moved aside to wait for my drink. I caught a glimpse of a uniformed policeman by the door. No one I knew. I started to get a bad feeling. This situation was starting to feel familiar to me, but I was usually on the other side of it. "Excuse me," I said to the young girl and held up a ten-dollar bill. "Your tip."

She looked confused and mildly annoyed by my money. "You already tipped me."

I set the bill on the counter. "Two things, though. Is there another exit?"

"No."

That bad feeling intensified. I pulled Rivera's business card from my pocket. "Could you call this man with the LDPD and tell him that Delacroix wants to know how to get rid of *une taupe?*"

"Taupe? Like the color?"

"Close enough." I took a sip of my *café au lait*, and it burned my lips. *Ah, Adrianna, where are you when I need you most?* I exhaled my disappointment and walked out of the place. Three uniformed police officers were waiting for me, one of whom I recognized. The two unknowns pointed their service weapons at my face and the third one, Blutshtälern himself, pointed a wand.

"Drop the coffee, Delacroix, and put your hands in the air," Blutshtälern commanded.

I looked at the burnt coffee I wanted so bad. What did they think I was going to do? Throw it at them?

"*Une minute, s'il vous plait.*" I took a drink of the coffee. It still burned.

"We don't please," Blutshtälern snarled. "You're under arrest for aiding and abetting a cop killer."

I took another drink, and an unseen fourth officer hit me from behind. He jerked my arms around and put on the cuffs; my cherished coffee splashing his pants. He jerked me toward the MWAT van, and I hoped Rivera would get my message in time. To do what, though, was still up in the air. I had a nasty feeling these guys wouldn't answer to Rivera, even if they were called out.

The door slid open and yet another officer dragged me into the van and sent me sprawling to the floor.

It was not properly equipped. No bench seats, or seats at all. Empty like a cargo van. Up front a heavy steel screen separated the driver, who sat motionless, silhouetted by the bright sunlight. I squirmed, trying to get my bearing and saw the man who dragged me in was not in uniform, and was now holding a syringe.

Blutshtälern clambered into the passenger seat and turned to grin at me. "You should have let me take that amulet; it would have saved you a lot of pain."

I squirmed away from the man with the needle, kicking at him. I was laying on a questionable surface in an awkward position, but capoeira is an art of defense that initiates attacks from awkward positions.

I gave a half-cocked roundhouse kick to his shoulder, and he staggered. I followed up with a thrust kick to his chest, shoving him away. But before I could get into position to do more, he flung himself at me. No finesse, but he managed to jab the needle into me. As he ducked away from me, I managed a very solid roundhouse kick to his head. He went down and lay still, moaning.

Blutshtälern chuckled as the van pulled into traffic. "Resisting arrest. And is kicking someone in the head assault? If we were really taking you in, you'd be racking up the charges."

I yanked the needle from my thigh, my body rapidly going numb and flung it at Blutshtälern's smug face. It hit the cage and dropped to the floor. "Where are you taking me?"

"Once we have ensured that there is no more demonic influence on you, your final destination will be the dump. But first..."

The driver turned around, and my first thought was the drugs were making me hallucinate.

Police Commander Aaron Cooper of Internal Affairs grinned at me. The expression distorted his face into something evil, or maybe it was the drugs.

"The McConnel requests your presence. Oh, and ah," he said. "Have a nice nap."

My last conscious thought was relief that they used drugs so I wouldn't have to deal with a third concussion.

* * *

I was aware of pain. I might not have been hit on the head, but whatever they injected me with left a pounding headache. My legs had gone beyond pins and needles and fire ripped through my muscles.

I opened my eyes and saw only darkness. Was I blind? I tried to move my head but to no effect. I tried my arms and legs and found them firmly bound. I became aware that I was sitting on a crude chair, one with a cold steel strap holding my head in place.

Cold air wafted between my knees, and I abruptly realized I was naked. So, it was to be torture, started by stripping away my dignity. I shivered in the dark, wondering how long I'd been left bound here, and how much longer they intended to leave me.

There was a whining creak behind me as a door scraped open. Ridiculously loud.

A light came on. Blinding, searing my vison. The intense illumination was amplified by the brilliant white walls. Every surface gleamed with a shiny, painful luminosity. I sat in the center of a wide room unfurnished except for a pair of short blackout curtains obscuring what I assumed to be a window. I heard the clunk of a door closing.

"Good. You're awake," Blutshtälern's grim voice came from behind me. "We can get started. Fuil, man the controls."

Blutshtälern came around the chair to stand before me. He was dressed in black with a roman collar. A purple stole lay draped around his shoulders, and he carried a chest. He set it on the ground in front of me, stood and crossed his arms. He studied me with a chilling mix of determination and excitement. I felt like a fly about to have its wings plucked off for science. "Do you denounce Satan and all his works?"

The Haitian *Voudon* tradition borrows heavily from the Catholic church, so I knew sort of where he was going.

He raised his chin, waiting for my answer.

"*Certainement*," I answered as I rolled my eyes

Blutshtälern was not amused by my bravado and held up his right forefinger. Pain lanced through my body as my muscles involuntarily convulsed. The chin strap, the metal and wood and wire all made sense now. I was sitting in a goddamn electric chair.

The demonologist, or more properly exorcist, fought to hide a smile. He enjoyed this.

"Do you denounce Satan and all his works?" he repeated, an incongruous sound of glee in his voice.

"Yes!" I spat.

"Too easy," he replied. He knelt and with exaggerated reverence opened the chest. His lips moved rapidly, but I could only hear the cadence of a prayer. He reached into the chest and produced a heavy, leatherbound Bible, then a gold cross easily a foot tall. He then pulled out a crucifix necklace and put it on as he mumbled under his breath, a little louder this time. I recognized Latin and realized it was the Lord's Prayer. Finally, he removed a holy water sprinkler and held it tight in his left hand. He stood, clutched the cross in his right hand and stepped toward me as he exclaimed, "*Cogit te Christi virtus, abite spurci spiritus!*" The drops of holy water splashed in my face.

Pain shot through my body, not from the water but from the chair, even worse that the last time. I felt my forehead burn where the metal strap pressed into my skin. "*Qu'est-ce que tu fais?*" I shouted, then switched back to English. "What the hell are you doing? I thought you combat demonologists had more effective, less violent techniques!"

He stepped back, crossed his arms and looked smug. "Relief is for those few possessed against their will. You have intentionally consorted with *vile* entities. We will need to mortify your flesh so that as you die, your soul will have all corruption exorcised and sent to God's glory. It is your only hope for absolution."

The door opened again, the grinding screech splitting my head. Another screech and it closed. Cooper's voice sounded, "Where are you at?"

"The beginning," Blutshtälern said with a quiet dignity.

"Good," Cooper replied in a cheery voice. "Then it'll be easy to start over. There are some things that must be done before you, what'd you call it? Mortify his flesh?"

"He is corrupt. He must die to save his soul."

"Yeah, we need him to die, too. But give us a few minutes, first," Cooper said in a soothing tone. "Why don't you and Fuil step out for food to give you strength, prepare you for the battle?"

I realized that Fuil was a proper name, not Blutshtälern calling him "fool."

The exorcist scowled and started to put the religious items back in the box.

"Just leave them," Cooper said with a wave as he came into my view.

Blutshtälern stood tall, then held up the first two fingers of his right hand.

Agony tore through my body. I cannot astral project, but for second, I thought I felt my spirit leave my body. I felt a moment of displaced peace before my psyche was sucked back to face the pain.

This time Blutshtälern did not try to hide his smile.

Cooper nodded approval, then moved out of the way so the exorcist could gather up his assistant and leave.

The door closed with that slow, maddening creak. I winced.

Cooper just stared at me, a satisfied grin on his face. He pulled that damn leather keychain from his pocket and rubbed it. I stared at it in a state of semi-shock, taking in details I'd never noticed before. The actual fob was tan and about the size of a business card.

"You know he's sincere, right?" Cooper chuckled. "He's *certain* that you have knowingly and willingly invited *evil* into you." He held up and waggled his fingers. "Wooh, evil!" he sang in a falsetto voice. "He *really* thinks he's working for the good guys. Ain't that rich?"

"Don't you think you are the good guys?"

"Don't be stupid," Cooper snapped. "Good guy, bad guy, that's just a bunch of archaic slang for the guy with the most power. None of that matters. But you know what does? Results. Results matter. You cannot be benevolent and achieve what we have. We're making a better future, for everyone."

"I think the women you traffic would disagree."

Cooper leaned over me and gave me a smug grin. "Sorry, I shoulda clarified. For everyone that matters. Those two-bit hookers oughta be grateful to us, anyway. We taught them a valuable life lesson."

I glared at him but finally said, "What?"

"That if you set yourself up to be used, you will be used." He smiled and leaned forward, his eyes running up and down my bound form, studying every detail. He got uncomfortably close; I could smell aftershave and toothpaste as he examined how I was bound to the chair. Satisfied, he studied my face, trying to raise my chin to see how tight the binding was. It did not move, so he tried side to side, still with no success.

"This will be easier if you just tell me where that whore and the amulet are."

"*Va te faire foutre,*" I growled, then snickered. "I honestly don't know."

"Great, I was hoping you'd say that," he pronounced with an excited titter. "It's much more fun this way." With his left hand still rubbing the leather fob, he took a marker out of his pocket and proceeded to draw. He drew on my face like a butcher draws cuts of meat. I felt the cold felt tip tracing lines along where my facial muscles attached to the bones. Then he stepped back to study his handiwork. He furrowed his brow and came back in to make a slow outline of my right eye, and I thought of the *Voudon* men of Samedi's, dancing with their stark face paint. Cooper gave a contemplative cluck as he finished. "'*Le beau est toujours bizarre,*' I think it went. Anyhow. My turn will come. Right now, The McConnel wants to see you."

Chapter Twenty-Six

Cooper took out his phone and texted something. A minute later the door behind me scraped open with that maddening creak. An unfamiliar female voice called out in a weak, subservient voice, "The exorcist and his acolyte are gone. Are you ready for The McConnel?"

Cooper's face tensed like he needed to carefully prepare himself. "Bring him it."

The door closed and Cooper looked down at me with something like...sympathy? Remorse? Fellowship? It was impossible to tell. "You will tell The McConnel everything you know. Everyone does."

I heard the door open again. Could they just go back to the electric shocks? That noise, far worse than mere fingernails on a chalkboard, seared into my brain. I puzzled at the sound of scraping feet and strained grunts, followed by a series of thumps, and a sound like a cough from a tuberculous victim's final days; dry, hoarse and ongoing.

Somehow the door continued to creak, setting my teeth on edge. "For fuck's sake, WD-40, Aaron, it's cheap. There's cash in my wallet, take it," I griped at my queued torturer. My complaint brought a weirdly congenial smile to his eyes, and he put a comforting hand on my shoulder.

"You damned idiot!" a woman's voice shouted, immediately followed by the sound of flesh striking flesh.

Cooper chuckled and shook his head.

Then there were more grunts and a raspy, coarse sound that I realized was someone, or something, cursing at someone.

A man walked into view. No, not a man. It was Macklin, the former vice sergeant; a Frankenstein's monster-like homunculus. Except now he did not look like the man I boxed against. It was

Macklin, physically, but gone were his arrogant sneer and his contemptuous gaze. His eyes were lifeless, hollow and he walked in a careless shamble. Only the faintest flicker of awareness kept him from looking like a zombie.

There were more grunts as something behind me moved.

I sat there shivering, partly from the cold, but more from what I imagined drew near. Just as in the old Lovecraft stories, the worst horrors dwelled in the undescribed darkness, those corners of the human imagination.

I clenched my mouth closed. I did not want Cooper to have the satisfaction of my fear.

My eyes went wide as the ensemble stepped into view. It was *un putain* sedan chair, carried by four women in sheer, translucent robes. One girl in the front had a bruised cheek that grew darker as I watched her quietly try to choke back sobs. I wrenched my gaze from the women to examine the denizen of the sedan chair as they sat it down.

It might have once been human, but now it was an emaciated thing. I was unsure if it was naked or wearing tight, weatherbeaten leather. Skin stretched over bones like pictures of the Auschwitz victims. I was gazing upon age manifest, stretched into such an unnatural length that its very form distorted like a rubber band pulled too tight. Or rather, a million rubber bands piled upon each other, all tugged nearly to snapping at once. I thought of the reanimated corpses brought back by Herbert West, screaming in horror at their own existence, crying for a return to their natural place among the dead.

The skin on the thing's head was thin and pearlescent where it wasn't pock-marked and looked just as decayed as the rest of it. Then the smell wafted over me. Dried, musty leather with an acrid undertone. Slowly, horribly, it pointed an aged, mottled finger at me.

"You," the thing rasped. Its beak-like mouth barely moved, and the words were quiet at first, but as it spoke the intensity of its language came through. "*You.*" It repeated and paused, studying me as if he could not understand that I was the reason he'd been called forth. I was beneath it. "You think I am ugly. I can see it your face." The thing's voice continued like the sound of crunching gravel. "I can see it in your eyes; you pathetic pile of skin and blood." He turned to the woman with the bruise swelling on her cheek and smacked his thin, dry lips. "Am I ugly?"

"No," the woman answered. "You are the McConnel, the most beautiful thing in the world. I love you."

Her sincerity terrified me. Was it the work of the missing amulet, or some darker magic?

The woman from front left of the sedan crossed her arms. "I love him more. He allows me to bathe him and worship his flesh."

"No," another woman shot back as she stepped from behind the sedan chair. "I love him most and he has selected me to bear his children."

Their overwhelming zeal chilled me as my head spun at the concept of the thing in front of me having children.

"No," the last woman said. "I love him the most." She looked at the misshapen mass with misty eyes of true love and she dropped to her knees before him. "Tonight, I will die for his pleasure." Her tone went beyond sincerity to breathless anticipation.

The other three women turned and gave a modest bow to the last. The woman with the bruised cheek, her eye swelling shut, muttered, "He should have chosen me."

From the corner of my eye, I saw Cooper grinning as he slapped Macklin on the shoulder, obviously enjoying the egregious display of subservient women.

The thing looked at me and sighed, flicking his fingers. "You're more competent than I thought, but not smart. If you were smart, you would join me."

I smiled and used my most chipper tone. "I can learn from my mistakes. Sign me up."

Cooper glared and stomped over to me. He rose a hand to strike me but froze as the creature—The McConnel—made a hissing noise like dried, rotting, logs crackling with fire. He was laughing. "I appreciate sarcasm. Very well. If you wish to join me," he leaned forward, "tell me where to find the repulsive whore and the pitiful amulet that has vexed me."

My turn to sigh. "I honestly don't know."

Cooper punched me. Hard. Pain exploded in my jaw and shot through my skull and continued as a horrible throbbing.

I spat out a chunk of tooth enamel along with blood from my split lip. "You should have had Macklin give you some lessons. You hit like a child; no proper follow-through."

He raised his foot and kicked me in the genitals. The pain was worse than the electrical shocks, but not nearly as much as my tooth.

Cooper turned to the creature and bowed his head. "May I?"

The creature murmured a harsh affirmative. Cooper moved out of my field of vision, then returned with a gilded box. He set it down, opened it, and removed the original amulet in all its gold and blue glory, the winged Isis amulet at the heart of the magic worked into the collar.; but On Cooper the assembly looked uncomfortably tight as he fought to get the amulet into position. He could not touch any part of the Isis amulet without pain because, like the clown, he was not bound to it. He loomed over me and smiled as he touched the amulet. His smile threatened to turn to a grimace, though, as I was sure icy pain shot up through his hand. Like touching a wet finger to frozen metal and having the skin stick for a second. He spoke in a subdued voice, almost like a mother soothing a child. "Where is Falcata and the other amulet?"

I felt the compulsion run through me. A physical force grabbed my whole being and threatened to crush and suffocate me; there was no way I could refuse to answer. This was not the way the clown used it; this was brutal precision in the hands of an expert. "I don't know," I gasped. "I made certain that I would not know or be able to guess." I felt my body relax as the compulsion faded and was replaced by a powerful, almost sexual, feeling of gratification.

"Where did you leave her?"

The compulsion hit me again and I answered, "Lincoln Heights. With the Fivers." Relief filled me and I craved that feeling of release. I wanted him to question me again, just to feel… *Merde*, the compulsion was addictive.

He touched it again. "Is that all you know?"

"Yes!" I blurted, seeking that rush of satisfaction.

Cooper crossed his arms and peered with more than a little disgust at the seat of my chair. "Well, you look like you're having such a good time, I guess I have to believe you."

"Wait, that is it? You are not going to turn me into one of his sycophants?" I was simultaneously disappointed, relieved, and terrified.

"You are not worth keeping," the creature said with his crumbling, rumbling laugh. "But you are worth having."

"Yeah," Cooper said with an evil glint in his eye. "See, The McConnel lives on death. He is where everything good goes to die." He jerked a thumb at the women. "Willing sacrifices are such a sugary snack, an occasional indulgence. He likes them young and sweet." He bit his lower lip and eyed me with scorn. "You, on the other hand, will make several full meals as we drag the life out of you."

I grimaced and tried to sound reasonable. "Just tell me, what *is* that thing?"

"You don't need to know, you just need—"

Cooper was interrupted by a dry, hackling cough.

Cooper glanced at the McConnel who flicked his fingers at me, apparently a signal to allow Cooper to answer.

Cooper looked like he couldn't believe I was being let in on the big secret, but he was also not going to disobey. "There is no word in any modern tongue that defines the glorious existence of The McConnel, but like all great heroes, he does have an origin story. He was an acolyte of Aleister Crowley. You know that Crowley died just six months after magic reawakened? In those short months there were black arts, rituals of unspeakable acts. Blood spilled to the nameless gods. You have no idea how I wish I could have been there. The McConnel was nearly one hundred years old at the time, but through these black workings he survived because his will was strong enough. Crowley's was weak, and so he died."

The rough, rumbling laughter came from the creature, evidently pleased to recall the events.

"If you want a name to call our patron by, take your pick. Black magician? Necromancer? I prefer lich." He gave the last word the German pronunciation, more like 'leek."

"A lich is not a real thing," I scoffed. "That is a D&D monster."

"The name fits," Cooper snapped defensively.

The creature groaned like a sewer grate being pushed into place. "Get on with it."

Cooper grimaced in dread as he touched the golden-winged Isis over his chest. "The second amulet, did you wear it?"

I clenched my jaws and tried to bite my tongue, but the words leaked out of the side of my mouth. "Yes," I squeaked and the high hit my body. *Mon Dieu.*

He touched it again. "Did you break the sympathetic bond?"

I fought but I also wanted so much to give the answer. "No."

Cooper grinned, showing his teeth; his face scrunched up, giving him a creepy rictus quality. "Now we are getting somewhere. The information is inside you, and I know the best way to get it out Master," he said with a sick sense of anticipation. "Splanchnomancy?"

I had no idea what the hell that was, but I was sure it would be unpleasant.

The creature paused in consideration. "Make it quick and ensure he lives through it."

Cooper went back to his box and produced a laminated map of Los Diablos. "You," he called to the girl with the bruised cheek. "You have a scrying stone, come here."

The young woman pulled a necklace from under her cotton shift and took it off as she walked over. She stood a foot away from me, completely oblivious to my pain and humiliation.

Now, from the box Cooper pulled out a leather bundle. He rolled it out to reveal a variety of knives. He selected a stubby, wickedly curved knife withe a brass piece set at the front of the handle to rest your thumb on for pressure to dig deep. An antique autopsy knife.

"This is how bad you need the new amulet? I'll get it for you." I wasn't sure if my words came for the compulsion or from terror. "You need it more than I do!"

"Nice try," The McConnel said.

"You are going to use Macklin, but you need the sliver you sent out. I'll help you!" I blubbered.

Cooper tapped his nose and grinned. "We'll get it back. And if not, it removed our greatest threats. For you. we are going to practice the old ways. Splanchnomancy, or as you may know of it, anthropomancy."

That I knew; the art of divination by reading signs in human entrails. "There are easier ways to use a sympathetic bond."

The creature croaked, "But not as much fun."

Cooper stepped closer and inspected the lines he drew earlier. "May I take my share now, as well? He can live a while without his face." He pulled that damned leather keychain from his pocket and rubbed it. "I had to stop hanging them in public, you know, but I get some satisfaction waving my trophies around in little ways."

The keychain. It was made from someone's face. The room spun as I realized what he was saying. "You?"

"*Duh.*" He rocked back and laughed. "You know what? I'm going to wait on your face. I really want you to see this and people are usually so busy screaming when I take my trophy, they don't appreciate the finer *points* of my art." He placed the blade against my flesh, directly under my sternum. Blood welled and trickled down my abdomen as the razor-sharp blade easily slit the skin. The blade must have some spell on it that brought more pain than the scalpel should have. He wiggled the blade and settled the sharp point to cut through my muscle. He tensed his shoulders to apply the necessary pressure.

Chapter Twenty-Seven

"Stop!" the bruised woman screamed, then clamped one hand over her mouth in mortification at interrupting.

Cooper jerked back, tearing my skin as he did. "What?"

I felt a trickle of blood down my stomach.

"Explain yourself," the lich growled.

The woman trembled and her voice was apologetic as she lifted the scrying stone dangling limp from its chain. "He has no sympathetic bonds. His flesh has no truth to reveal."

I remembered how Chelsea was shaking after our embrace and her insistence that I do not touch her again. *That's why*, I thought. *You stripped our sympathetic bonds. Good girl.*

Cooper shrugged. "No matter, his flesh will give me other answers." He lined the knife up again.

"No," the lich grunted. "He is young. Such taking is to be savored." He smiled and the low cackling laugh poured out of him. "You may begin the lingering death."

Cooper blanched, then looked down on me and chortled. "You will have preferred to be gutted." He wiped the blood from the blade on my bare skin. Before he put it away, he sprayed the steel with something and wiped it down with a smooth cotton cloth. Before, he was in a rush, but now he took his time.

He pulled an ampule from the box. From his roll of knives, he selected the strangest. I'd never seen a blade like it before. The handle was six inches long, but the blade was barely the length of a thumbnail. A heavy looking guard sat between the blade and handle.

Cooper sighed. "You know, you have powerful friends and a woman who loves you. It will take three or four days for you to die.

They *might* find you." He recited the lines sarcastically, without sincerity.

What was he playing at? Then it dawned on me. The torture needed to drag on. Dropped into a pit of despair, I might succumb too fast. Cooper was offering me hope to use as a weapon against me. I knew that, but against my will a flicker of hope moved through me.

He opened the ampule, and I paled as the stink wafted over me. The dark green ichor reeked of effluent and every dead thing rolled into one bottle of liquid.

The stench didn't seem to bother Cooper at all.

He casually dabbed a bit on a cloth and touched it to the bleeding wound on my stomach. Fire lanced through me. Not the sting of antiseptic, but of violation. Like he'd rubbed feces in my open wound.

Perhaps he had.

"Are you up to date on your tetanus inoculations?" he asked casually, like a family physician reviewing a chart.

"What?" I managed through clenched teeth. The broken one throbbed and I tried to relax my jaw.

He touched the amulet and repeated the question.

"Yes!" I screamed and hated myself for it. Ecstasy and misery swam through my conscious. The misery won.

"Ugh, you *would* make me work this whole damn time. If you succumbed to tetanus, I could basically take the time off and watch. The muscle spasms would be so strong they would shred you, snap your bones and tear all your little muscles. I wouldn't have to do a thing but butter the popcorn, ya know?" He leaned in close and whispered. "I find this part so tedious."

He removed the amulet, set it back in the box, took the weird knife and made a three inch long cut on my arm. He dabbed that nasty stuff from the bottle into it.

I whimpered with the pain.

The McConnel laughed.

"Is…that *thing* just going to sit there for three days?" I gasped, staring the monster before me down.

"Pretty much." He made another incision. "You might find this part interesting. I'm cutting to avoid your nerves. Wouldn't want you to lose feeling, now, would we? Is there anything like this practice in *Vodoun*?" He pronounced my religion's name like a native speaker. I hated him for it.

He dabbed the foul liquid into the wound again and my skin boiled from the inside. On top of the agony, that damn door opened. No one reacted. How could they not hear that horrendous, awful racket? I swear it was even louder than before. But the noise coalesced into a voice, a familiar voice in my head. *"We're here."*

A phone rang. Cooper paused and answered. "Yes?" he said, annoyed at the interruption. "What?" He jerked the phone way from his ear and addressed The McConnel. "We're being raided. MWAT has secured the lower floors."

"Pity," The McConnel sighed. "This room is heavily warded; they cannot find it with magic. The entrance is disguised by an intricate illusion spell." He leaned forward and snarled at Cooper. "What stupid thing did you do to bring them here?"

"What did I do?" Cooper cried in indignation. "I'm not the one with the entourage and the big truck."

Blutshtälern burst into the room. "They're right behind me!" He stopped, frozen at the sight of The McConnel.

"And you led them to us!" The McConnel screeched.

"Who are you?" Blutshtälern cried. *"What* are you?"

The lich addressed the women. "Kill the voodoo cop and this idiot!" He pointed at the confused exorcist.

The four girls turned as one and rushed Blutshtälern.

Blutshtälern went for his weapon and aimed it at The McConnel and pulled the trigger. Nothing happened. He stared down at his weapon it as if it had betrayed him. Then the three women were on him. They raked Blutshtälern's face with their fingernails, clawing for his eyes. He went down under the force of his attackers.

The woman with the bruise, her eye nearly swollen shut, split from the pile of violent flesh and sprinted toward me, pausing to grab the rolled bundle of knives.

Macklin just stood there, oblivious.

The bruised woman stood in front of me and drew the Victorian autopsy knife.

There was a scampering sound and a feline yowl as Pakhet, beautiful, sweet, angelic Pakhet, bolted past my chair and launched herself at my attacker's face. Pakhet landed and dug her claws in as the woman shrieked and scrabbled at the little beast with both hands.

The knife clattered to the floor at my feet.

I strained against my bonds, but it was useless.

The woman tore Pakhet away and slammed her into the floor, then held her hands to the deep slashes in her skin. Her face was furrowed with claw marks. Her lip was torn and blood spilled into her eyes as she screamed.

Pakhet lay still, momentarily stunned.

"Pakhet?" I called.

"Only for a few minutes! Cheslea gave me some strength."

The woman with the torn face stopped screaming and turned back to me.

"I've heard of bad hair days, but you're having a bad face day, lady," I groaned through the fire igniting through my body.

She looked at me, as if seeing me for the first time, and screeched like the devil was sitting in my place.

The door opened again, this time with just a slight scraping sound. I realized now that the sound I had been hearing, that horrible screeching…was a little magic cat screaming her guts out at top volume, but I had only heard it when the warded door was open.

"What is this?" Blutshtälern screamed as he fought to get the women off him. "I didn't sign up for this!"

"Forget them," the lich commanded the women. "Stop the intruders!"

One of the three women kicked the exorcist in the groin, and another wrestled his useless gun away while the third kicked him in the head. They left him stunned and rolling on the floor, his hand clutching his groin, and raced to the door. The fourth woman, blinded by her swollen eye and face wounds, seemed to forget me and stumbled after them.

Pakhet popped up and ran to me. Then she paused, considering what she could do to help me.

I heard the door burst open, and three MWAT officers in full tactical garb hustled through, the leader carrying a bullpup style assault rifle and a backpack. The two other MWAT guys had handguns.

The compelled woman, the one who would die for her master's pleasure, apparently, leveled her acquired gun at the leader's face and pulled at the trigger.

Still nothing happened.

She gave a little smirk, and the weapon clattered to the floor from her limp hand.

The MWAT leader responded by tasing her to the floor. She twitched a couple times at my feet, then passed out.

More officers swarmed into the room and within minutes the women and Blutshtälern were in handcuffs. And still Macklin just stood there. I almost felt sorry for him.

Almost.

I gritted my teeth and ignored the pain long enough to call the officer that almost got shot. "You okay?"

He gave me a double thumbs up. "Yeah. We figured the guns didn't work, but the tasers function just fine. A gamble we won, this time."

I looked at the bruised, bleeding woman bound in handcuffs. Her young face was blank. Without instructions, she was helpless.

I dropped my head to my chest and looked down at Pakhet. "I do not suppose you could get me a blanket or towel or something."

Pakhet licked a paw. "No big deal. I've seen you naked."

A hand touched the back of my neck and sweet relief swept through my body.

"But I haven't," Lenore teased from behind me as she used magic to soothe my pain. She was in full tactical gear and bent over to get a good look. "Doesn't look like I missed much."

"It's cold in here," I muttered. "That's a damn fine heal spell, you got there."

"Yes, but I can only keep it up for a few minutes." She released the band keeping my head immobile.

"That's what she said," I quipped. I felt giddy at my rescue as she freed me from the restraining straps.

Rivera was right behind her, and any humor evaporated. "Where is the amulet?"

"Cooper put it in his little box of horrors. Oh, and test that damn leather piece he packs around. I am sure it is human."

"What box? What leather?" Rivera demanded.

I looked and, indeed, Cooper's torture-rama kit it was gone. "What about Cooper? The McConnel?"

"What? You mean Cooper from Internal Affairs is The McConnel?" Rivera asked, puzzled.

"No! Cooper is the goddamn Trophy Hunter, *Jefe!* And he works for The McConnel. Just like that idiot." I nodded at Blutshtälern. "But that moron didn't know it. They were here," I stuttered as Lenore cut my hands free.

"Are you sure? When we stormed the room there was only you, the four women, Blutshtälern and that thing." He jerked a thumb at Macklin.

"The women, be as gentle as you can. I know what he did to them," I said as I chafed my wrists. Lenore's magic touch practically removed the pain boiling across my body but did nothing for the pain of the internal injuries. "Is there something to clean these wounds with?"

"We'll see." He shoved his hands in his pockets, furrowed his brow. "We got healers comin' up."

Another officer handed me a bottle of betadine and a pressure bandage.

Lenore spoke up. "That's a good start, but we need to get him to a full-service healer."

"Lenore," Rivera barked.

"Yes?" she answered while freeing my feet.

"Did they get out of here by magic?"

Lenore stood up, held her hands out and waggled her fingers. Then she put her hands on her hips and looked impressed. "Wow, even with all the wards I can't imagine how this level of magic could go undetected. This is High Magick. This power has to be generational. It would take over a century to lay down this work."

"The lich, The McConnel, is over two hundred years old," I explained.

"The what?" Lenore asked. I suspected she never played D&D.

"That is what Cooper called it. A black magician seeking immortality."

"And he got away with the amulet?" Rivera snapped.

Lenore crossed the room to open the black curtains. Behind them was a tiny door. She opened it and peered inside, then let out a low whistle. "They used a shrinking spell. This is a pneumatic tube, technology over a century old."

"The lich and Cooper?"

"Yep," Lenore said. "Looks like it."

"Damn," Rivera spat and turned to me, still sitting naked in an electric chair. "Oh, and thanks for the tip-off, but you could have just said 'mole.'"

Lenore stood. Also behind the curtains were my discarded clothes. She threw the pants at me. "You'll want these."

I took the clothing and responded to Rivera. "I was trying to be clever."

Rivera studied the bound exorcist. "I can't imagine when they could've used the amulet on Blutshtälern, I mean to completely take over someone of that power..."

"They didn't use the amulet. He was all in from the beginning."

Rivera cocked his head at me. "You're sure?"

"*Certainement*. Not malicious, just criminally stupid." I turned around to step into my pants and addressed Lenore over my shoulder. "Thank you for finding me."

She gave me a crooked grin. "Nothing to do with it, that was all your girlfriend. She was up in my head space like, 'Oh, my god! He's gonna die!' and would not leave me alone about it."

I looked down at Pakhet.

"The other girlfriend," the cat said. "And now I must take my

186

leave. I've exhausted the energy Chelsa gave me and at the end of my ability to control this body without losing my place in the prison. I must rest and deal with Shard."

"Shard?"

"It is the sliver of Nergal I now guard. Much easier. They must have carved off Nergal's least abhorrent part. With Chills' help I've made some peace with it. We're kinda on first name basis, now."

"Becoming friends?" I asked.

"That will never be possible. Shard must reunite with its totality. That totality is evil. Shard is merely amoral." Then the cat spasmed and meowed, just a meow. Halima was no longer there.

"Halima is downplaying her role in finding you." Rivera said and the tone of his voice carried respect. Little one led us right to this room. Cats have a keener sense of smell than dogs, but damned if you can count on the little *gatitas* to help."

"Oh, well. That's fine, then. That is so much better." I turned to Lenore. "So, Chelsea sent you?"

"Check your pockets," Lenore instructed.

I did and pulled out the keys to the unmarked car I checked out.

Lenore held up my suitcoat. I took it from her and found an unfamiliar key fob in the jacket picket.

"Your girl slipped a GPS tracker on you when I'm sure you kissy-kissed goodbye. The RNC was so sure we'd be using magic to find you; they didn't check for mundane means." She gave a little snort and twirled the fob on one finger. "Losers."

They didn't block wireless signals, I thought. *That's why the cell phones worked.*

Alarms blared overhead. A lot of them. Almost simultaneously Rivera's radio crackled with a panic-stricken voice. "Incendiaries are going off on the bottom floors! The whole building is on fire!"

Chapter Twenty-Eight

Tendrils of smoke streamed through the doorway, and I could see the orange light of flames. Rivera ran to the steel double door, looked out and slammed it shut. "Hallway and stairs are fully engaged." He pointed at one of the MWAT squad. "Stevens, the far wall."

The officer ran to it, tugging his gloves off. He ran his bare hands over the plaster surface.

"Cold?" Rivera snapped.

"Yes."

"Breaching charges."

The remaining two officers rushed to the wall. They moved fast, deliberate, well-rehearsed and stuck four widely spaced devices to the wall and ran back.

"Cover those girls," Rivera commanded his men. "Leni, cover Delacroix and Halima."

He pulled a clicker out of his tactical vest. I saw the flash a split second before the sound, and the pressure drummed into my ears. I saw very painful stars for a second as a piece of brick glanced my forehead.

Here we go, concussion number three. Or is it four? I wondered as I held my head in misery.

"Sorry," Lenore said. "Shield spell failed."

Blood streamed down the side of Lenore's face.

Rivera looked over the edge of the breach. The charges were set perfectly, blowing out a seven-foot hole through the dry wall and masonry, leaving support girders on either side intact. A brick building stood across the wide alleyway. "Forty feet down to the street. Clear for now."

Randell, the squad leader with the backpack, pulled out a nylon rope and looked around the room.

"Tie off on the electric chair," I called to him. "It is bolted to the floor."

In seconds he had a bowline knot in place and the rope flung out over the edge.

The steel doors made an alarming bonging noise.

"Delacroix, you know how to buddy rappel?"

"*Oui,* but what about them?" I waved at the bound prisoners and Macklin.

"Stevens, go. Secure the far end," Rivera commanded.

Another officer twisted the rope into a carabiner on the back of Stevens's tactical harness, and he ran through the breach headfirst, Australian style.

Rivera tore his gaze away from the breach and scowled at the prisoners.

"We can't leave them!" I insisted.

There was another ringing rattle as the steel doors buckled from the heat.

"Wasn't going to," Rivera said calmly.

I could almost see the gears turning in his head as he tried to figure out what to do.

At that moment a swan flew in through the breach. It barely touched down before the air shimmered and Hildegarde stood before us in her feathered cloak.

"What are you doing here?" I asked in shock.

"She's working with us," Rivera answered. "Lenore got Hildegarde and three swans to help track your GPS signal. Cheaper than the two helicopters we had looking for you."

"You all need to get out of here!" Hildegarde chastised us like she'd caught us raiding the cookies in her pantry.

"We're trying," Lenore replied testily. "*Jefe?* I can get the girls and Macklin out of here, but you're not going to like it."

"Magic?" Rivera said and scowled. "On the fly? Oh, sure, I mean you've already had your fail for the mission, right? Your next three spells should be great, that's how it works, right?"

What *Jefe* was saying was that it is a statistical fact that even high-level mages fail their spell cast 25% of the time when under pressure.

The building gave a deep, ominous groan and the floors shuddered.

We were definitely under pressure.

"It's a prepared spell."

Okay that drops the failure rate to 10%, I thought.

"What is it? Flight? Teleportation?"

Lenore gave him a grossed out look. "God, no. We'd have a better chance at jumping out the hole and flapping our arms really hard. No. I never leave home without a boing boing, and mine's got three layers."

Even better odds.

"Is that the thing you do with the kids on picnic day?" I asked.

"That's why I have it prepared."

"A boing boing?" Hildegarde said. "With more than two people? Someone's going to break a leg, or worse."

"Got a better idea?" Lenore shot back.

"No, but I can make *your* idea a better one," Hildegarde said, ignoring Lenore's testy tone. "But it will be messy. We swans have to bathe every month. Do you know what type of bath we prefer?"

Lenore held her hand up to her mouth. "Oh, my god. The genius! This—I—I don't think it's ever been done before!"

The steel doors banged like a physical force hit them.

"Fine, Randell, uncuff the girls, not him." Rivera pointed to Blutshtälern. "Jackson, go join Stevens."

Jackson ran to the rope and twisted it into a carabiner on the front of his harness and went over the edge in a classic rappel.

The four women did not react to being released. They just sat there, empty eyed. In fact, they looked more like Macklin. "Stand up," I commanded, hoping they were so used to obeying they would not stop to think. They stood.

"I only prepared one spell," Lenore said. "We will have to jump together."

"Jump?" Blutshtälern bellowed in disbelief.

I leaned closer, looming over the exorcist. "O ye of little faith," I said.

The noise from the overheated door grew more insistent.

Okay, I was a little concerned about our predicament. Actually, very concerned. But I had faith...

"I need some water!" Lenore shouted over the sound of stressed metal.

Randell handed her a collapsable canteen as he hooked up to the rope.

A sudden fear came over me and I stopped him. "One second. Pakhet! Damn, Cocopuff."

The feline ran to me. I scooped her up and tried to get her into Randell's backpack, but she stuck her legs out in all directions, thrashing at the air. "Okay, Pakhet. I hope you can hear me. Tell Cocopuff she can ride in the backpack or burn." The animal stopped flailing, and I put her in the pack. "Take care of her," I appealed to Randell with rising desperation in my voice.

Randell nodded and rappelled down the side of the building.

"Delacroix, get over here! It's your turn to jump!" Rivera commanded.

"*Non*, I'm going with them." Magic is complex and inconstant. But there is one consistent rule: the success of a spell is directly proportional to the confidence of the wielder. My decision to go with Lenore was meant to bolster her self-confidence. Then I realized I should not have bothered. It was Lenore, her ego was just fine. She thought she could mind-wrestle ancient demons on a Tuesday.

The room grew hotter and the floor rumbled. The floors below were collapsing with mighty, shuddering booms. If the door gave way, it would create a chimney effect and draw all the smoke and flames into the room in one explosive wave of fire.

Lenore and Hildegarde stood motionless at the edge of the breach. Lenore took a deep breath and poured out the water.

Rivera herded the prisoners to the breach. The empty eyed group stoically obeyed his commands.

I shoved Blutshtälern toward the breach. "When I give the order, you will jump or burn. And frankly, I do not care which."

Rivera and his last man hooked each other up to the rope like this wasn't their first carabiner rodeo. The final tactical officer ran headfirst through the breach with Rivera hot on his heels.

Meanwhile, Lenore and Hildegarde lined up everyone not able or willing to rappel. The door banged louder as it warped in the heat. The room shook and small bit of ceiling tile drifted down like some improbable snowstorm.

I wrapped my arms around Macklin, lifted him just off the floor and screamed. "Jump!" with all the force of command I could muster.

Lenore shoved Blutshtälern toward the window. In a second, everyone was through but Hildegarde, me and my homunculus friend.

I said a quick prayer to Great Aunt Chery, known for her wild escapades, looked deep into Hildegarde's reassuring eyes, and leapt.

Someone once told me that the only fear people are born with is fear of falling. This fall would take about three seconds. It felt like twice that time had passed, and nothing was happening. Then suddenly I felt light-headed and panicked as my stomach rose to my throat. I was plunging to the ground.

Then I was at a foam party. Clouds of bubbles surrounded me. They were tiny, frothy, but they also possessed a definite physical substance. I felt my momentum slowing and I let out a breath I did not know I was holding. I let go of Macklin just before we hit the ground. I bounced and landed harder than I would like, but no damage. Everyone else landed more squarely in the spell and were still bouncing.

There was a cracking sound above and the magic column of bubbles collapsed. The street looked like a mass bubble bath, which apparently swan maidens are adept at producing. Added to Lenore's trampoline spell, the result was messy; we were all soaked with slimy soap, but safe. A bird screeched overhead, and I looked up to see Hildegarde jump as flames raged out of the opening, scorching her tail feathers. There were no bubbles to save her, but before she hit the ground she transformed and broke her fall with her wings. As her webbed feet hit the pavement, she took her human shape, and staggered. "'Scuse me," she said as she wobbled. "Back and forth like that is hard."

We did not bother to cuff the girls or Macklin. The MWAT told them where to go and they followed orders. Blutshtälern, however, required persuasion of the handcuff kind.

As fire crews swept around the building and we were corralled back, I tagged Rivera's shoulder. "Tell me you know where Chelsea is and that you were wrong about her being dead meat."

"If it's so important to you, *si*, I was wrong. And she's perfectly OK. In protective custody. She's safe, but unconscious. I took a lot out of her to give power to the cat." Rivera said.

"What?" I gasped.

"Calm down." River held up placating hands. "She'll sleep it off and she has real protection."

"*Jefe.*" I ran my fingers through my hair. My sides split with pain, the world spun, and my hair, short as it was, was littered with knots. "Your people brought me here."

"I need you to trust me." He tapped his chest for emphasis. "*I* have her in a safe house with your other friend, Leslie."

I cringed, that would not end well.

"My two best people are with them. Falcata does a very good disguise, by the way, fooled me. But she turned herself in to me when you were grabbed. See, when she slipped that tracker on you, she also put in a mood charm. One that leveraged her empath ability and would alert her if you were frightened or in pain."

"She is resourceful."

Rivera put a hand on my shoulder. "She cares about you, almost as much as she cares about her little one-woman war. You two could make a powerful partnership. Now, calm down, find a medic to look at you, and let me and my men do our job. We're really quite good at it."

Rivera started to steer me toward the nearest ambulance.

"And then you will take me to Chelsea?"

"If you have a message, give it to the cat. Randell's taking her over. Falcata wants that cat back ASAP."

"Then, Randell can take me."

"Not right now," Rivera said in a stern tone. "We have to find Cooper and The McConnel."

At that moment a shadow crossed Rivera's face. We both looked up to see a black swan nosedive towards us, slowing with powerful wings to transform as she lighted before us.

The warrior goddess stood before me with crossed arms and steely eyes.

"Hello Nandi," I greeted her. "I hope you are well. Thank you for your help."

"Hildegarde gave us a full account of what you did for her. We are in your debt."

"Rest assured, the debt is paid in full," I replied.

"No," Nandi said. "You misunderstand me. I do not want a transactional relationship. No quid pro quo. You have proven yourself a friend to my bevy. If you need our help, do not hesitate to call."

"Thank you, and if you or yours need help, we are here."

"Cool." Her accent changed. It was posh before, but now it became an East London cockney. "Besides, it were wicked fun. All flyin' about the city, an' all. Now we're friends and all I can relax. Keepin' up that Tolkien speech is exhaustin'."

Rivera broke into our conversation. "We need to go."

"Where?" Nandi asked.

I waved my hand around. "Wherever we need to. We have a necromancer and a prolific serial killer on the loose."

"Oy," Nandi said, a wickedly mischievous look in her eyes. "I tink I can help you wit dat."

Chapter Twenty-Nine

"How?" I asked.

"What kind o' necromancer?" Nandi asked. "Does he reanimate dead things, use corpses for divination or does tha guvnah kill to stay alive?"

"That last one. Though I don't think he is human, anymore."

"Oy, that kind o' right bastard should be easy to find." Nandi frowned in thought. "You got any of its victims?"

"We have several victims connected to his organization, the RNC," Rivera said.

"Where?" I asked. "The cemetery?"

Rivera grimaced. "We have standing orders to exhume them if we need more evidence."

That's not creepy at all, I thought.

"If it's what you say it is, then it'll wanna be present at as many deaths as possible. But did any ah the poor blightahs drown, by any old chance? And, ah, if any of 'em are birds in the figurative sense, could yeh check their downstairs to see if the floor's never been pulled up, you take what I mean?" Nandi pointed at her crotch.

"Sexist," Rivera said with a smirk.

Nandi smiled, displaying perfect white teeth. "Oye could learn ta like this one."

"Are you going to make a harp?" Hildegarde asked breathlessly. She did not wait for an answer. "Can I help?!" She bounced on the balls of her feet. "Can I? Can I? Can I?"

Nandi placed a steadying hand and on the bobbing swan maiden. "Yes, young Hildegarde," she replied in the posh accent with well-practiced patience. It dawned on me she must use the posh accent

194

whenever speaking as the official swan queen.

Hildegarde brought her fists up and made small punching motions in the air.

"Several of them drowned," Rivera replied, "They like to waterboard anyone they think is a snitch." He grimaced. "Female? A few, but given the nature of the RNC's crimes, little chance of a virgin."

"We'll work wit what we 'ave," Nandi slipped back to her more comfortable accent.

"*Jefe!*" Randall Randell called out. "What about Ester Jones? Her body's still in the morgue."

"That's complicated," Rivera said. "Ester was intersex. She had vestigial male anatomy, but also ovaries."

Nandi gave a look of consideration. "Blimey, works fo'me."

Rivera seemed to chew it over. "We think the RNC snatched her and then killed her because of her condition, can't be sure she drowned, but we found her in the San Gabriel River, stuck behind a bridge strut. Pretty decomposed."

"We'll know if she drowned." Nandi turned to the younger swan. "It's going to take more than us two. We'll have to reach out to The Bonny Swans."

Hildegarde's face fell. "Do we have to?"

"What are The Bonny Swans?" I asked

Before Nandi could reply, Hildegarde blurted, "Bunch of stuck-up old birdies."

Nandi put her hand back on Hildegarde's shoulder and said in her posh mode, "They are not that bad." She turned to me. "They are aloof, among the elder of our kind. The keepers of Swan lore. Centuries of tradition."

"Centuries?" I asked. "But there has only been magic for less than a hundred years."

"Oy, yeah, but swans been around." Nandi smiled. "Bring the body to Echo Lake. Come on Hildy. Let's talk to the bonnies."

Hildegarde nodded glumly and morphed into her swan form. Nani followed and the pair ran down the street, trumpeting at people to get out of the way before they fought their way up into the air.

Rivera screwed his face up as he watched them depart, then turned Lenore. "Did I just hear them say they're gonna make a harp outta Ester Jones? Did I hear that right?"

Lenore nodded with a hint of a smile.

"Will the family allow that?"

Randell shrugged. "Her father's family disowned her when Ethan transitioned to Ester. She was alternating back and forth between the streets and a youth shelter Picked her up for trespassing. Sleeping in a factory."

I sighed. I felt for the poor girl. It was a common story. I didn't just feel sorry; I felt a dull ache growing. Then my sides clinched and I staggered, clutching my guts.

The lingering death was definitely lingering. In me.

Lenore stepped toward me and laid her hand on the back of my neck, soothing most of the pain. "It's going to take a few days to get that shit out of your system."

"Can you get me an amulet to block the pain?"

"Sure," she said, but then her eyes hardened. "If you can stay in the hospital ICU for a week. You need to listen to your body. You could seriously injure yourself without realizing."

"I need to be operational."

"I have a charm you can use…but you won't like it."

"Stop yammering," Rivera cut in. "Let's go get the body."

* * *

"Body" was a relative term. Decomposition was well along and even sealed in a heavy-duty body bag, it was unpleasant. I do not know why I've always needed to dampen down my empathy and treat corpses as objects. They are people and deserve respect, but thinking of the lives cut short keeps me up at night.

We transported Ester in the same van I was abducted in, the stripped down MWAT cargo van.

It was dark when we drove to the lake. Rivera, Lenore and I were all jammed in the front seat so Lenore could lay hands on me. When not keeping the pain at bay, Lenore was weaving together a white cotton cord heavier than yarn and muttering under her breath. The words were faint, and she slipped into an unknown tongue. She spoke a few sharp words in that foreign language. Then she announced, "It is done."

Rivera smirked. "He's not going to like it."

"Give me your wrist," Lenore directed.

I complied. She held my wrist tight, her eyes closed. "The rot is receding, but you may not realize it for some time. This will help." She tied the woven cored around my wrist. The residual pain vanished, but my body itched, all over.

"New pain will feel like pain, but the infection will just itch. As my healing touch wears off, you will itch more. Like whole body poison ivy. And it's, uh, it's not a dental spell, you may notice. So don't sue me," she said with a grin and elbowed me.

My side bloomed with itchiness where she jabbed.

I waved away her explanation. "*Ma grand-mére* taught me how to deal with a busted tooth. I have oil of cloves at home."

"Heads up. We're here," Rivera said as he turned into the park entrance. The evening sky glowed with the city lights. Most nights you could only see the brightest stars, certainly not the Milky Way I remember from Haiti. When we stopped the car Hildegarde and Nandi were waiting, along with two other women dressed in swan feather cloaks, accompanied by four swans. Two of the birds and one of the women wore blue silk bands around their necks. They had a stretcher woven from willow tree twigs. The weaving was tight and elegant. We hauled the body bag out and set it on the stretcher.

"To the side, please." Nandi pointed.

We did as instructed. The two maidens we did not know knelt beside the body bag. One reached for the zipper.

"You may not want to do that," I stuttered. "The body is badly decomposed. We cleaned it, but it is still…"

"It was not embalmed?"

"No." Lenore said.

"Good." The woman ignored me and opened the bag. She and her sisters ignored the smell as it spilled into the night air. The two reverently scooped up the corpse and with tender care put the grisly figure on the woven stretcher. Four maidens stood around the body, softly weeping. They all knew the tragedy of life cut short.

"Poor child," Nandi said. "She should not be seen like this."

The four maiden joined hands and bowed their heads. The body shimmered and turned into a beautiful woman with golden hair clad in a lovely red dress. The glamour spell was so powerful it even disguised the scent.

Ester looked at peace, as if merely sleeping.

"This is how she would want to be seen and remembered," Nandi said.

The four powerfully built women raised the stretcher and bore it on their shoulders. They turned to the lake. I started to follow.

"No." Nandi put up her hand. "This is our rite. No outsiders, and especially no males are permitted."

"But what are you going to do, exactly?"

Lenore touched my arm. "Let them do their thing."

"Meet us there." Nandi pointed to the lake shore. "Tomorrow, mid-morning."

I tapped Rivera on the shoulder.

"Lemme guess, 'Where's my girlfriend?' Am I right?"

"Well, where is she?" I asked as I realized I was scratching my arm, which was somehow making my back itch worse.

"I can't tell you that," he replied through a yawn.

"We have burners. Her's is turned off. Did your people take it?"

"Don't think so, don't see why they would. Let me check in with my guys," he sighed. "Likely, she just turned it off before she gave her strength to the cat 'cause she knew you'd be ringing it off the stand. She's safe. You get some rest

* * *

I dropped Lenore at her place and took the van to my apartment building. Once there, I pulled out the burner I shared with Chelsea. It went straight to voicemail, again.

I sat in my apartment and realized how lonely I was. No cat, or woman or catwoman. I treated my tooth with oil of cloves and poured myself a stiff shot of dark rum. Rivera was right. He'd talk to his guys and everything would be fine. I could try to get some sleep. I eyed the bottle. Maybe one more shot to help me sleep. Or a hot shower to dull the itch.

My phone rang. "Yes?"

On the other end I heard sounds of frantic motion, then Rivera's voice, as if he were turning back to the phone to speak. "I'll be at your place in ten minutes. My people aren't answering, either."

The rum that was sitting so comfortably in me turned sour.

I hit the end call and dashed out of my apartment and down the stairs. Seven minutes later, a patrol car skidded to a halt by the curb, lights and siren blazing. Rivera shoved the door open, frantically waving at me. I jumped in and he tore off, killing the siren and lights as he did.

"I have her stashed her at my best safe house." He drove recklessly through the late-night traffic. We pulled into a residential neighborhood, and he slowed down, did a few quick turns down side streets to ensure we were not being followed, then pulled up to a nondescript split-level house. It was brick with brown shutters and gables. Rivera hotfooted to the door and knocked. We heard a muffled shout. Rivera unlocked the door, and we rushed in. An MWAT officer I did not know was handcuffed at the bottom of the stairs, holding pressure on a bleeding graze to his thigh. His equipment belt lay on the floor, radio smashed. He looked up at Rivera. "Crap."

"Right, what the fuck, Williams? Where's Randell?"

"He's in the bathroom. Dead. She shot him."

"What happened?" I demanded while Rivera called for backup and medical.

"I don't know, she was pacing around talking to that cat."

"She was conscious? Rivera demanded.

Williams hesitated. "Yeah, yeah. She woke up.

He looked up at me. "I know it's not just a cat. She was frustrated that the cat was not answering. She was manic, pacing and talking, then suddenly she sat down, rubbing her hands together. Then she jumped up, all sunshine and said she had to go to the bathroom. When she was gone a long time, Randell went to check on her and she shot him, then came downstairs and got the drop on me. Had me give her my equipment belt and my gun. She cuffed me then she said, 'so you won't follow me,' then she shot me in the leg and was gone."

"These are your best guys?" I snarked at Rivera, then scowled at Williams. "You said all sunshine? You mean like she was happy to do that to you?"

He nodded.

"How did she go? By car? On foot?"

The officer shrugged.

"What are you thinking?" Rivera asked me.

I pulled him to the kitchen and spoke quietly. "I think he is a goddamned liar, and not a particularly good one. If he is cuffed down here, how does he know Randell is dead? Where did she get the gun? Did you let her bring one?"

"No, we searched her."

"Where is Leslie?"

Rivera rubbed his jaw. "She should be here. I trust Williams, though."

"I don't. Let's go check on Randell. Maybe he's still alive."

Rivera looked convinced. "Trust but verify. I like it. Lead the way."

We came back from the kitchen and Williams was gone.

"Fuck," Rivera spat.

I ran to the door, my service gun drawn and peered onto the street.

No sign of him. I looked back at Rivera. "He must've known I was suspicious."

Rivera shoved past me. His own men betraying him was getting too personal. "We need to find that bastard and make him tell us what really happened." He paused. "Christ, Randell."

We ran upstairs but he was dead.

\.

* * *

I ended up at the station slumped in an office chair while reports flooded in from Rivera's trusted officers. I needed sleep, but all I could do was scratch and think about Chelsea. My imagination ran wild with the possibilities of what they were doing to her, a mix of my own torture experience, my knowledge of Samedi's curses, and wild fears.

Lenore burst into the office and snatched my phone, that I had been listlessly staring at, away. "Turn around."

"What?"

She grabbed my shoulder and physically spun me in my chair, and then her fingernails raked my back. The itch was receding, but the scratching felt almost orgasmic. I moaned.

"That's enough for now. Thank you."

"Del, you have no idea how many times I've offered to scratch an itch for you."

"What?"

"Oblivious much? Now, come on. Let's go see the swans." She took one look at me, gave a curt wave of her finger and about-faced to the front door. I followed on her heels.

At Echo Park, a weird mist covered the north part of the lake waters. In the distance, the only swans visible were the swan pedal boats.

Lenore yawned, covering her mouth with her hand. She did not sleep much either. "Guess we're early. They did say midmorning, not dawn."

"9 a.m. is hardly dawn," I said with a calm I did not feel.

"You're early." Hildegarde's voice came from the mist. "But we're ready." She and Nandi stepped out of the mist as it dissipated behind them. Both wore their feathered cloaks, black and white, but Hildegarde now wore a blue silk ribbon around her throat. Her usual playful attitude was muted. She carried a silver tray with something so beautiful it took me a moment to realize how macabre it was.

She sat the tray on the ground by a large stone.

"Wow," Lenore said in appreciation. "A swan harp. A real fricken swan harp."

I looked at what should have been a grisly sight. The harp body was carved from a human breastbone; the golden strings were spun from Ester's hair and her fingerbones made the tuning pegs. Every surface was gilded; every detail accomplished with meticulous care and reverence.

"Wow. Such precision. Do you make many of these?" Lenore asked.

"The Bonnies knew all about the harps," Hildegarde explained. "But this is only the second one in a century, to our knowledge. I did most of the work. I didn't know I could." She touched the blue ribbon

200

on her throat, her face a mixture of pride and apprehension.

"Oy," Nandi interjected, "the cheeky bird outdid herself. Oy lost a bet. Thought she'd make a cock-up of it. 'stead they made her a bloody Bonny."

"I know for a fact you didn't bet against me." Hildegarde's voice held a hint of mischief.

"Do we need to play it?" I asked.

"No, silly." Hildegarde took the harp from the tray and set it on the stone, eyeing it with calm anticipation. Nothing happened. Unperturbed she rotated the harp about an inch. Nothing happened.

"What is it supposed to do?" I asked.

She did not answer. On the seventh turn upon the stone, the harp sang on its own, the voice a somber contralto.

> *"My father scorned me, a man I could not be.*
> *Faithless mother reviled her daughter, me.*
> *No safe place to lay my head.*
> *No easy way to earn my bread.*
> *Taken in the night,*
> *By men I could not fight.*
> *But when they saw my nature sure,*
> *They deemed me repulsively impure.*
> *They turned me to the thing dark,*
> *Whose vile evil left its burning mark*
> *The McConnel took its pleasure*
> *By inflicting pain beyond measure."*

The singing paused, then it repeated the simplistic verses. Lenore, knowing what to expect, pulled a map and compass from her bag and measured the direction the harp pointed.

"The harp will only sing when facing the one responsible for the death," Hildegarde said. "The magic is super complex, I mean so much I need to learn, but the harp is easy to use. Take it a mile west and repeat what I did."

"And the directions will triangulate the position of the McConnel," I summed up.

Lenore looked at her map and pulled out her phone. "*Jefe*, we have the harp and the first azimuth, meet us at the east side of Dodger Stadium."

* * *

Rivera was waiting when we got there, along with four armored assault vehicles. Lenore wasted no time finding a stone to set the harp on. She faced it south. After a breath she turned it an inch toward the west. The contralto voice sounded as the harp repeated its song.

Lenore checked her map and triangulated. "Crap." She handed it to Rivera.

"Crap," he repeated. "The lines meet in the center of the south wing of the Los Diablos convention center. What's going on there?"

Lenore had her phone out. "Three different events. Double crap. One of them is a 'spontaneous' rally in support of Marlon Meadows." She swiped over to a news site and scrolled down. "There's got to be hundreds of people already on site."

I was terrified that The McConnel had got to Chelsea and Leslie. They might both be dead, or worse, under its control. I remembered how addictive following his commands could be. I turned to stare at the distance. "How many people can it tell to kill us?"

Chapter Thirty

"There is no 'us,'" Rivera said with a grim finality. "You two," he indicated me and Lenore, "are not going anywhere."

Lenore bristled. "You need me."

"As much as I need another ex-wife. I know you're invested, but this needs to be a precision operation. I will only use the remaining MWAT trained agents. They've trained together; they know each other's strengths and weakness. They know each other well enough to finish each other's statements. So, I need you at the station and out of the way."

"So you can walk into another ambush?" Lenore countered.

For a second his eyes burned with fire, but then he gave her a wan smile. "Fair enough. But I'm not going to get you two involved this time."

He didn't say any goodbyes, just packed up his team and rolled off.

"Well, fuck him," Lenore spat.

The burner phone I shared with Chelsea buzzed in my pocket. I almost ripped the fabric getting it out. "Chelsea, *mon dieu,* I was hoping you would call."

Silence teetered on the other end and then I heard a low bass chuckle.

"Falcata is such a pretty thing. Such a cute face."

My blood chilled at the sound of Cooper's voice.

"That Leslie Modeste though, she's not my type. I honestly see no reason you would be with her. Not very pretty, but she'll make a couple of sturdy keychains." I could feel the grin through the phone. "I'll get a lotta mileage outta her, anyway."

"Where are you?" I demanded.

The chuckle resumed. "Tell me, Del. How safe can a safehouse be if a safehouse ain't that safe because your fucking buddy doesn't do his homework? I just keep dancing circles around your pathetic wannabe Sherlock Holmes friend. You know how I cracked that safehouse, Del? Because I'm the one that set it up, and here's a little slice of bacon for ya. It's not the first time I've cracked it for a little *skin*. Anyhow. The girls and the damned cat are with me. I think I have just about everyone you care about, so don't screw with me. Oh, wait, don't you have a gramma somewhere?"

I gripped the burner so hard I felt the plastic give a little pop. I imagined that was the bones in Cooper's neck. "What do you want?"

"Why, you. You come to me unarmed and bring Welles, and I'll be a good boy and release the hostages."

"Bullshit." I stuck to English, his mention of *ma grand-mère* had me shaking with rage and fear. He couldn't get to her, right?

"What, you don't take me at my word? Look, Leslie has no idea what is happening. And Falcata? She has no evidence against me, nothing more than her word against mine, and she's a certified cop killer." He tried to sound sincere, but I wasn't buying it. "So, if you don't show up, I will make certain that they know the reason I am hurting them is that you were too much of a coward." He paused in thought. "I won't kill both the girls, mind you. Falcata's gotta go, but Leslie...how long will she want to live without a face?"

I didn't let him bait me. "What do you want with Lenore?"

"Not gonna hurt her. I just need her magic to tie up some loose ends."

"Where do we meet you?"

That infuriating chuckle again. "Drive to Venice Boulevard around South Pembroke. I'll have a spotter watching for you. When I see you are there, and not followed, I will call again."

"You could just tell us to meet you at the convention center," I snapped back, hoping to eek some intel out of him.

"Ah, ah, ah," he said in a voice brimming with malicious mirth. "I'm not at the convention center, so you better hurry, Del...because there is definitely more than one way to skin a cat and I'm gonna start *real* soon. Meow, meow, little buddy." He hung up.

I bristled with impotent rage.

"Well?" Lenore asked.

"That was Cooper. He says he has Modeste, Chelsea and Halima. He says he will release them if we come to him. He specifically wants you. He claims you will not be harmed."

"Right," Lenore replied, her face unreadable. "Guess it's off to the convention center for a fun old time for me, then. I'm gonna love being a lobotomized jewelry rack."

I opened my mouth to protest.

"Think it through. Cooper's not a magic user. We know The McConnel is at the convention center, if he is not there, he is double-crossing the old bastard. He'll need a powerful Talent. Without Macklin, I'll be his huckleberry."

"I've smelled magic on Cooper before, and the amulet burned him."

"Oh, yeah, he has some latent Talent, but he doesn't practice. He can detect magic, but only if he is looking for it. Magic is not second nature to him."

"Not a magic user?" I mused. "Meet me at the car."

"Where are you going?"

"I need to make a call for some advice."

Lenore grimaced at me. She dropped her poker face to allow me to see indecision, then she shrugged and headed to the parking lot.

As I walked away from her, I hit the speed dial on my phone.

* * *

Lenore was sitting in my unmarked car with the windows down, blasting "Everybody Wants to Rule the World" by Tears for Fears. She was singing along in her loudest voice and added "especially me!" after every refrain.

Maybe she's a sociopath, after all.

I dropped into the driver's seat and turned the volume down before starting the engine.

"Did you have to call your therapist or something?" Lenore asked as she turned the volume back up.

"What?" I asked. I had just gone in to the station to pee.

"The phone call you just made," Lenore retorted.

I started to reply that I didn't go in to make a phone call when a searing pain jolted through my skull. "Gah!" I gasped. The pain was intense, like a lightning bolt. I wasn't prone to headaches, and the last time I'd felt anything remotely like this was—

"Hey, wait a minute!" Lenore snapped and grabbed my head to yank my face close to hers. The pain subsided as Lenore stared deep into my eyes. I felt her *presence* invade my mind as a wicked smile bloomed across her face. "Oooohhh. Well played, homie. Okay, okay." She let me go and I shook my head to clear the residual pain. "Lead on, maestro. What's the plan?"

"We're going to do as instructed," I said as we turned into the street and entered LD's best traffic.

"Alright, I'm in. I don't know what you're up to, you don't know what you're up to, but I got faith," she said as she rolled down the window and let the blaring heat invade our air-conditioned space. "I gotta say, I respect that kinda balls, I really do."

I glanced at her as I avoided rearending the car in front of us. There were times I felt we were not having the same conversation. "Did you just heal my headache or try to violate my privacy for fun

Lenore let out a disgusted sigh. "Del, would it hurt your feelings if I said I took a peek and didn't find anything?"

"Perhaps I kept my mind blank to avoid giving you information you do not need."

"That'd be the smartest thing you've done today." She looked out the window and grinned and waved at someone I couldn't see.

The burner phone rang. Lenore answered it and put it on speaker. "Heya, hot stuff. How's your Cronenberg craft night going? Should I have brought my glue gun?"

"Go south on Flower until you pass Highway 22. You will see a building with storefronts. Pull into the parking lot. You are being monitored, physically and mystically. Do not try to contact anyone." There was a very distinct click.

"Well, they're no fun," Lenore groused.

I had to meander back to Flower and drove both under and over the freeway before we made our destination.

There was a tiny parking lot and three shops in the building.

I parked and instantly a team of hex-kiddies appeared. The oldest wore a black bandana around his head, maybe sixteen. Maybe.

They swarmed around the car, competing to look inside for liftables and were very disappointed. After a minute, bandana boy tapped at my window

"Must be the right place," I muttered, lowering it. Bandana boy held out his hand, palm up. Up close I had to make two revisions. First, closer to age fourteen than sixteen. And female.

"What?"

"You supposed to tip for service," she smirked.

I sighed and handed her a fiver. She just stood there, looking at me like I was an idiot. I added a ten. Her eyes darted to the other kiddies. Then I just gave her all I had. Odds were, I wouldn't be needing it.

She looked satisfied, like we'd just made a completely legit transaction and was now all business. She pointed down the street. "Alright, mister. So whatcha gonna do is, you gonna go south, like one more block. They a building just like this on the right, but at the end is, like, an office door. That's where you're goin'. They're waitin' on ya, and they the type I wouldn't make wait." She leaned closer, her head almost in the window and she eyed both me and Lenore appraisingly. "Hey. I tell you what. Take me to an ATM and I'll tell you how to get far enough way you don't hafta go see 'em."

"No, thank you," I replied, hitting the window button.

"Suit yo'self, but you gonna regret it," she said, and the kids slid away just as abruptly as they arrived.

I gathered my courage and pulled back onto Flower and easily found the next location. Almost identical to the last, except at the end there were three concrete steps leading to an oaken office door. I parked the car, exited without comment and waited for Lenore to get out. We walked to the three steps. There was a small brass plate on the locked door that said, "Bovine and Carr, Attorneys at Law." Below that there was a dusty, beige doorbell with a speaker beside it. I tried the door, but it was locked tight, so I rang.

A nasally female voice came through the tinny speaker. "May I help you?" she asked in an irritated tone.

I looked at Lenore, who shrugged.

"We are supposed to meet someone here."

"Do you have an appointment?" she said, still sounding peeved.

"No, we were *summoned,*" Lenore retorted.

"Summoned?" she replied, sounding confused. "One minute while I check the calendar. What did you say your name was?'

"Detective Delacroix and Mage Lenore Welles."

"Oh," she said in disgust. "I see you were penciled in for a counseling session. You need to go around to the left. There will be steps going to the basement. Have a nice day."

"Counseling?"

The speaker clicked off.

"Wow, that must be some amazing nail filing sesh we just interrupted," Lenore grumbled as she studied the cloudless sky above us.

I followed her gaze. "See something?"

"Nothing at all." She smiled and waved at the steps. "After you."

I led the way around and down to a distressed steel door. I got the feeling it was worn intentionally to create an ominous ambience. No buzzer, so I raised my hand to knock; but before my knuckles hit the metal we were greeted by an unholy cacophony as worn hinges that shrieked open to reveal a stooped older man, looking to be in his eighties. He had a fringe of unkempt white hair combed over a liver spotted scalp. The rest of his skin was sallow, and his milky blue eyes were locked in a nearsighted squint. In contrast, he wore a finely tailored black suit.

"There you are," he said, eagerly rubbing his hands. His tone was a mild rebuke, as if we were late. "Come on in," he said in a brusque, businesslike voice.

Once inside, we could see a small basement room fitted out like a professional office, with a wide steel door at the far end that resembled a garage entrance. Laying on the floor were two limp bodies, Leslie and. Pakhet paced in steel cage along the wall wearing the copy amulet I had made, but the winged Isis hung on a nail in the wall above the cage. I could see the tiny gold scarab with it and imagined it twitched in anger. So, the pacing feline must be Cocopuff and Halima was confined to her prison with the Shard.

Before I could rush to Chelsea's side, the old man admonished me. "Oh, stop. The women are fine, only under enchantment. As long as you do not touch them, they will wake up right as rain, once our business is concluded.

Now, one quick question." He held out an illicit lie detector charm. "Were you followed?"

"No," I answered truthfully. The charm sputtered for a second and went green.

He held it to Lenore. "Now you. Were you followed?"

"I know of no plan to have us followed. I neither saw nor detected anyone following us."

The charm went green without hesitation.

"Very good. Here, put these on." He handed us wrist straps, each bearing piece of cold iron.

Lenore looked at the piece skeptically. "I thought I was here to do magic."

"And I can't do magic," I protested.

"Yes, yes, yes. Precautions, protocols, you know?" He smiled at Lenore. "We will need you in due time, now be a good girl and put that on."

She sighed and complied.

The man moved behind the desk and sat down. He motioned for us to sit, as well. "Now, down to business." He rubbed his hands, in resignation.

"And what business is that?" I asked.

The man blinked. "End of life planning, of course. You may refer to me as The Undertaker. I prefer funeral director, but my boss likes the cruder term." He pulled some papers from a drawer. "This is a standard contract. I've filled out most areas, but I am required—" his lips curled in a very obvious counterfeit smile, "—required to take some of your wishes into account. I am afraid I can't offer an open casket option. The client has left very specific instructions." He grimaced. "Personally, I take no pleasure in the process. I would prefer to kill you cleanly, but the client has specified an extended experience. We'll have to use energizing charms to keep you going. But the good news for both of us is, we are only contractually required to continue for twelve hours. Now, are there any body parts, except the face of course, that you wish to keep intact until death?"

"I don't see that it matters."

He stuck out his lower lip and made a note. "Religious requirements?"

"*Non.*"

He passed the paper over, along with a pen. "Right. Just sign here and we can get started."

I didn't move. "Release the hostages first."

"In good time. The client specified that you should be restrained and when Ms. Welles, here, finishes her bit, the designated hostages will be released."

"What do you mean by 'designated' hostages?"

"Just legal speak for our contract, I assure you." He stood up. "Now, if you will please remove your jacket and tie." He drew something from a drawer and unrolled it to reveal a leather apron. He pulled it over his head and tied the back with deft movements one wouldn't expect from such arthritic-looking fingers.

I stood but left my jacket on.

"Suit yourself," The Undertaker said, "but it is a nice jacket. A pity if I have to cut it off."

I relented and removed it.

He nodded and produced a black velvet hood and dragged it over his head. It looked tailored to fit, with mirror lensed goggles. Satisfied, he pressed a button on his desk and the steal door opened to reveal a mostly empty, chamber beyond, tiled in dark red. Blood red. It reeked of disinfectant. The prominent feature was a sturdy steel chair bolted to the ground in the center middle of the room with a video camera focused on it. Along the far side were two more doors and a large cabinet.

On the slick floor by the far was a body wrapped in a tarpaulin bound with a rough jute rope.

"And that?" I pointed at the wrapped figure.

"Prior client. The old man pulled out a pocket watch. "He's not dead, yet…" He put his watch away. "Please, be seated." He waved to the chair.

It was in very good shape; highly polished and the steel and leather restraints looked new.

"Well, at least this is an upgrade to the last electric chair I as tortured in," I said with forced cheerfulness.

"Only the very best for our clients," The Undertaker said to me before turning to Lenore. "You can wait outside. This will not be pleasant. I'll call you in when necessary."

"No," Lenore said, stretching out the word as if in thought. "I'm gonna watch."

"Suit yourself." The Undertaker sounded peeved. He tapped the video camera. "Detective Delacroix, do you wish a copy of this to be sent to someone? I mean for an observer to verify your death. It would not be suitable for loved ones."

"*Non.*" I did not move to the chair as the reality of my imminent death enveloped me.

"Sir, if you do not sit, I will be forced to harm hostages. That rather undoes your purpose in coming here, doesn't it?"

I complied.

The Undertaker scurried to me and in less than a minute I was secured to the chair. Unlike my last experience, I had a lot of wriggle room. Perhaps so he could access different parts of my body.

Do not get the idea that I was not afraid. I was as terrified as a mouse being fed to a boa constrictor. My knees shook uncontrollably, and my palms sweat. I took a deep breath.

"Oh dear, what have we here?" He tugged at the cotton charm on my wrist. "This will never do." A razor knife appeared in his hand as he cut the charm away.

For a second, I had relief from the persistent itch, but then fire lanced through my body.

"I think we are ready." The Undertaker addressed the camera, "You may enter, now."

Chapter Thirty-One

The left door opened, and Cooper strode into the room with a huge grin on his face, followed by a man with an opulent black box. Deep red velvet covered the side panels and solid gold fastenings held the lid in place. Cooper lifted the winged Isis from Pakhet's replacement collar with quiet reverence and a touch of fear. A moment of hope soared through me. He had the wrong amulet.

"Aw, *Coops*," Lenore said with disdain. "You got the wrong one, ya ding dong. If you wanna use the Shard, and I assume you do, you gotta have the smaller, gold scarab."

I glowered at Lenore, and she shrugged. "Hey, next time don't pick a sociopath as your second in a duel of wits. Ooh, wait. Next time. You're about to die." She gave me a cartoonish grimace.

"Are you sure?" Cooper demanded, studying the copy.

"Don't be a dweeb, Coops. I know you can sense magic. Any in that amulet?"

"I-I-I thought it was shielded," he stammered.

Lenore rolled her eyes. "Just go get the little one."

Cooper rushed to the outer office and returned with the correct amulet in his hand.

His companion placed the box on the floor and opened it to reveal the original collar, with the winged Isis amulet.

A palpable sensation of longing rushed through the air. The two pieces of Nergal were so close now I could feel them reaching out to each other.

Cooper stared at me as he snapped at The Undertaker. "Leave us."

The Undertaker scurried back to his unsullied office and closed the door with a sigh of relief.

My mind raced to find a way to keep him talking. "I thought you worked for The McConnel."

Cooper rolled his eyes and made a grand, sweeping gesture. "That old guy wants to rule the world, make his will the only law of the land; do you see how pointless that is? All that work, and what does it get you? Even with the amulet's mass compulsion, there's gonna be resistance. Why bother becoming immortal if you're just going to spend the rest of eternity always looking over your shoulder? No, me? I'm all about the simple life. See, I'm not really convinced even with the two pieces reunited that I could overwhelm The McConnel through compulsion. He's somewhat of a master of it, if you haven't noticed. But I bet it will distract him just long enough for me to shoot him and go back to the *little* things that really bring me pleasure. I'll never have to hide my trophies again, with this thing. Hell, maybe I'll have 'em put up in the Met. They'll love it, 'cause I'll make 'em." He pulled out and rubbed the leather piece from his pocket. "In the meantime, McConnel can parade around thinking he's got the real deal."

"Does McConnel really think he has the genuine article? Wouldn't he know the difference?"

"That old wreck talks a big game about, 'Oh, I used to know Aleister Crowley back in the day, blah blah blah,' but the truth is he's too afraid to touch it himself, and too paranoid to give it to another magic user. Like you, he's forgotten there is another replica in play."

"The one Ms. Modeste detected in the museum."

Cooper touched his finger to the side of his nose. "You know, you are not so stupid." He clapped his hands together as he relished his impending work. "Alright, no more chit-chat. We are ready. First, Ms. Welles, free up the Shard so it can return to the main amulet."

Lenore hesitated, tugging at the cold iron strap.

Cooper waved her down. "Go ahead and take it off. I know I don't have to tell you what will happen if I detect any magic missiles aimed at me. You know just how petty and sadistic I can be."

"I know," Lenore said calmly as she unfastened the cold iron.

Cooper turned back to me, leaning his hand against the headrest by my ear. "When she's done with that, I'll do a light mindwipe on your ex and then Welles can take her and cat. It'll just be me, you and Chelsea. We're on a first name basis, here, right?"

"You said you'd let them go; I stipulated all of them!" I cried as I struggled against my bonds., I felt leather and chain biting into my skin, flaying me, but I did not care.

"'Designated' hostages, dumbass." Cooper leaned over me and stared gleefully into my eyes. I could smell his aftershave and the scent of his Talent, small though it was. "I'd love to sell your dumb ass a car sometime. Look, Del. Falcata knows way too much, and I paid The Undertaker for full services, we don't want that to go to waste." He picked up a small, wicked looking knife. "Besides, did you really think I was gonna let that pretty face go to waste?"

I howled in Cooper's face, and he squeezed his eyes shut, barely containing his laughter.

Okay, my plan was off the rails. I had to get it back on track.

Lenore moaned and I looked over to see her cradling the little amulet, eyes rolled back up in her head.

Merde. If I lived, how was I going to explain her behavior to HR? Whatever.

"What about Welles?" I asked. "She knows more than Falcata. You're just gonna let her walk? I think you're gonna use the amulet to cow her and flay her, too," I said in a voice loud enough I was sure Lenore could hear.

"Oh, come on," he laughed as he continued to present his tools to me, one by one, setting them out on a long, black velvet cloth. He walked over, grabbed my chin, pressed his cheek to mine as he wrenched my gaze over to Lenore and whispered heavy in my ear. "I think Ms. Welles knows which side her bread is buttered on. But you, you are a puzzle worth solving. Thoroughly. I might just let The Undertaker soften you up a bit, then mindwipe you. Hell, I'll make you worship me. Well, I don't actually have that kind of fine control with the amulet yet. You may end up demented, a risk I'm willing to take." He shrugged. "Or maybe I'll get your best bud over here to help me."

I screamed as hard as I could.

"Go ahead. No one can hear you."

"Wait!" I screamed and Cooper returned his amused grin back at me. "Why the faces?"

Cooper sneered. "All those people had it coming. Liars and two-faced bitches. I was just peeling away the lie to show the world who they really were."

"But the display, that is part—"

"Oh please, you know damn well I still display them." He brandished the leather keyholder. "Right under your sanctimonious noses." Then he stepped to the unconscious Chelsea and easily lifted her limp form to set her up against the wall, facing me. With a tenderness that made a mockery of compassion, he caressed her soft cheek. He sighed and brought up the tiny blade. Even as he stroked her cheek with his left hand, he started making tiny cuts across her forehead. Thin rivulets of blood streamed along her scalp.

There was a part of me that was thankful Chelsea would not awaken to this horror.

Cooper stopped. "This will not do. Ms. Welles, I need assistance. She needs to be responsive."

"Busy!" Lenore sang out as I howled again and fought my restraints until it hurt. "The Egyptian's a tough one but I just about got her loose and the Shard will fly. Interrupt me now and that thing might decide to kill us both."

"Fine," Cooper snapped. "We'll give the whore a break. I'll take care of Ms. Modeste, alright?"

"Whatever," Lenore sang back. "I'm busy."

Cooper put away his knife and reached for the original amulet. His face hardened as he accepted the pain of holding the amulet.

The lights blinked, then the second door in the back blew open in eerie silence.

A crackling voice filled the room, like dry leaves whipping in a wind that swirled around us. "I knew from the beginning you would betray me."

Two men rushed through the door; one brandishing a wand and the other a Beretta M9 semiautomatic pistol.

The McConnel rolled into the room in an extravagant Victorian wheelchair this time, pushed by two strong blondes who might be twins. They stared unfocused with hollow, expressionless eyes.

Cooper froze, Nergal's amulet in his hands. Lenore kept up what she was doing. Both antagonists ignored her.

"Sir," Cooper wheedled. "I was only trying to help you get the Shard back. By re-uniting them a safe distance from you. I wouldn't want anything bad to happen to you."

The McConnel laughed, a sound like a dry spasmatic cough. "Don't even try such a ludicrous lie. I've been following you with my mind since you ran from the warehouse saying you were going to deal with that." It pointed at me.

"But I—"

"You actually thought I wouldn't notice you steal the amulet. But I felt the magic leave with you. You play political games, Mr. Cooper, you may expect political prizes. You will die for my pleasure tonight. As gamey and foul as you are." One of the women put her hand on his shoulder. "You will be an apt appetizer." He squeezed the hand on his shoulder. "She will be my sweet dessert." He looked at me as if assessing me for the first time. His eyes took on a hungry look. "And you will be the *plat du jour* I have longed for." He smacked his dry, crackly lips. "But I can be generous. I will let Ms. Falcata and the

214

others go. See? In many ways, I'm not so bad as this weasel." He pointed a claw-like finger at Cooper. "He was going to dispense with her, but I show you mercy. Who is the kinder master, then? Besides, she is still cooking. There will be something fascinatingly delicious about her in a year or two. Best to let such sweet fruits ripen." The McConnel turned to his mage. "Freeze him, so he has to watch."

The mage flicked his wand and Cooper froze, as though his entire body were on pause. Dead still, not even breathing. I saw his hand at the small of his back, on his gun.

The man with the nine-millimeter blew away Cooper's right knee, then strode over to the immobile body, magically still upright, removed Coopers weapon, and blew away Cooper's left knee.

The McConnel gave a slow clap. "Oh, you are seasoning it up for me."

The man with the wand twitched, and Cooper dropped to the floor, writhing in agony.

Lenore's words were suddenly lodged quite loudly in my head. *I thought you had a plan. Where is the cavalry?*

I did the unthinkable and let her mind in without constraint. *I don't know.*

You're so lucky that McConnel guy is so gross. Our minds were still touching as she broadcasted, and the words overwhelmed my entire being. *Bobby, now would be a good time.*

The McConnel whipped his head around and stared at us, his beak-like mouth hinged open in shock.

Oh, boy.

Rushing feet stamped beyond the door to the office and we heard several large somethings get stuck to the door's panels. After a second of tense silence, the door exploded.

"Fall back!" cackled The McConnel.

The two men rushed to his side as the women fought to spin the unwieldy wheelchair. As they tried to push it back toward the door, I saw two things in quick succession. The first was a spark bounce across the tiled floor that looked an awful lot like a magical flashbang, followed by the oblong shape of a traditional stun grenade.

I squeezed by eyes shut just in time.

Voices, these with the surly confidence of career law enforcement, called out an all clear. Then four men in MWAT uniforms burst through the door Cooper originally used, followed by two men in the brown robes of the Nogs.

More MWAT and Nogs poured in from the front office. One of the Nogs cast a spell at Cooper and he went limp on the floor.

"It took you long enough!" Lenore griped. "I was about to have to switch sides."

"Loose ends," Rivera called out as he entered.

"Oh, yeah," Lenore retorted. "But Bobby followed us, and he should've gotten you here sooner."

"LD traffic's a bitch, you know that," Bobby said.

The McConnel must have seen a chance to retake the amulet. He threw himself from its chair, brittle bones cracking on the hard floor as it slithered with unnatural speed and tackled Lenore.

"No!" she shrieked as he seized the small amulet from her grasp. "It's not stable! You ding dong!" The ancient lich shoved her away and made to break the soft gold of the scarab.

"Now we all die!" it screeched.

"You first," Kaufman said and casually pistol-whipped the creature. Its skull visibly dented as thin watery blood trickled over the mottled skin. The lich collapsed, fingers still twitching at the amulet. Two Nogs closed in, and I could feel them try to drain the magic energy from the scarab.

They were too late. I also felt magic rush into the amulet and build exponentially.

Then I smelled death.

Chapter Thirty-Two

Rivera and the Nogs tensed in the magic backdraft. A noise like an approaching freight train filled the room. My ears were not recovered from the flash bang and the new noise was excruciating.

Two MWAT officers led Macklin in. Before I could ask why, Jason Mangel rushed in with his toolbox and rummaged through it. "I got something…might absorb all this potential magic energy…"

"Doubt it!" Kaufman shouted, his arms raised before him as though he was holding back a collapsing wall.

Rivera stepped forward gingerly, as if he expected any motion to detonate a landmine under his feet. "Right now, that little amulet is a live bomb, a *big* one. It'll make the storage unit incident look like a kiddy pool. We can't outrun the blast." Rivera looked at each of us in "We have to get the Shard back into the main amulet without releasing Nergal."

"Halima," I interrupted with a shout as the thundering sound drew near. "Let me touch it. I can persuade her to—"

"What we need to do," Kaufman screamed above the din, "is rip out the Egyptian and put her in here." He tapped the homunculus.

Rivera held up his hand to silence my objections. "McConnel weakened the containment, she's being consumed every second we stall. What's left of her is the only thing keeping it from exploding. We have to get the Shard out before it finishes. It won't release its grip easily."

"We have once chance to rip her out." Kaufman turned to me. "Look, I know you care for her, but we have to literally tear the Egyptian out, and there's no telling how much of her we will get."

One of the Nogs brought Macklin's body up and stood it by the amulet.

"Stand back!" Kaufman commanded. "This is our only chance!"

Rivera nodded and backed away,

"I got something that will help!" Jason Mangel exclaimed as he triumphantly held up a little contraption that looked like a bearing compass taped to a spray bottle and a…small jawbone.

I saw Kaufman's brow furrow, but he nodded. No time to ask how Mangel thought it would help.

The room seemed to accelerate around me, then a hum of energy nearly drowned out the roaring sound of magic being sucked in before it morphed into a screech like a jet taking off. The McConnel was right about one thing. We were all about to die.

A team of Nogs swarmed around the amulet while two of the MWAT officers took hold of Macklin's body. Mangel joined them and clipped a small electronic box to the creature's ear. "Give it twenty seconds."

Rivera didn't have time to argue, he gritted his teeth

I felt Lenore grab my wrist, You're going to want this."

The cord was back on my wrist. Adrenaline had dulled the pain, but now the itch was back.

Time paused a millisecond and the room went deathly quiet. The lack of sound became far more unsettling than the overpowering shriek.

A stupid thought flitted about my brain. "She won't be happy being a man."

Lenore punched me on the arm, and I realized I'd spoken out loud. "Del, don't be a doofus. It's a homunculus, it can be any gender it wants. It might take a month to get the appropriate bits."

Rivera glared at her.

Lenore shrugged. "Okay, three months if you need everything ethically sourced. Which you really *don't*."

"This is it!" Rivera announced in low, even voice. screamed at me. "We're doing this on the fly, and you know how finicky magic gets without preplanning."

I had no illusions about the situation. If this went wrong and I ran, I'd only die tired.

"Bobby, where you want me?" Lenore asked.

"On the amulet."

Lenore pushed aside two Nogs and laid her hand on the scarab. She didn't scream, but light erupted and I could smell flesh burning.

The McConnell chuckled, still somehow alive.

Kaufman put the original amulet on the homunculus. "Now, Welles! Bring her to me!"

She stood. Electricity crackled around her hand as she moved in slow agony. She stopped in front of Macklin's body.

"On the count of three, grab ahold of as much of the Egyptian as you can and tear it out. You're gonna have to get a tight psychic hold on the subject, but you have to release the amulet before the Shard escapes, or it will kill you."

"Don't tell me how to do magic!" Lenore snapped. "I play with these forces as a warmup exercise." She bellowed, "One! Three—" She jammed the amulets together and laughed even as smoke oozed from her closed fist.

I couldn't tell if it was confidence or a fatalistic acceptance.

The energy hum I felt came back as a painful vibration that rattled the fillings in my teeth.

With a pained scream, Lenore threw the amulet down.

Mangel's device lit up so bright the world seemed to turn purple as I clenched my eyes shut.

My ears popped. Sensations rolled over my consciousness, and then everything went quiet.

I slowly opened my eyes, blinking to clear my vision. The room was frozen in an awkward tableau, everyone in a pose of shielding their faces against nothing. I let out a breath I didn't know I was holding and the tableau collapsed.

Lenore cursed quietly and crumpled; her face knitted in pain. Mangel retrieved something from his toolbox and rushed to her. I watched him frantically dabbing the electrical pulses still crackling under her skin. Even as he manically dabbed, Lenore's skin re-charred under his fingers. Mangel's actions made me think of someone trying to put aloe gel on a radiation burn.

I turned my attention to Macklin.

The homunculus twitched.

"Halima?" I ventured.

The figure suddenly brought its hands up to the side of its head, tapping as if to check that the head was really there. Peels of semi-manic laughter filled air. "I'm free, I'm free!" The homunculus giggled, bouncing on the balls of its feet.

"Halima?" I asked again.

The figure danced a graceless jig and chuckled in a way that was suddenly horribly familiar. "I've learned my lesson, okay, guys?" it said in the high-pitched whine I remembered all too well. "No black magic. None." It crossed its heart. "I'll take the punishment, any punishment. From now on I'll behave."

"Not Halima," Rivera muttered.

"*Non*," I said. "That is Westley, the clown."

"The Egyptian must be back in the large amulet," Rivera said.

"You mean Cleopatra?" Westley said. "I saw her. I sorta…pushed her out of the way when I saw an opening in the…the…I don't know, man, I'm just glad to be out of there. You all saved me! You're my heroes!"

I held my fingers to my forehead. "She won't abandon Nergal. It is her duty. But we have to get her out." The words came out of my mouth as a reflex. "And put *him* back in!"

"Not possible," Rivera said with a sad shake of his head. "First, we don't know how much of her has been subsumed into Nergal. Second, even if there is just a little left of her, she has to stay in place as a plug. Third, it is unethical to put someone in against their will.

Lenore rolled her eyes. "I'll do it."

Westley balanced even as Rivers snapped, "No you won't. With the Shard restored, Nergal is back to his full power. If we free her, we risk releasing him."

I knew he was right, but I wanted to scream.

"I have a thought," Kaufman said.

Chapter Thirty-Three

Kaufman turned to the deflated form of McConnel. "Brothers, take him back to his chair."

Two Nogs lifted the broken pieces of the lich and set them in the elaborate wheelchair.

Kaufman regarded the remains, still twitching with malevolent energy. "You are barely animate. The only joy you get from living is in dominating, annihilating and humiliating others. Why do you want to live?"

The lich cleared its throat; at least, that was what I thought the grinding noise was. Harsh words grated out of the remains of its mouth. "A life of spite is still a life." Somehow the broken thing managed to sound smug.

"You are going to jail, I'm going to personally make sure of it," Rivera said calmly, but then his voice dropped to a threatening snarl. "How long do you think you will live in prison, banned from using magic?" Contempt filled his words.

Kaufman added, "I don't think you will make it through processing."

"Make your point, little man," The McConnel spat.

Kaufman stepped over to the pair of amulets and with gloved hands lifted the ancient one. "But here is another prison you could go to. One where you will live forever and not be vexed by your broken body."

The McConnel made a dry cackling sound of humor. "You would team me with an evil god?"

"You think Nergal will be happy about a sidekick? Can there be two mega-geniuses in the same room?" I pointed out.

"You are a fool," The McConnel said arrogantly, "but I am not. I'll take your bribe, little man, but you've not heard the last of me."

I gave a questioning glance to Rivera, who made a gesture like washing his hands.

Kaufman's walked over to the broken necromancer. "Here it is." He fastened the collar around its neck. Mangel picked up the smaller amulet and started to put it on the lich.

"Wait a minute," I protested. "We are going to put Halima into that thing's body? She deserves better."

"No," Kaufman said as he took the smaller scarab amulet from the quantum mechanic and placed it on the sunken remains. "I made this as a home for her and with the right help, it will call her out." He looked down at Lenore who was still bandaging her hand.

"You go right ahead Bobby," she said without interest.

"Oh, come on, Leni, you know you miss working magic with me. One last time. I promise it will be more fun than that trip to Hawaii."

Lenore stared at him as if trying to tell if he was serious. She stuck out her lower lip and her mouth twitch with mirth. "Oh yeah," Lenore brightened with happy memories. "The Big Island. Good times. I told you I could get that volcano to erupt." Despite the obvious pain, there was a twinkle in her eye.

"Yeah, you did. A shame about the village."

"Hey, no one was killed." Lenore sounded defensive. "Besides, between FEEBLE grants and local charities, that village is really nice now."

Kaufman gave Lenore the smile of an old friend. "Leni. I need your help."

"I'll help, if…" She trailed off.

Kaufman sighed. "Yes?"

"If you promise this will not be our last magic together, that you will assist me in some future working."

Kaufman sighed. "Nothing illegal, fatal or soul destroying?"

"Cross my heart." She made the gesture.

Kaufman did the same and I sensed the magic that passed between then. The promises were now bound by their alchemy.

The pair stood over the dry heap of The McConnel and joined hands.

"I'll pull Halima from one amulet to the other at the same time you put McConnel in," Kaufman said cheerfully.

"On three," Lenore specified.

"I'll count," Kaufman said.

Lenore stuck out her tongue at him.

"Can I hook this up first?" Mangel held up what looked like a brass compass.

Kaufman waved his annoyed approval.

Mangel used an alligator clip to hold the device to The McConnel's body.

When Mangel backed away, Kaufman stared into Lenore's eyes. It felt like they might be about to say wedding vows. "One. Two."

Both mages tensed.

"Three."

Lenore gasped, but it was a sound of pleasure, not pain.

The figure of The McConnel blasted apart like a pile of dried leaves covering a firecracker.

Kaufman stood somber; his head bowed.

Lenore shook with laughter. "What a rush!" she said gleefully. "You knew I'd get that…essence." She shivered. "Didn't you? Of course, you're too stuck up to take any pleasure in it."

"It is all yours," Kaufman said with a quiet smile.

"Bobby, I knew you still cared."

"Was it done?" I blurted out.

"Oh, yeah," Lenore said with a dismissive wave at the macabre pile. "You can grab girlfriend number two, here."

I picked the scarab it out of the dried remains and held it in my hands. "Halima?"

Foreign words filled my head, but I understood the conflicting emotions; both terrified and optimistic. "English, please."

"*Oui, français*, Del?"

I grinned. "*Oui*, or French will do"

"Oh, thank the universe. Where am I?"

"You are back in your little amulet. I'll take you to Chelsea." I paused. "Rivera?" I Pointed at the wrapped body. They said he was still alive."

"Who is it?" Rivera asked.

I do not know," I said. "The undertaker just said it was his last client. Wait a minute, where is the undertaker? The guy who runs this pl ace, he was in the outer office. Old man, nice suit."

Rivera called out, "Anybody see anything?"

No replies, everyone just shook their heads.

Rivera waved an over an officer who cut the rough rope.

"He's breathing, but in bad shape, we need a healer." Another officer, wearing the caduceus of a combat medic rushed over.

I heard a noise and saw MWAT officers carrying in containment equipment. The main apparatus looked like a chest freezer with wards scrawled across it. The thing smelled of burning rubber, foul and robust. Mangel took charge and put his little device and the original collar into it, and slammed the lid closed. All of the scent of the amulet vanished.

"You know," I addressed Rivera. "The McConnel is already planning its escape."

"The McConnel was planning his escape when Kaufman started talking. We'll make sure he stays put." He smiled. "We have our ways."

I gave him a side-eye, unsure if I wanted to know the details.

"Look who we found," The medic called. And helped Ted Gruber sit up.

"I told you she didn't kill him, or anyone."

"Simmer down Voodoo. There will be an investigation, but right now, she's in the clear."

I heard Halima in my head. "Thats a relief." I held the scarab up to the light and it sparkled. Cocopuff stirred in her cage and started a pitiful round of meows. She probably missed Halima as her wet food hookup. I stepped over the unconscious Leslie toward Chelsea. I carefully put the scarab necklace around her neck.

"Wake up, my love, we have company," I whispered in her ear, and gave her temple a light kiss.

Her eyes flew open wide with a harsh intake of breath. She stared at me like she didn't understand what she was looking at.

"Chelsea?"

Her eyes darted about. "No, it's me, Halima. Chills is still asleep. I will endeavor to waken her. I just wanted to tell you how thankful I am to be back with her." Her eyes drooped. "With you."

"Nice to have you back," I said cautiously. "I hope the Shard didn't hurt you."

"No, it only took what I gave freely. I think now that it is reunited with the greater entity, there will be changes."

"How so?"

"What do I have, that I can give so freely?"

"Uhh…"

Halima looked at me with Chelsea's eyes. They were full of kindness. "Empathy. A concept completely alien to the entity." The shared body relaxed, then jerked back awake. Those same blue eyes looked up at me, now baffled. "Del? You're alive."

Her hands flew to her neck and seized the amulet. The joy on her face was incredible. I could tell she was talking to Halima, and I imagined them like two schoolgirls who have missed each other and cannot help, on an internal level, squealing, dancing and hugging.

224

Chelsea's eyes regained focus. She leaned back against the wall and touched the drying blood on her forehead.

I stayed her hand. "Cooper cut you, a little. The wounds are deep, but small. You won't even need stitches."

Chelsea blinked at Leslie and reached down to check her neck for a pulse. Leslie moaned and her eyes fluttered. She woke slowly, like from a very long slumber. She whimpered, like she used to when I knew she was having bad dreams and rolled over.

"Hey, Rivera, make sure this one gets home," Chelsea commanded.

He nodded.

I examined Chelsea. Even though the amulet was touching her skin, she kept a tight grip on it.

"Is Cocopuff okay?" Chelsea nodded toward the cage. "He didn't hurt her, did he?"

"She's fine." I opened the cage and the little one rushed Chelsea, weaving between her legs. She stooped to pet the cat. "I'll brush you out and feed you when we get home, good? So much tuna, little one, all the wet food. We'll eat all of it."

The cat backed off and I put my hand back on Chelsea's shoulder and led her toward the door, Cocopuff right behind us.

She kept probing her face.

"Everything okay?"

"Yeah." She looked up at me, perplexed. "Can I go home, now?" She added quietly, "Home with you?"

Epilog

"Hey, Delacroix!" Rivera called out.

"*Oui?*"

"Get over here with Lenore."

I touched Chelsea on the shoulder as an assurance I would be right back.

One of the MWAT officers had somehow managed to manifest cups of that mana from heaven—cheap, instant coffee. Rivera offered me a cup. "That was a ballsy move, Delacroix. How's your head?"

I took a drink of the astringent, bitter amazingness. "I'm okay. No concussions, this time. I lucked out, considering."

Rivera looked from me to Lenore, then Kaufman. "It ain't worn off, yet, has it?"

Concern gripped me. "What hasn't?"

Kaufman clapped me on the shoulder. "You don't remember, Del, but you placed a phone call right before you and Leni came here."

I blinked at Lenore. "That's what you meant. But how did you know?"

Lenore gave me a crooked grin. "When I said I peeked into your mind and didn't find anything, that's what I meant. Bobby's the only mage I know good enough, and cocky enough, to do a mindwipe by phone. Besides me, of course. And besides, I saw the wheels turning in your head the moment I told you Cooper wasn't a real magic user. I knew you'd called your boyfriend."

"I still don't remember."

"It'll come back," Kaufman said.

Lenore continued, "I didn't know what you planned, and I didn't want to know. But it was the aversion spell that gave it all away, if you wanna know, Bobby. I couldn't look for the drone following us, but the spell let me know it was there."

I heard a loud groan and saw the medic help Gruber to his feet. He gave me a tentative wave.

I waved back and called, "Glad you are okay."

He gave me a thumbs up.

Rivera smiled. "I bet this makes you look forward to night shift."

"It will be a relief," I admitted.

"I think I got bad news for ya, then." Rivera said. "You and Welles make too good a team. I want the pair of you working on a special project for me. Right up your alley. Zombies."

I cringed. I have already had too much to do with zombies.

"Don't make that face, I think you can do some good."

I was not so sure.

Rivera jerked a thumb at the door. "Take your lady friend home and take the next two days off. Then 8 a.m. in my office. I won't yell at ya like the cap. In fact," Rivera gave my arm a friendly squeeze, "I'll have donuts."

I sighed and nodded and went back to Chelsea.

She appeared to be having an animated discussion with herself.

"You and Halima back together, then?" I asked warily.

Chelsea beamed a smile. "Yeah, our bond is stronger than ever." She placed my hand on her shoulder. "She's teaching me how to love. I really think I'm understanding."

"So, you are in love with her?" I said carefully.

"On levels I didn't know existed."

I stepped away from her, my head sinking to my chest. "I am so happy for you, and I won't get in the way. I hope—"

"God, you are a dumbass. Seriously."

"What?"

"Did I not *just* ask you to take me home with you? What was I gonna do there, play Smash Brothers with my spirit sister—No, hush, Hallie, I will explain video games later— Del, I swear you need to be hit with a clue by four sometimes."

Chills," Halima's voice filled my mind. "Could you put me back on the cat, there are times I need my own body,"

"In a minute." Chelsea stepped close and grabbed both my shoulders. "I love Halima, we are closer than sisters. But *she* loves you, and me. What she is teaching me is how to love *you*." She threw up her hands in mock exasperation. "I don't know if it will work, but least I have a guide and I'm willing to try."

"I hope the cat thing doesn't make this awkward."

Chelsea gave dismissive wave. "Back in the day I had a client with a severe Neko fetish."

"What is a Neko?"

Chelsea raised her to my cheek and gave it a tender pat. "Oh you sweet summer child. I'm going to enjoy corrupting you."

She kissed me and I felt love, the warmth of true connection and commitment, pouring between the two of us.

The MWAT officers made whistles and Mangel clapped.

She pulled back sharply. "Okay, this is going to be a little awkward."

"I am sorry, what?"

"Halima felt me kiss you. She wants a turn."

The End

Connect With Me Online. I am eager to hear your thoughts.
Email me at: gmandragora@gmail.com

Like my page on Facebook:
http://www.facebook.com/GeoffreyMandragora